NANNY NEGOTIATIONS

THE BROTHERHOOD: LEGACY

MERRY FARMER

NANNY NEGOTIATIONS

Copyright ©2023 by Merry Farmer

This ebook is licensed for your personal enjoyment only. This ebook may not be re-sold or given away to other people. If you would like to share this book with another person, please purchase an additional copy for each recipient. If you're reading this book and did not purchase it, or it was not purchased for your use only, then please return to your digital retailer and purchase your own copy. Thank you for respecting the hard work of this author.

This book is a work of fiction. Names, characters, places, and incidents are products of the author's imagination or are used fictitiously. Any resemblance to actual events or locales or persons, living or dead, is entirely coincidental.

Cover design by Erin Dameron-Hill (who is completely fabulous)

ASIN: B0CBS5KNTM

Paperback: 9798852139917

Click here for a complete list of other works by Merry Farmer.

If you'd like to be the first to learn about when the next books in the series come out and more, please sign up for my newsletter here: http://eepurl.com/RQ-KX

ONE

THE CHAMELEON CLUB was the last place on earth Heath Manfred would have chosen for a business meeting. It was one of those ancient, creaking gentlemen's clubs that had been around since his grandfather's grandfather's grandfather's time. Or maybe it would be better to say his granduncle's granduncle's granduncle's time, since the membership of the club was restricted to men who loved other men. It hadn't changed in all those years, except for allowing women who loved other women to become members in the seventies.

It was still housed in the painfully discreet building across Park Lane from Hyde Park. Most people passing thought it was a hotel. It had survived the Blitz in the forties relatively intact, and survived the AIDS crisis in the eighties and nineties with slightly more casualties. Heath was convinced that it would survive for another two hundred years and more, like all the other entrenched markers of British society that may or may not have been useful anymore. At least The Brotherhood, the organization that owned The Chameleon Club, was actively involved in charitable causes and advocating for equal rights around the world, unlike the membership of too many other ancient clubs in London.

Heath let out a sigh as he stared up at the club's discreet, grey edifice. He was stalling. There was never any point in stalling. He needed to get his head out of his ass and just go in and meet with Gerry, and everything would be alright. It wasn't like the members of the Chameleon Club read the tabloids or listened to celebrity divorce gossip anyhow. They were far too civilized for that. It wasn't like any of them would remember he was a member of The Brotherhood either.

"Stop being a dick," he muttered to himself and pulled open the heavy entrance door.

Stepping back into the Chameleon Club after nearly ten years of avoiding the place was surreal. Everything looked the same. The entryway had the same, polished wood and barely noticeable security cameras and metal detectors. Heath was fairly certain that the same besuited security guard that had been there during his university days stood in front of the second doorway he would have to pass through to get to the club itself. And the man didn't look like he'd aged a day in all those years.

"Good afternoon, Mr. Manfred," the guard greeted him with a calm smile, confirming his suspicions. "It's nice to have you back again."

So much for going unrecognized.

"Thank you," Heath nodded to the man, fighting the flush of heat that rose up his neck to his face as he emptied his pockets and took off his coat to send everything through the metal detector. "It's been a while," he said, making casual conversation as he walked through the scanner.

"It has, sir," the guard made casual conversation. He turned to gather Heath's things from the detector, then twisted to hand everything back. "I was sorry to hear about your troubles with Miss Stone."

Mortification spilled through Heath. So the stuffy old Chameleon Club was full of gossip about his life too, was it? Typical.

"Thank you," Heath said, smiling tightly at the man.

"Mr. Tyburn is waiting for you in the dining room, I believe," the guard said.

Heath had forgotten how omniscient the staff of the club was. He couldn't tell if it creeped him out or if it made things easier.

He nodded to the man as he refastened his watch, then headed into the heart of the club. Nothing had changed with the building or its decoration, but everything had changed with him. His footsteps echoed on the marble floor of the front hall as he crossed to the corridor that would take him to the dining room. The high ceilings and plain walls amplified the sound and made Heath feel like he was in a museum. That or on his way to the headmaster's office to have his hand smacked for whatever wrong thing he'd done now.

He could hear the gentle buzz of dozens of conversations coming from the main dining room before he reached it. The dining room was more of a ballroom where tables and chairs could be set up or taken down to adapt the room to whatever function The Brotherhood needed it for. Breakfast, lunch, and dinner were served there to the members every day. Heath had taken advantage of the free food on numerous occasions during his time at Imperial College London, when he was too hungover and debauched to cook for himself, or to be seen in public in that condition.

The sheepishness of those old feelings swirled around him as he stepped into the vast room with its Victorian decorations and crystal chandeliers. He glanced around at the other members of the club, searching for Gerry, and trying not to feel like the club was some sort of aging queen in tweed and sequins, who would embrace him with a false smile while inwardly sneering at him for daring to show his face where he didn't belong.

"Heath, over here."

Heath turned at the sound of Gerry's voice to find his colleague seated at one of the smaller tables by the windows that ran along the far end of the room. As relieved as Heath was to find Gerry, he hated having to walk through rows of tables of men and women who all looked at him like they *knew*.

"Gerry," he said with a curt nod as he reached the table and quickly slipped into a seat.

Gerry laughed at him. "You have no idea how fun it was to watch you squirm as you walked in here."

Heath frowned at him. "Thank you for making me feel so comfortable," he said, picking up the menu card next to the place he'd taken as a server rushed over to fill his water glass. He added, "Dick," under his breath, then shot a withering look across the table.

Gerry laughed again. "Come on," he teased. "You said you were a member, so I thought, why not discuss business in a companionable setting over first-class cuisine?" He sent the server a flirty smile and a wink when the young man finished filling Heath's glass.

Heath ordered his lunch quickly so the young man could escape from Gerry's horrid flirting, then said, "I thought the rules of the club stated that members can't hit on or date the staff. Did they change that?"

"No," Gerry said, waving the whole thing away as if it were a fly trying to get to his soup. "I don't mean anything by it. It's just fun."

Heath arched an eyebrow at that and reached for his water. "I'm not sure they see it as fun."

Gerry shrugged. "I'm not really serious about it. Alec knows that. We have an understanding."

"I just bet you do," Heath muttered before taking a drink of water.

Gerry chuckled. He waited until Heath had put his glass down and glanced nervously around to see how many sets of eyes were on him before saying, "You are a member, right?"

"Yes," Heath admitted, rubbing the back of his neck and not looking at Gerry directly.

"Then why are you looking around as if you expect the police to come in and drag you out for trespassing at any moment?"

Heath cleared his throat, then looked at his friend. "I haven't been here for nearly ten years," he confessed. "I wasn't sure I would be welcome anymore, since having a high profile marriage."

"High profile divorce, you mean," Gerry said.

Heath let out a breath and stared flatly at Gerry. "Thank you for reminding me," he said, then reached nervously for his glass again.

Gerry relaxed into a sympathetic shrug. "Gemma was an attention-seeking shrew. She was after your Hollywood connections. Everyone knew it from the beginning."

"I didn't know it," Heath said, then sipped his water. The cooling ice wasn't helping like he'd hoped it would. "I was in love," he muttered before putting the glass down.

Gerry winced. "Is that why you don't want to be here?" he asked. "You do know that The Brotherhood has no problem at all with bi and pan members."

Heath flushed hot and snapped a guilty look to Gerry. "It was just a phase at uni," he said. "I was just carrying on with the tried and true, nineteenth century tradition of fucking around with my college mates. Once Gemma came along, I didn't look at another man, or another woman, for that matter, that way again."

"Mm-hmm," Gerry hummed. The smirk he wore told Heath he didn't believe a word of that. "If that's true, then why did you keep up your membership in The Brotherhood?"

Heath huffed out a breath and sagged back in his chair. "Is this really why you brought me here for the meeting? To grill me about my sexual past? To dredge up that astoundingly brief time in my life when I was wild and wanton and didn't think about the consequences of my actions?"

Gerry laughed. "Spoken like a true aristocrat," he said, affecting a heightened upper-class accent.

Heath stared at Gerry. "We are not amused."

That only made Gerry laugh harder.

The moment was saved as the server returned with Heath's lunch. Gerry flirted with the young man a little more, and fortunately, the man really didn't seem to mind. Heath started eating, hoping that the more distance he put between the previous conversation and whatever they discussed next, the less embarrassing Gerry's topic of conversation would be.

He was in luck.

"It looks like things are going to move forward with the After the War series," he said, everything about him more serious. "Brad and Olivia are finally satisfied with the scripts for season one, and as soon as we get a greenlight from the co-producers in LA, they want to move on with scouting locations."

Heath heaved an inward sigh of relief. Business at last. The production company he and Gerry worked for was one of the most prestigious in the UK, and for almost a year now, the two of them had been working, along with the writer and potential showrunner, to adapt the memoirs of an early nineteenth century duke—who had hosted a house party of decommissioned, gay naval officers after the Napoleonic Wars—into a television show for one of the top streaming services. Heath held a high position in the corporate end of the production company, and Gerry was one of the producers in charge of developing new series. The idea had generated a lot of interest in the industry, but they still needed financing to make the series a reality.

"Which is why it's going to take a trip out to LA to win the support we need," Gerry finished up after a good twenty minutes of eating and talking.

Heath shrugged, feeling infinitely more at ease, now that he'd eaten. "I'll schedule a few meetings for next month," he said.

Gerry eyed him with a smirk. "Will the divorce be final by then?"

Heath swallowed his last bite awkwardly. "The divorce was final yesterday," he said, reaching for his water to force the bitterness down.

Gerry's expression changed, like something else had occurred to him. "Are you okay with leaving Eugenie to make the trip to LA?"

Heath winced. His daughter, Eugenie, was the center of his completely off-kilter universe and the one thing he didn't know how to manage along with the rest of his career. "I'll think of something," he said.

As if that were a call to the Universe to mess his life up a little more, a hand landed on his shoulder as a voice behind him said, "Heath. How ironic to see you at the Chameleon Club the day after your divorce was finalized."

Heath scowled, then twisted to look up at his older brother and the shit-eating grin the bastard wore.

"Oakley," Heath sighed, shrugging Oakley's hand away.

"Is that any way to greet family?" Oakley asked, helping himself to one of the free chairs at the table.

"It wasn't my idea to come here," Heath defended himself, trying not to sound like the sullen brat Oakley always accused him of being. It was hard not to be sullen when your older brother was brilliant, gorgeous, insanely wealthy, and a fucking earl on top of all that.

Oakley laughed. "I won't tell Mom and Dad that you've

decided to follow in my footsteps after all and that they have to rely on Marmie to carry on the family line."

Heath sent his brother a withering look. Oakley had been unapologetically gay since the day he was born. That hadn't stopped their mother from bemoaning the fact that he hadn't settled down and started a family. The moment Elton John and David Furnish had announced the birth of their first son via a surrogate, she had latched onto all the possibilities for the grandchildren she thought she'd never have. And when Gemma had given birth to Eugenie, she'd practically lost her mind spoiling her granddaughter.

But Eugenie was a girl. The family's title was entailed through the male line, like some pitiful Jane Austen novel, Oakley was too popular in certain crowds to settle down anytime soon, and with Gemma making a splash all over Europe with her new boy-toy, Heath's chances of producing a male heir were close to zero. That left Marmaduke, the third son, with the burden of making the family proud.

"I didn't come here on purpose," Heath insisted, fighting to hold his own against Oakley's teasing. "Gerry wanted to meet here to discuss the new series we've been working on."

"Right," Oakley said with a sly grin. "And it's pure coincidence that your ex-wife is all over social media, celebrating her freedom, as she calls it, with that bit of human excrement she left you for."

Heath sighed, heating with anger and embarrassment. "Did you want something, dear brother?" he asked, glaring at Oakley. "Or did you just come over here to make fun of me?"

"I just wanted to make certain you're alright," Oakley said with a suddenly sympathetic smile.

Heath grit his teeth, then let out a breath. That was the problem with Oakley. He annoyed the hell out of Heath and pestered him to the point where Heath wanted to punch him, then he made a complete turn-around and acted like the caring and concerned brother Heath needed him to be.

"I'll be fine," he sighed, rubbing a hand over his face. "Now that the whole thing is done, Eugenie and I can move on with our lives."

"How is Eugenie taking it?" Oakley asked.

Heath shrugged. "She's three. She's more upset about losing her Peppa Pig blanket than Gemma walking out on her."

Oakley hummed. "Gemma was never particularly maternal."

"Gemma only cares about herself and her career," Heath grumbled. "She doesn't care that she has a beautiful, funny, adorable little girl with the biggest, sweetest heart."

"I love how much you love her," Gerry said with a smile.

"She's my daughter," Heath said. "She's the best thing that has ever happened to me and my reason for being."

"How is my darling niece?" Oakley asked. "Mum said something about the nanny quitting?"

Heath sighed. "The nanny did quit, but it had nothing to do with the divorce or anything. She had family obligations she needed to take care of. On top of everything else, I need to find another nanny."

Being reminded of that filled Heath with a deep sense of dread. He'd put out some feelers and had a few applications, but Gemma had stupidly mentioned on social media that her daughter needed a minder, and Heath was now inundated with fans and fortune-hunters who were applying for the position for all the wrong reasons.

"You shouldn't have a problem finding someone to care for Eugenie," Oakley said. "She's a darling."

"She is, but I am," Heath said. "Having trouble finding a reliable, qualified, non-predatory woman to take the position, that is."

Oakley winced. "Celebrity has its pitfalls, I suppose."

"Gemma has her pitfalls," Heath grumbled. "I won't trust my daughter to just anyone."

"Where is she now?" Oakley asked.

Heath sent his brother a mock sullen look. "Mother has her."

"Oh, God," Oakley said, his eyes going wide. "When you get her back, she's going to be wearing a floral dress with a tiny cardigan, pearls, and an Alice band."

"She's only three," Gerry laughed.

Both Heath and Oakley glanced to him with somber looks. "You don't know Mother," Heath said.

That only made Gerry laugh more. "I swear, it doesn't matter how much progress the rest of the world has made, you nobs keep thinking it's the Victorian era or something."

"We do not," Oakley said, stealing a crisp off the side of Heath's plate. "It's at least the Edwardian era by this point for Mum and Dad."

"Mum still hasn't recovered from watching Downton Abbey," Heath sighed. "I'm half convinced she's waiting for Dad to die so she can walk around calling herself the Dowager Marchioness and talking down to people, like Maggie Smith."

Gerry laughed uproariously. "Well, I can't help you with that problem," he said, entirely too amused with the situation, "but I can help you with finding a nanny."

"You can?" Heath perked up a little.

Gerry nodded. "My sister runs an employment service that places nannies and private nurses and people like that. I can give her a call and have her send over someone who is not only vetted and qualified, but who will be utterly discreet."

Heath wanted to shout in victory. "I would love that," he said. "Could you have her set something up with my assistant, Sara? If I'm going to have to make a trip to LA next month, I'm going to need all my time finalizing things for the series on our end and setting them up on the Hollywood end. I won't have time to sort through nanny CVs."

"Absolutely," Gerry agreed with a nod.

"That series about the gay sailors is going forward, then?" Oakley asked with an interested grin.

"We're working on it," Heath said. "And it's gay naval officers at the end of the Napoleonic Wars, not gay sailors."

"Isn't it the same thing?" Oakley asked with the look he wore when he was teasing Heath just to get under his skin.

"Fuck off," Heath told him. He placed his hands on the table and stood. "Now, if you'll excuse me, since I don't really belong here, I should leave before they have me thrown out for liking breasts."

Oakley laughed. "Right. That's why you're leaving." He eyed Heath like he'd told a gigantic, blatant lie. "You're not running out of here like your arse is on fire because you're afraid to deal with your love of cock."

Heath glared at his brother. "I'm not the one featured in the tabloids with a new, empty-headed, wannabe model half my age every other week."

Oakley shrugged. "What can I say? I have a type."

Heath rolled his eyes and shook his head as he gathered up his things to leave.

He took one step away from the table before Oakley grabbed his wrist and said, "Call me if you need a shoulder to cry on. I love you."

Dammit, every time! The bastard couldn't just let him feel one thing toward him.

"Thanks, Oak," he sighed. "I'm alright. Really."

Oakley squeezed his wrist, then let it go.

"I'll get your nanny situation resolved by tomorrow," Gerry said as Heath walked away from the table.

Heath smiled in thanks and waved at him before walking through the gauntlet of tables and other members at the club. He truly was grateful for Gerry helping him out. And if he was honest, the other club members looked at him with sympathy and understanding, not revulsion or derision. But then, that was what The Brotherhood was all about. For nearly two centuries, its members had pledged themselves to help each other out of every sort of crisis a gay man could get into.

That was why he'd joined in the first place all those years ago, not for the free food. He loved the idea of an underground network of queer people helping other queer people. Even if his brief experiment in dating men was well behind him.

TWO

THERE WERE things in life that Aubrey Kelly just didn't want to think about. How badly he'd done in school was one of them. The reason why he had stuffed up his interview at the only university that had been interested in him was another. And how pitiful it would be to move back in with his parents at the ripe old age of twenty-five if he didn't land the job he'd been sent to interview for was another. That was the biggie.

But as he glanced at his phone, checking the address the agency had sent him to, then up at the actual house that address was attached to in front of him, he had the horrible feeling that there was no way in fuck whoever lived in the stately, Georgian townhouse would ever hire a guy like him to be a nanny to his child.

The home in Mayfair was like something out of a Georgette Heyer novel. And he fucking hated Georgette Heyer, what with all her questionable historical research and thinly veiled antisemitism. The whiteness of the townhouse's façade was just so white and so perfect, with black accents here and there that marked it as belonging to someone who wanted you to know that they didn't want you to know they had money.

Aubrey swallowed the sick feeling that had been building in him and pulled himself together. Janice wouldn't have sent him to Mr. Heath Manfred's house to interview for the nanny position if she didn't think he was fully capable of the job. And despite some of the sins of his past, he had five solid years of working for some pretty important people under his belt. He could handle this.

Summoning his courage, he stepped up to the door and pressed the bell. And, of course, it rang deep in the house with an understated, classical chime that indicated the owner of the house not only had money, they had an ancient family line to back it up.

And here Aubrey was, just some guy from Porthleven who would end up working at his cousin's day nursery while living with his parents if he didn't land this job. Because opportunities like the ones he'd been lucky enough to have so far and like the job in front of him didn't come along every day. He couldn't wait for another position like this to open when he had bills piling up to the point where they might topple his wobbly kitchen table.

No pressure. None at all.

The silence as he waited for someone to answer the door was killing him. Places like this probably had butlers and maids and, fuck, it probably had footmen. Aubrey wondered where the hell they were if they weren't answering the door. He knew nothing about service, but if the nanny position fell through, maybe he could get a job with Mr. Manfred as a footman. Three of his great-grandparents had been in service, he flattered himself to think that he was attractive enough for the job, and if the butler at this place was as negligent as—

Aubrey's spiraling thoughts were cut off as a shadow appeared on the other side of the frosted glass cutout in the door, and he held his breath as a lock was turned and the door opened.

And then he burst into an embarrassing cough as the most gorgeous man he'd ever seen opened the door and stared right at him. The man was tall, with broad shoulders and a body that looked fit as fuck, even in the suit he wore. His deep maroon tie made him seem warm somehow, as did the slight, natural tan of his skin and his chocolate-brown eyes. His brown hair was just a bit too long, and made Aubrey want to comb his fingers through it to keep it from falling in his face. Best of all, the man's lips were—

"Can I help you?" the vision before him asked in a terse tone.

Aubrey recovered from his cough, shoved his phone into his back pocket, and said, "I'm here to interview for the nanny position."

He thought he'd managed that bit far better than he could have. His voice hadn't cracked at all, and he'd kept his Cornish accent to a bare minimum.

But the man in front of him said, "Are you certain?"

Aubrey blinked. Was he certain? He wasn't certain of anything, except that the man in front of him was born to wear a suit. Although Aubrey wouldn't have minded peeling him out of his suit either.

"I think so," he said, trying a smile to see if that helped. He had a feeling it just made him look like he had gas. "I'm Aubrey Kelly?" He extended a hand, just in case the god inside the house would deign to shake it.

He did not shake it. The man frowned a little and said, "I thought Aubrey Kelly was a woman."

"Ah," Aubrey said, disappointed. "Common mistake. It's my parent's fault, really. They're artistic, you see. I was named after Aubrey Beardsley. Which is ironic, when you consider…."

Aubrey made himself shut up before he went too far. He'd always made certain his CV stated that he was gay, just so there were no surprises with prospective employers, but if the man in front of him hadn't even been aware he was male, he probably hadn't read his CV at all. Unless he actually *was* a butler and Mr. Manfred was sitting back in a wood-paneled office somewhere, smoking a pipe while reading the latest review of the opera or something. Or maybe taking snuff.

"Sorry," the man said, stepping back and gesturing for Aubrey to come inside. "My assistant only put your name on my calendar when she scheduled this interview. I assumed, and I shouldn't have."

That answered Aubrey's question about whether he was speaking to a butler.

"It's not a problem," he said, breathing too heavily instead of laughing as he stepped into the house. "Are you Mr. Manfred?"

The man looked at him strangely as he shut and locked the door once Aubrey had stepped into the foyer. "I am," he said, moving ahead of Aubrey and gesturing for him to follow him down the hall. "I'm surprised you didn't recognize me, since my picture has been all over the tabloids for the last year or so."

Aubrey bit his lip as he followed Mr. Manfred down the hall to, unsurprisingly, a wood-paneled office loaded with books. There was even something he swore was an enameled snuffbox on the end table beside a leather-upholstered couch. He really had walked into some sort of historical drama, hadn't he.

"I have to admit, I haven't been keeping up with celebrity gossip," he said, feeling like he'd already destroyed all his chances of getting the job. "My last placement was with a family who insisted their children be kept away from television and tablets and social media. I can't say I'm really invested in any of it myself, although I have a few social media accounts that I don't really keep up with. Although you probably checked them all out, since you're thinking of hiring me."

Mr. Manfred moved to the room's huge desk, but instead of sitting behind it like a judge, he leaned against the front and crossed his arms. Aubrey wasn't sure which was more intimidating.

"I haven't surfed through your social media accounts," he said. "I didn't even realize you were a man."

Aubrey tried not to wince or flush with embarrassment. "Good point." He really was in danger of stuffing the interview all the fuck up.

"Have a seat and tell me a little about yourself," Mr. Manfred said, gesturing to one of the leather-upholstered chairs in front of the desk. They matched the sofa, because of course they did. "I might have missed the detail about you being male, but my assistant did send me your CV, so I know a little about your education and your previous employment."

"Ah, yes, my education," Aubrey said, taking a seat as directed.

He wasn't sure he liked it, since Mr. Manfred now towered above him. Although that wasn't such a bad thing either. With his imposing frame and no-nonsense expression, Mr. Manfred was exactly the sort Aubrey liked towering over him. Not that he was particularly kinky, but that wouldn't have stopped him from calling Mr. Manfred "Daddy" if he asked.

"Here's the thing about my education," he went on, his voice squeaking for a moment as he tried to clear the naughty thoughts about his prospective employer from his head. He squirmed against the too-slippery leather of the chair, trying to find a comfortable way to sit and hide what could possibly happen below his belt, if Mr. Manfred kept staring at him with that stern look. "My grades were awful, I'll admit it," he said. "I barely squeaked by with enough A-levels for the Early Childhood Care program where I earned my certificate. But if you did look at my employment history, I think you'll see that the families I've worked for were pleased with me. I certainly loved the kids I've worked with."

"Yes, your letters of recommendation were exceptional," Mr. Manfred said. He glanced down just a little bit and colored slightly. "Or so my assistant tells me. You were her top choice of all who applied."

Aubrey opened his mouth to say more to sell himself, but Mr. Manfred stood straight and rushed on with, "You must excuse me, Mr. Kelly. I'm making a mess of this entire interview process." He moved to sit in the chair beside Aubrey's. "I've just come out of a long and bitter divorce process, and the production company I work for is in the process of finalizing negotiations for a high-budget television series. I can assure you that my daughter, Eugenie, is my number one priority, but—"

"No, you don't have to explain," Aubrey said, spurred to action by the man's sudden show of vulnerability. He shifted in his chair again, leaning more toward Mr. Manfred. "I absolutely understand the sort of pressures that high-achieving people have on them. That's why you lot hire nannies to begin with."

A moment later, he realized how his words must have sounded.

"I mean," he went on, wincing and closing his eyes for a moment. "That's not how I meant it at all."

"I think I know what you meant, Mr. Kelly," Mr. Manfred said with a kind smile.

So kind, in fact, that Aubrey blurted, "You can just call me Aubrey. I don't stand on ceremony."

Again, he wanted to grimace and slap himself. Mr. Manfred was someone important. Aubrey had read the job description Janice sent him, though he hadn't realized Storm

Productions was a film studio. He'd thought they had something to do with emergency preparedness. And it was clear from the house and the room they were in that Mr. Manfred's people were the crustiest of the upper-crust on top of that. People like that definitely used "mister" when addressing others.

But Mr. Manfred said, "Thank you, Aubrey. And you can call me Heath."

He said it, but Aubrey wasn't so sure he meant it. A funny sort of look came to…Heath's eyes, as if he couldn't quite believe he'd given a pleb like Aubrey permission to address him by his given name.

Or maybe it was something else. Heath did seem to stare at him for just a hair too long before shaking his head and saying, "My one and only concern is for my daughter. Eugenie is three, and very interested in the world. I am hoping to find a nanny who can encourage her curiosity of the world around her and who can keep up with her. She can be a handful."

He paused, glancing down for a moment, then looked up and met Aubrey's eyes with an unnerving amount of seriousness.

"Her mother, my wife—my ex-wife—Gemma, never really showed much interest in her," he continued in a quiet, hurt voice. "Gemma is a high-profile model and would-be actress. Everyone said she only wanted me for—"

Even though he stopped, Aubrey's mind filled in the entire story for him. And it wasn't good. No wonder Heath had a hurt, awkward, uncomfortable feeling about him. It was almost like the man was looking for some sort of reassurance.

"Are you concerned that Eugenie's mother might try to interfere with her?" he asked, as businesslike as if he were at the boardroom table with Heath instead of a cozy office.

"No!" Heath's eyes went wide. "Part of me wishes

Gemma would take more interest in Eugenie. I'm worried about how it might affect her once she gets older and needs her mother."

As quickly as he'd said that, he snapped his mouth shut and looked sullen. Then he cleared his throat and went on.

"I love my daughter, you see," he said, sounding artificially upper-class now, like it was expected that he wouldn't adore his own child. "I want her to have everything her heart desires. Which is why I want to be certain I choose the right person to look after her when I cannot."

"I understand completely," Aubrey said. "And I can assure you, I will care for Eugenie like she's my own. I don't mind helping out around the house either, although with a place like this and you being who you are, I don't know if you need someone to help with the washing up." Aubrey smiled as his joke.

Heath didn't smile. He looked borderline affronted. "I don't employ servants," he said.

"Oh…er…um…I shouldn't have assumed," Aubrey stammered and flushed with embarrassed heat.

Heath's expression pinched, and he said, "Well, I guess that's not really true. I'm proposing to hire you, after all. And I do have a cleaner that comes twice a week. But I do all my own cooking and washing up."

Aubrey fought not to grin at the way Heath spoke with so much pride. The two of them definitely came from massively different worlds, that much was certain. Growing up in his world meant that Aubrey had had to do the washing up—and the dusting and the Hoovering—as regular chores to earn his weekly 50p.

"In that case," Aubrey said with a grin, "I can definitely help with the washing up. I'll even do the shopping and tuck Eugenie in at night. And I promise I'll keep my room tidy as well or you can give me a demerit."

He grinned at his little joke, but Heath's expression fell, like he'd said something wrong.

Before Aubrey could find out how he'd cocked up this time, a stately woman with grey hair, who looked to be in her sixties, came marching into the room, a smartly dressed, fussy toddler in her arms.

"Heath, you'll have to take her back now," the woman said, marching right over to the chairs and plunking the toddler onto Heath's lap before he could stand. "Bunny's garden party starts in an hour, and you know the traffic between here and Kensington is horrid at this time of day. I wouldn't mind being late, or skipping the event entirely, but Trudy's grandson is going to be there and I have to—oh, hello. Who are you?" She blinked rapidly at Aubrey as she straightened from handing the toddler—who Aubrey assumed was Eugenie—over.

Aubrey was so blown over by the whirlwind of the woman that he could only gape at her in amazement.

"Mother, this is Aubrey Kelly," Heath answered for him as the fussy girl on his lap burrowed into him for a tearful hug, despite the fact he was wearing a suit. "He's come to interview for the nanny position."

"Have you?" Heath's mother asked, surveying Aubrey as if she wasn't sure her son had the right understanding of the situation.

"I have, madam," Aubrey answered her with ridiculous formality. He instantly felt like an idiot.

Then again, the woman wore pearls, and one generally addressed matrons wearing pearls formally.

Heath's mother hummed as she continued studying him. "With hair that red, your people must be Irish."

"Cornish, ma'am," Aubrey answered.

"Mother, don't intimidate the poor man," Heath said with a sigh. He was struggling to keep Eugenie on his lap. She'd had her hug from Papa, and now she was wriggling to get down. "We don't want to frighten Aubrey away before he's even had his first day."

Aubrey's breath caught. That made it sound like he was hired. Thank God! His troubles would be over, and happy days would be here again.

"Well, I'll leave you to it, then," Heath's mother said, glancing suspiciously between Heath and Aubrey. Aubrey wasn't sure he liked the sparkle in the woman's eyes. "Send me a copy of his CV, will you?" she asked her son as she started out of the room. "I'll have my contact at Scotland Yard investigate him."

Aubrey nearly choked on his own spit. "Investigate me?" His voice rose to an embarrassing squeak.

Heath rolled his eyes. "Don't listen to her. She's probably been watching some detective show or something. My mother watches entirely too much telly."

"That's rather convenient, since you work for a film company."

Aubrey's observation went unanswered as Eugenie managed to wriggle free of her papa. But instead of chasing after her grandmother, like Aubrey expected her to do, she walked right over to stand in front of Aubrey, gazing up at him with wide, curious, innocent eyes.

"Well, hello, you," Aubrey said, bursting into a smile. He held his arms open, giving her the option to come closer to him or back away, and asked, "And what's your name?"

"Genie," the adorable little princess said, beaming up at him.

"Genie," Aubrey repeated, as if it were the most wonderful thing he'd ever heard. "That's the perfect name for a princess. And you're dressed like a princess today, too." He glanced over her frilly, pink frock and cream-colored cardigan that he swore was cashmere.

"My mother likes to dress her up," Heath said. Aubrey

could hear him roll his eyes, even though his attention was focused on Eugenie.

Eugenie, grabbed at the skirt of her overly formal dress and held it out. "It's pink. I like pink."

"So it is, and so you do," Aubrey said. "I like pink, too. And purple. And glitter. Unicorns aren't half bad either."

He reached for the cuff of his trousers and pulled it up enough to reveal he was wearing pink socks with unicorns on them. That had been a deliberate choice, since he knew his potential charge would be a little girl.

Eugenie laughed at the sight of Aubrey's socks. She then did the very best thing she could have done, given the interview situation. She held up her arms, asking Aubrey to pick her up.

Aubrey glanced to Heath. "Is it alright? I don't want to presume or do anything you don't approve of."

That was the right thing to say. Heath smiled. And frankly, the man looked like heaven when he smiled. "Go ahead."

Aubrey turned back to Eugenie and lifted the girl into his lap. She seemed instantly smitten with him. Or maybe just smitten with his hair. Once she was high enough, she reached and touched the hair just above Aubrey's ear, almost like she had to make certain it was real.

"Yes, I'm a ginger," he told her, unable to wipe the smile from his face. "I hope you can forgive me for that."

Eugenie just giggled shyly, then slumped against Aubrey's arm, half burying her face against him.

"Well then," Heath said. "It would appear that Eugenie has made her choice. You're hired, Mr. Kelly."

Joy bloomed in Aubrey, and with it, a huge amount of relief. "Fantastic," he said, still smiling at his new charge. "When would you like me to move in?"

When the answer didn't come right away, Aubrey shifted to check with Heath.

Heath's smile was gone.

Aubrey's heart sank.

"I'm…I'm afraid it's not a live-in situation," Heath said, looking worried to the point of panic. "I thought that was made clear."

Aubrey winced. "I'm sorry, I thought Janice was going to make certain I had a live-in situation. It's just that I don't really have a place to live at the moment, and I can't really afford anywhere in London, with rents being what they are these days. I'm sorry, sweetheart," he said to Eugenie.

Eugenie must have figured out that something wasn't right with the grown-ups. Her shy smile had gone, and she looked as though she could burst into tears at any second.

"I'll talk to Janice and let her know you need someone with their own place," Aubrey went on, having trouble keeping the disappointment out of his voice. "I'm sure she can—"

"I suppose we could make it work," Heath blurted. The panicked look he wore seemed worse instead of better. "This is a big house with plenty of unused rooms. We'll work something out. You could stay here on a trial basis, and if it's too uncomfortable, we'll decide on something else."

Aubrey blinked in surprise. "Really? You're willing to take a chance on me?"

Heath held perfectly still for a moment. Pink splashes painted his handsome face. It occurred to Aubrey that he wouldn't mind living under the same roof with someone who was so suave and in charge one moment, and so vulnerable and emotional the next. Given the little Aubrey knew about the man from the fifteen minutes they'd been talking, especially the bit about the divorce, he wondered if Heath really needed a friend and minder the same way his daughter did.

"We'll give it a try," he said at last, clearing his throat and looking as though he was trying to hold himself together. "If worse comes to worst…." He didn't finish the sentence, he just looked from Aubrey to Eugenie then back again. "We'll give it a try."

"Fantastic," Aubrey said, smiling. "I won't let you down."

He definitely wouldn't. Because even though the job was as Eugenie's nanny, Aubrey couldn't shake the feeling that Heath needed him, too.

THREE

WHAT HAD HE BEEN THINKING?

Those words ran through Heath's mind several times in the next two days, as he converted one of the second-floor guestrooms into a proper bedroom for Aubrey. That involved ordering new linens and curtains that didn't look like they'd been purchased when the house had been constructed in the 18th century, and sending his assistant, Sara, to pick them up and deliver them to the house. He also ordered a new wardrobe for the room and considered a new and bigger bed.

The whole time, he told himself that he was simply completing a task he should have done ages ago, and that it did not give him a little zip of joy to think about ensconcing handsome, clever, engaging Aubrey Kelly in his house. He may have even caught himself thinking that he wouldn't need to purchase lightbulbs for the room, because Aubrey's smile lit everything up around him.

What had he bloody well been thinking?

Gerry was the one who actually asked that question on the morning when Aubrey had said he would arrive with all his belongings.

"I didn't think you liked strangers in your personal

space," he said over the phone, as Heath paced the length of the hallway, Eugenie in one arm, his mobile held up to his ear with the other.

"I don't," Heath said, bouncing Eugenie slightly, like he had when she was an infant, as if that would avoid the meltdown she seemed inches away from having.

"I thought the nanny job was just a daytime thing and that you like to take care of Eugenie yourself at night and on the weekends," Gerry went on.

"I do," Heath insisted.

"So what happened to change that?"

Heath sighed and would have rubbed a hand over his face, if he'd had one to spare. What had happened? The interview had been going so well. He'd been taken aback by the fact that Aubrey was male, but then mostly embarrassed that he hadn't looked closely enough at his CV or letters of recommendation to see that. On paper, Aubrey was a gem, and Heath was certain that, in no time, he would count himself lucky to have found the man.

But that was the problem. Aubrey Kelly was a gem. There was something about the man that was comfortable and charming. His entire bearing was electric. Being around him had made Heath feel as though there was actually joy in the world after all. Eugenie had taken to Aubrey instantly, and in Heath's limited experience of children so far, they were astute judges of character. His daughter's excitement over the new arrival in her life alone was enough to convince him to hire Aubrey on the spot.

But if he were honest with himself, it was Aubrey's dancing, green eyes and his shockingly ginger hair that had grabbed his attention. It was the man's fit body and the graceful way he moved. It was his high cheekbones and the dusting of freckles across his cheeks and the curve of his lips.

Bloody hell. It was all The Brotherhood's fault. If he hadn't gone to the Chameleon Club the other day and soaked in that comfortable, accepting atmosphere, he never would have remembered the follies of his university days. He wouldn't have even considered being attracted to a man again.

That was it, though. He *was* attracted to Aubrey, and in a moment of desperation, thanks to the instant connection he'd seen between Aubrey and Eugenie, he'd done something wildly out of character. And now he had a stranger moving into his house.

"Heath? Heath, are you still there?"

Gerry's question made Heath realize that he'd come to a stop in the middle of the hall and was staring at nothing as his heart thumped in his chest. He was a massive fool, and if he didn't pull himself together, the world would know it.

"Sorry. Eugenie needed my attention for a moment," he lied. Although Genie was wriggling and squirming to get down. He put her down, then followed her when she ran into her playroom at the back of the house.

Gerry laughed. "Sure. Blame your daughter so that you don't have to answer my question."

"He couldn't take the job unless I gave him a place to live," Heath blurted. "And he was so good with Eugenie that I couldn't let him slip away."

"He's hot, isn't he," Gerry asked, a smirk in his voice.

Heath let out a breath and pinched the bridge of his nose. "That is neither here nor there."

"Yeah, he's hot," Gerry laughed.

"The last thing I need right now, with the ink not even dry on my divorce papers," Heath said, pacing the playroom a little as Eugenie dove onto her mountain of stuffed animals—most of them purchased by his mother, "is to get involved with anyone. Especially a man. The press would eat that up. Besides, we have the series to deal with first and—"

Before he could finish inventing a list of excuses as to why he had no interest in Aubrey Kelly beyond the care the man would take of his daughter, the doorbell rang. With it, Heath's breath caught and his insides tensed.

What the actual fuck was he thinking?

"I'll call you back, Gerry," he said, pulling his phone away from his face.

Heath heard Gerry's sardonic, "Sure, you will," before he tapped to end the call.

He shook his head and shoved his phone into his back pocket as he started for the hall. He spared a quick look for Eugenie, but figured as long as he kept the playroom in sight and within earshot as he answered the door, she would be alright.

He, however, might not be alright.

The moment he opened the door to find Aubrey standing on the porch, a massive duffle over one shoulder and two large boxes stacked next to him, Aubrey burst into a wide smile. And Heath's insides felt like they might burst with it.

"Good morning, sir," Aubrey greeted him with just enough cheek to send a wave of heat up Heath's neck to his face. "Should I come in through the servants' entrance, or will you permit me to enter through the front door?"

Heath was very much afraid that the look he gave Aubrey would make it seem like he had indigestion, when in fact he was simply trying not to smile at the joke. Trying and failing.

"Let me help with your things," he said instead, stepping out to lift one of the boxes as Aubrey stepped into the house.

The box was heavy, but Heath lifted it without too much difficulty. He didn't think that was anything exceptional, but the look of semi-adoration that Aubrey gave him as he brought it into the house was in danger of causing semi-something else.

"You don't have to help with those," Aubrey said as he shrugged the duffle off his shoulder and dashed out to bring in the other box. "It's all my stuff, and therefore not your responsibility."

"It's no problem," Heath insisted, shutting the door once Aubrey had himself and his belongings inside.

There was something significant about shutting the door on the outside world and creating a private space in his home that had Aubrey as a part of it. Heath tried to ignore the way his heart pounded over the mad decision he'd made, but he couldn't.

"I've put aside a bedroom for you on the second floor," he said, starting down the hall. "Let me just fetch Eugenie and we'll show you.

"Sounds good to me," Aubrey said.

Heath tried not to think about how much he liked the hint of a Cornish accent in Aubrey's tenor voice—like he was some sort of naughty pirate trying to hide his identity—or how rich and friendly the sound was.

Eugenie didn't want to come away from her stuffies at first, but as soon as Heath told her that her new nanny had arrived, she bolted from the playroom and raced down the hall to greet him. Aubrey had his duffle over his shoulder again and one of the boxes in his arms, but that didn't stop Eugenie from crashing into one of his legs and hugging him.

Fortunately, Aubrey laughed instead of shouting and dropping things, like Heath would have done. "Well, hello, princess," he said with a smile. "I guess you do remember me after all. Have you come to help me move in?"

Eugenie grinned up at him and nodded, still just a little bit shy, even though she clearly adored Aubrey.

"I hope your room has everything you need," Heath said, still feeling like he'd done something completely barmy as he picked up the other box and started carrying it up the stairs, Aubrey and Eugenie behind him. "If you think it needs anything, just let me know."

"I'm sure it'll be fine," Aubrey said, smiling down at Eugenie. "It doesn't take much for me to be happy."

Heath nodded as he turned the corner on the first floor

and started down the hall to the stairs leading up to the second floor.

"That's my room just there," he said, nodding to the room at the front of the house, just at the base of the stairs.

A second later, he cursed himself for pointing it out. It wasn't like Aubrey would need to know where he laid his head at night or anything.

"Duly noted," Aubrey said, then followed Heath up to the second floor.

Heath cleared his throat and fought down his embarrassment. "Eugenie's room is this one right at the top of the stairs. I still sometimes keep her door and my door open at night so I can hear everything going on inside. It's better than any of those baby monitor things."

"Makes sense," Aubrey said, smiling down at Eugenie over the top of his box.

"And I've put you on this floor so that you can be close to her too, in case she needs anything at night and I'm not there," Heath went on, taking Aubrey down the hall to the room directly above his bedroom.

"So it looks like I'm topping you, then," Aubrey said as they entered the room.

Heath nearly dropped the box he carried on his foot. He barely made it over to the bed to let it spill out of his arms there.

"I'm sorry, I'm sorry," Aubrey apologized with a laugh. "It was a badly timed joke. I take it back."

Heath was so beyond any ability to speak that he just cleared his throat and moved to scoop Eugenie into his arms, like a shield, as Aubrey dumped his things onto the bed. "The other advantage of this room," he said, mortified that his voice came out all gruff and grumbly, "is that it has an en suite. Gemma had that done four years ago, just after we were married. She insisted it would be useful for guests, but really, she used this room herself when she was having a snit, which was most of the time for the past few years."

Aubrey sobered in a hurry. So much so that Heath was afraid he'd shocked or upset the man.

"Sorry," Aubrey said, his face pinching awkwardly. Heath couldn't tell if he was sorry for Gemma or still sorry that he'd made a joke.

"Don't worry about it," he said, still looking at Eugenie. He couldn't keep using his daughter to hide, though, so he forced himself to face Aubrey like a man. "We'll just leave you to settle in," he said, immediately backing down on his determination to face Aubrey and his impulses by fleeing the room.

"Thanks for this," Aubrey called after him. "I know it wasn't what you were expecting, but I'm genuinely grateful."

"It's no problem," Heath called from the top of the stairs.

He hurried down as fast as he could, finally breathing once there was some space between him and Aubrey.

"Daddy, I want to play with Nanny," Eugenie protested, trying to wriggle away from him again.

"Yes, I know, sweetheart," Heath said as his phone began to ring and vibrate in his back pocket. "But we have to give Nanny Aubrey some time to unpack and settle in."

Eugenie whined at that and continued to squirm. Heath reached for his phone and saw that it was Gerry again. He frowned and huffed, but Gerry was as likely to be calling about work as he was about anything else, so Heath had to answer.

"This had better be about work," he said, heading into his bedroom with Eugenie instead of all the way downstairs. He could hear Aubrey shuffling and bumping around above him, which brought images to his head that he didn't need at that moment.

"It is about work," Gerry said. There was a smile in his brief pause before he said, "But before that, was that the hot, new nanny arriving earlier? Is that why I was summarily dismissed?"

Heath let out a heavy breath, not least of which was because the moment he sat on his bed, Eugenie escaped from his grasp, darted into the hall, and raced up the stairs to be with Aubrey again.

"He has arrived," Heath said, as though announcing the arrival of the king.

Gerry laughed. "And?"

Above him, Heath heard Aubrey's muffled voice say, "Hello, princess. Have you come to help me unpack?"

Despite his annoyance and discomfort over so many things, part of Heath loosened and relaxed. Eugenie would be fine. That was the only thing that mattered.

"And he is hot," he grumbled to Gerry, then quickly added, "There. Are you satisfied?"

Gerry laughed louder. "Yes. Very. And if you play your cards right, you will be too."

Heath stared flatly at the hallway in front of him. "I'm not interested in dating, Gerry, and I haven't been interested in men in years."

"Mm-hmm." Gerry's answer infuriated him. At least the man had the decency to move on with, "I've just heard back from Bryce Films. They're interested in hearing our proposal for *After the War*, but they won't be able to meet with us in person until next month."

Something in Heath's soul seemed to fall into place as he talked to Gerry about work while listening to Aubrey and Eugenie thump around in the room above him. He would have thought that hearing other noises in the house, especially knowing who was making those noises, would be a major distraction. Instead, the indistinct sound of Aubrey and Eugenie talking to each other and making friends was a signal that all was well, that his daughter was taken care of, and that he could focus on business.

Gerry had a lot to say, and Heath had opinions on all of it. As exciting as it was to think that Hollywood was interested in their decidedly niche project, Heath was loath to jump at the first offer that came their way. There were other studios interested in partnering with Storm Productions to make *After the War* a reality, and it was essential that they got into bed with the right company.

Of course, getting into bed with anyone was not the imagery Heath needed, considering what was going on in his house. He still thought he was half-mad to let Aubrey move in. As soon as he finished talking business with Gerry, he headed back upstairs so that he could have a discussion with Aubrey about house rules and how they would all deport themselves.

That intention, and every other intention he could have had, was immediately blown out of the water when he saw the state Aubrey's room was in after only a few moments. True, Aubrey was only just moving in, but there were clothes everywhere, wrinkled and bunched instead of folded and neat, a pile of books on the dresser had already toppled over, and one of the potted ferns that Heath had set in the window well had been knocked over, and dirt spilled everywhere.

"I've only been gone ten minutes," he blurted before he could stop himself.

Aubrey snapped back from where he'd been hanging things in the wardrobe. Heath was certain he would have said something to defend himself, but from the pile of clothing on the bed, Eugenie said, "Daddy, look!"

Heath did look, and to his horror, his daughter held up a short strip of condoms in rainbow-covered wrappers.

"Sh—" Aubrey leapt toward Eugenie. "Those aren't for playing with, princess," he said, carefully taking the condoms away from her. "How did you find those anyhow?" He snatched up a plain, black toiletries case, stuffed the condoms back in, and zipped it closed.

Heath was too stunned to react. To any of it. He would be a hypocrite for holding the condoms against Aubrey, because Eugenie had found his own supply before, too. He was far more taken aback by the sheer volume of mess that Aubrey had managed to create in such a short time.

"I will understand entirely if you've just changed your mind about hiring me," Aubrey said with embarrassed seriousness.

The last thing Heath wanted was to banish Aubrey from his life, though that came as a surprise to him.

He shook himself and moved to the bed in an attempt to pick up Eugenie. "She doesn't know what they are, she was probably just drawn in by the rainbows," he said. Eugenie evaded his reach, clamoring over the pile of clothes in what looked like an attempt to get Aubrey to defend her.

"I'm so, so sorry about that," Aubrey said, holding the toiletry bag behind his back, since Eugenie had spotted it.

"How is it possible for you to have made such a mess so quickly?" Heath asked, looking around at the room. "Do you even know how to fold clothes?"

"Of course, I do!" Aubrey answered. He sidestepped to put the toiletry bag on top of the wardrobe, then moved to the bed to pick a pre-meltdown Eugenie up. "It's just that a lot of this needs washing."

Heath's brow shot up. "You brought your dirty laundry to me?"

Aubrey's mouth twitched into a grin. "You were bound to discover it all anyhow, if you did a background check on me."

Heath blinked. Then he got the joke. His heart melted a little. People generally didn't joke with him, but Aubrey had teased him multiple times since entering his house. He should not like that so much. He should not be straining against his trousers just because a cheeky red-head was trying to make him smile.

"I did perform a background check on you," he said with exaggerated grimness.

Aubrey lost his grin. He swallowed, then said, "And?"

Heath met his gaze and held it, fighting with everything he had not to smile. He'd had Sara run a brief, criminal background check, and she'd said there was nothing to report, but he hadn't pored over police records or anything himself. Aubrey didn't know that, though. So Heath let the silence drag on and on, until a flush appeared on Aubrey's handsome face and his eyes grew wide with anticipation.

Finally, he said, "And the washing machine is in the kitchen. The washing pods are in the cupboard beside the drier."

Aubrey gulped like he was swallowing a laugh, then said, "Yes, sir." His emerald eyes danced with humor.

The whole exchange made Heath deeply regret allowing Aubrey to move into his house…because he felt he was very much in danger of having to rethink everything he thought he knew about himself.

Still telling himself he was merely playing along with a joke, he stood taller and nodded at Aubrey. "I apologize for the short notice, but I have to go to the office."

"I don't mind," Aubrey said with a smile. "It'll give Eugenie and me a chance to get to know each other better. She can help me unpack, and maybe find all my other unmentionable belongings." Heath's face heated, and Aubrey rushed to add, "I'm just joking again. I can assure you, I keep my fleshlight in a locked box."

He was still joking, but the idea of Aubrey indulging in a little "self-care" had Heath flushing even hotter. He cleared his throat and said, "When I return, I expect this room to be spotlessly tidy."

"Yes, sir," Aubrey said, practically quivering, he was trying so hard not to laugh. Heath thought it was entirely likely that he was holding back from asking if he'd be spanked if his room wasn't tidy.

Or maybe those were Heath's own thoughts.

The joke was over. He couldn't go on like that. Aubrey was his employee now, and he had a responsibility to both him and to Eugenie. It would be unfair of him to do anything that got in the way of his daughter's care.

"Will you be alright looking out for Eugenie as you get settled?" he asked in a much more reasonable tone. "I could call my mother to take her for the afternoon."

"No, we'll be fine," Aubrey said, completely relaxed again. "Won't we, princess?"

"Yes!" Eugenie declared.

The moment was broken. Heath nodded, said goodbye, and retreated into the hall and down the stairs before he could say or do anything else that would embarrass the shit out of him. But as he headed out to go into work, the same words kept echoing over and over in his head: what had he done?

FOUR

AFTER TWO WEEKS of living under Heath's roof, Aubrey had no idea how he was still employed.

"Could you please remember to put the milk back when you take it out for tea?" Heath asked him in a strained voice at breakfast on a rainy Monday. He plucked the carton from the counter and put it back into the fridge with an irritated sigh.

Even though Aubrey wasn't done with it yet.

"I'll remember next time," he said with a tight smile as he settled Eugenie into her booster seat at the table.

"And why is there pancake batter all over my counter when you haven't even made the pancakes yet?" Heath asked on, rubbing his forehead.

Aubrey bit his lip to stop himself from making some sort of clever retort. In the last two weeks, he'd discovered that Heath didn't always respond well to his attempts to make every awkward situation better with humor.

And there had been a lot of awkward situations.

As it turned out, living with a man who hadn't been expecting anyone to live with him any time soon was more of a challenge than Aubrey had anticipated. In his last two placements, he'd had suites to himself that were separate from the families whose kids he'd been caring for. That had meant he'd been able to listen to his music or stay up late or walk from the bathroom to the bedroom naked.

In Heath's house, all he had was a room and a bathroom, right in the middle of the family space. And Heath's bedroom was immediately below his. Which meant within shouting distance. Shouting had happened on his second night there, when he'd turned up the volume of his favorite Ed Sheeran song so he could dance along…at ten o'clock at night. That had earned him a shout from below, followed by a few calmer, but much more embarrassing words at the breakfast table the next day.

Then there was the confusion about where his mail should be sent. Heath had seemed surprised when he'd opened his mail to find a few catalogs of a slightly, but not very, delicate nature staring back at him. They hadn't completely figured out what Aubrey should do with his free time, since the only space in the house was communal space, which meant they were all on top of each other when Heath was at home.

And despite what Aubrey gathered was Heath's immense wealth, not to mention his occupation, the man only had one television in the house. Two weeks, and they'd already argued over whether to watch *The Chase* or *Pointless* in the evenings. Watching *Pointless* every weekday was a hill Aubrey would die on, because Alexander Armstrong was a dish.

But that was all nothing to the time Aubrey had bounded down the stairs, bright and early, on a Saturday, intending to go out for a run, only to nearly slam into Heath coming out of his bedroom wearing nothing but a towel. The man was built like a god, with a broad chest, slim waist, and plenty of hair on his chest that Aubrey wanted to grab hold of and bury his face in. It had not helped matters at all that he'd been wearing only a loose-fitting tank-top and running shorts that hid very little.

At least that encounter had answered Aubrey's suspicions about Heath's sexuality. No one could hide the truth when they ogled like that.

"Please clean this mess up before I get home," Heath sighed, stepping away from the kitchen counter with an irritated sigh.

Aubrey sent him a wary look once he had Eugenie safe in her chair. "Are you sure you're feeling alright?" he asked as he went to the hob to test whether the griddle was hot enough yet.

"I'm fine," Heath snapped distractedly, grabbing his suit coat from the back of his chair. "Just a little tickle in my throat is all. It'll pass."

The way he frowned and rubbed his throat as he spoke told Aubrey that it was not just a little tickle, and it would not pass. It wasn't really his place to say anything, though. He was Eugenie's nanny, not Heath's. If Heath thought he was well enough to work, then who was he to contradict him?

"Take care," he called after Heath all the same, waving at his back as he retreated down the hall. Once the back door shut, Aubrey turned to Eugenie and said, "I think we should make a quick trip out for throat lozenges and cough syrup after pancakes, just in case."

"Pancakes!" Eugenie shouted with glee, taking what she wanted from his statement.

They had their pancakes with blueberries—a specialty of Aubrey's—then Aubrey made certain that he cleaned the kitchen to a state of pristine perfection as Eugenie played with crayons at the table. For good measure, Aubrey tidied up the living room and Eugenie's playroom as well, and even vacuumed Heath's study, though he felt like an intruder every time he so much as looked at it. Just because he'd made it past the Dreaded Hallway Encounter of Near Nakedness last week didn't mean he was in the clear entirely. He needed to make absolutely certain he earned his keep.

Because, frankly, he loved his new job. And he was damn good at it. Eugenie was a darling, and they'd bonded nearly at once. He was comfortable in the overly fine Mayfair house, despite feeling like an impostor. For once in his life, he felt like he was where he was meant to be, doing the things he was best at. And he still harbored hope deep within him that he and Heath could at least become friends.

He didn't dare think about anything more than that, even if his cock had woken him several times over the last few days, begging him to indulge in a few inappropriate nanny and lord of the manor fantasies.

Once the house was tidied, Aubrey took Eugenie out for a walk to the nearest chemist's shop to pick up everything he anticipated Heath would need. And, of course, a few sweeties for Eugenie. And for him. Because he was the best nanny in the world, after all.

Those feelings took a dent when he and Eugenie decided to stroll through Hyde Park before heading home, and Eugenie tripped while chasing after a duck. Aubrey's head had been turned for less than three seconds as he'd checked out a staggeringly fit man with his shirt unbuttoned nearly all the way who had to be Italian. Eugenie had bolted, the duck had taken flight, and he'd ended up with one sobbing, grass-stained little girl whom he'd scooped up and carried home while pushing her stroller with his free hand.

Unloading the stroller once they got home resulted in half-eaten snacks, scuffed shoes, and their purchases from the chemist's spread all over the foyer. Since Eugenie had recovered by then and was adamant about playing with her zoo, as she called the obscene number of stuffed animals her grandmama had given her, Aubrey ended up abandoning everything from their walk to follow her.

He managed to change her out of her stained clothes and

into something clean, but by the time the back door opened and a decidedly ill-looking Heath walked into the playroom just as lunch was served, he hadn't had a chance to deal with the dirty clothes.

"What in God's name is all of this?" Heath demanded hoarsely. His color was high, but Aubrey suspected it wasn't because he was angry.

He leapt up from where he had settled Aubrey at her child-sized table with a jelly sandwich he'd cut into bite-size pieces and rushed to Heath.

"You realize you aren't supposed to come home until the end of the workday," he said, moving straight into placing the back of his hand on Heath's forehead to test for a fever. "It's not fair not to give me time to turn the pumpkin into a carriage and the mice into footmen before you return."

Heath sighed in irritation. He was burning up. The way he swallowed gingerly told Aubrey everything he needed to know about how he was feeling, so he didn't ask.

"Come along with you," he said, spinning Heath and pushing him out the door. "Go upstairs and change into something comfortable. Stay in bed if you need to, and I'll bring you up some soup and an ice lolly for your throat."

"I'm fine," Heath lied, his shoulders dropping. "I just came home for lunch. I'm going back to work after."

"No, you are not," Aubrey insisted, turning him once they reached the stairs and giving the small of his back a push to get him to walk up. "In the two weeks I've known you, you haven't once come home for lunch. You're ill, Heath, admit it."

Heath was most definitely ill, because instead of answering back or protesting and attempting to go about his business, he merely held up his middle finger to Aubrey without looking at him and continued up the stairs to his bedroom.

The gesture was so unlike the serious, stodgy Heath that

Aubrey had come to know in the past fortnight that Aubrey snorted into laughter. He shouldn't have been happy. It was utterly wrong of him to be so giddy when his employer was ill and could potentially bring him and Eugenie down with him.

On the other hand, it was as if his moment to shine had come and he was about to get exactly the opportunity to knock Heath's socks off with his ability to care that he'd hoped would save his position.

"Where is Daddy?" Eugenie asked as Aubrey headed back into the playroom to clean up everything he'd let slide earlier.

"He went upstairs to bed, princess," he said, pausing to rest a hand on Eugenie's head for a moment. "I think he's caught a cold."

"I can make it better," she said, all innocent smiles and hope.

"I'm sure you can, but we have to be careful not to catch it."

Aubrey was serious about that. As Eugenie finished her lunch, he raced around, cleaning surfaces and checking to make certain they had enough soup, tea, and ice lollies to last Heath through the first phase of his cold. He went so far as to set up the living room so that the cushions were plumped, a blanket was at the ready for tucking Heath in, the remote was within reach of Heath's spot, and all the medicines they'd bought on their trip out were at the ready, but out of Eugenie's reach.

In the middle of doing all that, Aubrey's phone rang.

"Who could be calling now?" he asked Eugenie—who had abandoned her lunch in favor of following Aubrey around and "helping".

He wasn't surprised when he pulled his phone from his back pocket and saw the word "Mum" on the screen.

"Hello, Mum," he answered the call, still moving around

the living room to make sure it was ready for Heath...if he hadn't already fallen asleep in his room.

Without so much as greeting him, his mother launched into, "Do you know who your new employer is?"

"Yes, Mum," Aubrey laughed. "He's Heath Manfred." He winked at Eugenie as she moved one of the pillows he'd just placed on the sofa to the other end.

"Yes, but do you know who Heath Manfred is?" his mother asked.

"Of course I do," Aubrey said, putting the pillow back as soon as Eugenie had abandoned it to dash across the hall to her playroom. "He's my employer."

His mother made a scoffing sound. "Since you're going to be like that, I'm just going to tell you what I've found out."

Aubrey craned his neck to look into the playroom so he could be certain Eugenie was alright. "Thank you, Mum. I'd prefer it that way."

"It isn't so much who *he* is," his mother went on in her best gossiping tone as Eugenie returned to the room with her arms full of stuffed animals, "it's who he was married to." As Eugenie proceeded to arrange stuffies on the sofa, his mother said, "Heath was married to Gemma Stone. You know, that model who always seems to be photographed while she's bending over to tie her shoes, even though she's wearing some designer monstrosity?"

Aubrey smirked. He knew exactly what his mother meant. Heath's ex actually liked it when paparazzi snapped pics down the front of her blouse. Aubrey had always figured she had some sort of a backroom deal with a lacy bra company to expose their products, as it were.

"I know he was married to Gemma Stone, yes," Aubrey said as he took Eugenie's hand and headed to the kitchen to make some tea.

"Yes, well, did you know that she left him for that funny, foreign actor fellow?" his mother went on.

Aubrey had, indeed, studied up on all the dirt that had been spread around about Heath, thanks to the divorce. He'd been more interested in trying to figure out if Heath had ever been romantically linked to a man, though. For purely professional purposes, of course.

"Honestly, Mum, I don't give a rip about those sorts of things," he said, glancing down at Eugenie as she headed straight for the cupboard where snacks were kept. If she hadn't've been there, he'd've used a much stronger word than "rip".

"Well," his mother said, "I just thought you should know that there is, apparently, trouble in paradise. Gemma has been spotted at several nightclubs and private parties *alone*."

Aubrey frowned, feeling far too protective of Heath for only knowing the man two weeks. But it also wasn't really his business. His main concern in that moment was filling the kettle and stopping Eugenie from tearing into the fruit snacks.

"As far as I understand it, divorced women are allowed to party these days," Aubrey said, steering Eugenie away from the snacks and over to where her crayons were still scattered over the table. He was glad Heath hadn't seen that. "They might not have been allowed to in your day," he went on.

"Ha, ha," his mother cut him off sarcastically before he could finish the sentence. "No, dear," she went on. "I'm not telling you this because it's idle gossip. I'm telling you because women like Gemma Stone know where their bread is buttered. If she's broken up with this new flame, there's a chance she'll show up on your doorstep again. You are her daughter's nanny, after all."

Aubrey froze in the middle of pulling mugs down from the shelf. He hadn't thought about that. He wondered if Heath had some sort of plan in place in case Gemma decided to try to walk back into his life. He needed to find out what the custody agreement between them was, and fast.

But not that fast. As his mother went on with, "I just

thought you should know," Heath appeared in the kitchen doorway. He was dressed in sweats and sock feet, and his face was pinched into a look of absolute misery.

"Mum, I've got to go," he said quickly. "I love you and I'll talk to you later."

He barely heard her "Goodbye, love," as he ended the call and put his phone on the counter.

"How bad is your throat?" he asked Heath, heading to the fridge. "We went out and bought lozenges and cold medicine today, but one of these might help, too."

It was a lucky thing that they already had ice lollies in the freezer for Eugenie. Aubrey grabbed one, opened it, and handed it straight over to Heath. He then turned Heath by his shoulders and marched him down the hall to the living room.

"You're not to do anything or worry about anything for the next few days, until this gets better," he said. "Eat your ice lolly, and suck on one of these."

As Heath sat, stunned, on the pillow and stuffed animal laden sofa, Aubrey took the package of lozenges from the top of the shelf where he'd stored the medicines and handed them over.

"I'm making tea," he continued, "which, hopefully, will help. I'll get you some paracetamol, too, and there's the remote." He pointed to the side of the sofa. "Let me know if there's anything else you need while you're going through the worst of it. Eugenie will probably want to nurse you through, but if you're worried she'll catch it, I'll do my best to keep her occupied while you sleep. Any questions?"

Heath just stared at him as if he'd grown another head. He then blinked and said, "I was just coming downstairs to get a glass of water and ask if we have any paracetamol."

Aubrey grinned broadly, then pulled a few tissues from the box he'd moved to the table beside the sofa. He used them to wipe Heath's hand where the ice lolly had melted, then straightened.

"Aren't you lucky that you hired me and let me move in?" he asked. Then, for good measure, he winked.

Heath blinked in return, but more like a squirrel in headlights than a man who was flirting with his capable and attractive nanny.

Aubrey eased up a little with a laugh. "Don't worry about a thing, Heath," he said, leaning in to grab a corner of the blanket so he could spread it over Heath's legs. "Just focus on getting through this cold. With any luck, it'll be a light one. I've got everything else taken care of."

"Thank you," Heath said, starting to come out of his shock. He licked at the drips on his hand, then gingerly sucked the tip of his ice lolly.

Aubrey had to turn away, because the images that came to his head were not of Heath sucking an ice lolly.

"I'll fetch the paracetamol and be right back," he said as he hurried out of the room.

It was probably wrong of him to feel so happy with Heath obviously on the downward spiral of a virus, but for the first time since coming to work for the man, Aubrey felt like he was finally in a position where he could prove to Heath that he'd made the right decision and that he was an asset to his life.

FIVE

HEATH HATED BEING SICK. Hated it with a passion. There was nothing worse than being physically and mentally unable to function, especially when he knew it was a microscopic organism that had taken him down. He wasn't sure which was worse, the sore throat and headache phase of a cold or the congestion and volcano of snot phase that he ended up in the day after he'd come home from work early.

He'd had no intention of leaving the office, particularly not in the middle of such a tricky time for *After the War*. There was a lot of negotiating still to be done, and he was the point person for the whole thing. But the moment Sara had seen him wincing as he swallowed and rubbing his neck now and then to check if his lymph nodes were swollen, she had ever so kindly, in her iron fist in a velvet glove sort of way, insisted that he go home.

And that was where Aubrey had taken over.

"It feels like your fever has gone down a bit," Aubrey said, as he crouched beside the sofa, resting the back of his hand on Heath's forehead. "I could get the thermometer if you'd like to know for sure." He paused, grinned in that impish way he had that Heath exhausted himself trying to ignore, then added, "But you won't like where I stick it to take your temperature."

"Or maybe I will," he mumbled when Aubrey twisted away to check on Eugenie as she dropped one of her toys at the other side of the room.

Aubrey turned back to him so fast that Heath was deeply worried he's spoken that thought louder than he'd intended to. He was ill, and that meant his defenses were down and he wasn't thinking straight. He should be able to catch thoughts like that and stop them from running away from him.

"How about some tea?" Aubrey asked as he stood. He didn't say anything or tease Heath, but the way he was trying not to smile and the sparkle in his emerald eyes was a dead giveaway that he'd heard Heath after all.

"Tea would be lovely," Heath muttered, wriggling a bit to settle in his blanket nest.

Aubrey leaned over him, like a good nanny would, and tucked him in. He even brushed his fingers through Heath's hair, though that might have been an accident.

Heath tried to breathe in through his nose—which was flat impossible—hoping to catch Aubrey's clean, masculine scent. He didn't know why he was so eager and pitiful when it came to grasping onto sensual markers of Aubrey like that. He'd never been such a ninny with Gemma, or any of the other women he'd dated. Or the men he'd fooled around with at uni either. It had to be the cold germs.

"Watch Eugenie for me," Aubrey said with a bright smile as he headed for the door. Eugenie turned to him at the sound of her name, so Aubrey added, "Take care of your daddy for me while I make tea, princess."

Aubrey left, and Eugenie immediately got up from the council of toys she'd set up around her to scramble over to the sofa. She knelt in front of Heath and patted his head lightly in imitation of what she must have seen Aubrey do.

"Daddy's sick," she said with a small pout.

"Yes, I am, darling," Heath said, reaching out from under the fuzzy blanket Aubrey had covered him with. "But Nanny Aubrey is taking good care of me."

Eugenie smiled, and Heath smiled in response. In response to what, he wasn't quite certain. Eugenie was precious, of course, but it was Aubrey and the care that the man had shown him in the last twenty-four hours that had Heath feeling like suffering through a cold might not be the very worst thing in the world after all.

Aubrey's behavior toward him since he'd come home went against every stereotype Heath had ingrained in him. Too many years of toxic social training had convinced him that men were not caring and nurturing. They were strong and took charge of things. They ignored petty things, like germs, to get the job done under any circumstances. Which was why he should be toughing it out in the office, loaded up with decongestants and paracetamol.

But he was happy where he was, cocooned in a fuzzy blanket, *Escape to the Country* playing on the telly, letting another man take care of him.

"Here you are," Aubrey said several minutes later—Heath wasn't certain how many, since he'd drifted off a bit when Eugenie returned to her toys. "Tea as promised."

Heath sent his sweet carer a wobbly smile and pushed himself to sit up so he could accept he mug when Aubrey handed it to him.

"You don't have to take care of me like this," he said in a thick, stuffy voice as Aubrey settled onto the sofa beside him with his own mug. "I wouldn't be offended if you took Eugenie out for the day to avoid my germs. I'm sure my mother would welcome you at her house."

Aubrey made a frightened sound and said, "Your mother terrifies me."

Heath chuckled and curled over his mug so he could

breathe in the steam a little. "She terrifies everyone. That's her job."

"There you go, then," Aubrey said with a nod. "I'll stay right here, because taking care of you is my job."

"It is not," Heath protested, making a face that was probably too much. Bloody hell, he hated the way being ill made him lose his dignity.

"Is so," Aubrey argued, shoving Heath's side.

Heath had moved to take a sip of his tea, and he was lucky the shove didn't cause him to spill any. He swatted weakly at Aubrey in retaliation anyhow.

Which was the wrong thing to do, because it made Aubrey laugh.

Aubrey's laughter did things to him that he didn't want to think about.

Except he did think about them, about how nice it would be if he could curl up in Aubrey's arms and let go until he felt stronger again. He thought about curling up in those arms once he was well again too, but those thoughts were even more terrifying.

God, he hated being sick! He had no resistance to anything when he had a cold.

"You really don't have to do any of this," he said after a few silent moments of sipping tea and watching the couple from Dorchester, who had another child on the way and needed a bigger house, tour the inevitable converted chapel in Hampshire that the presenter on the telly had taken them to. "I'm perfectly capable of caring for myself when I'm sick."

"Heath," Aubrey said with a flat look. "That's the nineth time since this morning that you've told me I don't have to do this. If I didn't want to be here taking care of you, I would have told you to sod off and gone about my business ages ago."

Heath managed to smile, even as his nose dripped from drinking the warm tea. "Thank you," he said as he set his mug on the table by the sofa and reached for a handful of tissues. "You've no idea what this means to me."

He blew his nose loudly and squelchily. It was embarrassing, really. His head and his heart were as mixed up as he'd ever known them to be, and even if he had been inclined to flirt with Aubrey, in the state he was in, he was the least sexy thing on the planet.

As he finished blowing his nose, Aubrey got up to fetch the small rubbish bin he'd brought in earlier for used tissues and made a show of trying to brush all of the ones Heath had just dropped on his blanket away using his elbow so he didn't touch them.

"You don't have to—"

"Ah-ah!" Aubrey cut him off, pointing a finger. "Stop telling me what I don't have to do." He finished clearing away the tissues, then sat by Heath's side again, maybe a little closer than before. "Just thank your lucky stars that I'm here."

"I do," Heath said. Admitting that filled him with shivers that had nothing to do with fever.

Aubrey smiled at him and patted his blanketed legs. "What did you do when you were sick before?" he asked. "I bet your wife didn't take care of you like this."

"She didn't," Heath said with a little more passion than he'd intended. He sighed, sagged back into his pillows, and said, "Gemma only took care of herself. I don't know why I didn't see that before I married her. She never really took care of Eugenie either."

Aubrey dragged his eyes away from the tele and smiled sympathetically at Heath. "I don't really know much about her. That whole world has never appealed to me."

"What, modeling or women?" Heath asked, immediately cursing himself for asking too intimate a question.

Aubrey burst into a broad smile. "Both," he said. "It was always men for me. When I was born, I came out of my mother and never looked back." He paused, his smile turning into a wicked grin. "How about you?"

Heath caught his breath—which was a far more noticeable gesture than he wanted it to be, considering how blocked his nose was. He supposed he'd known this moment would come eventually. Part of him had hoped he could avoid sharing such intimate details with Eugenie's nanny, particularly since those details could very definitely change everything.

Aubrey had been so kind and compassionate while caring for him, though. It didn't seem right to withhold things from the man. And after over two weeks of living together, Heath was reasonably certain Aubrey had already guessed the truth.

"I looked back," he said, carrying on with the metaphor. "But I also looked forward."

Aubrey arched one eyebrow. "And how does that work, exactly?"

Heath sighed. "I suppose I'm bi," he said, giving up his pride and the urge to keep his past a secret. He wriggled down into his blankets and pillows a little more, as if he could shield himself from whatever scorn Aubrey, and the world he moved in, would heap on him.

"You suppose?" Aubrey asked. If Heath wasn't mistaken, he had a glimmer of excitement in his eyes.

Heath pursed his lips, sniffled, reached for a tissue, and did everything else he could think of to stall before saying, "I noticed both the girls and the boys in school, but I didn't think much about it. I was more interested in my A-levels and making the cricket team to worry about dating." He paused, slipping into an introspective state that was somehow heightened by the germs pulsing through him, then continued with, "I suppose not dating before university was my way of avoiding the truth."

"You're very good at avoiding things," Aubrey said with a teasing grin.

Heath narrowed his eyes at him, then blew his nose with particular vigor. Aubrey chuckled, which did absolutely nothing to calm the buzz his confessions had created.

"I dated at university," he said. "Michelle Forester, and then Calvin Bruce. Although, honestly, I wouldn't call what I did with either of them dating so much as—"

"Bonking like bunnies to see how it felt?" Aubrey finished the sentence with a grin. He peeked at Eugenie, and Heath had the feeling, like he always had, that Aubrey would have used different words if Eugenie hadn't been there.

He sighed. "Yes, that's exactly what it was."

"And?" Aubrey prompted him with a sinful grin.

Heath glared at him and his teasing. "And I discovered I liked both."

"Top or bottom?" Aubrey asked, his eyes dancing ridiculously.

"Fuck you," Heath muttered before he could stop himself. Fortunately, Eugenie hadn't noticed.

"That answers my question," Aubrey laughed.

Heath would have pulled a hand out from under his blanket to show Aubrey his middle finger if Eugenie hadn't chosen that moment to glance over to the sofa to see what the grown-ups were laughing about.

"Would you like to watch cartoons, darling?" Heath asked, reaching for the remote instead.

"Peppa! Peppa!" Eugenie erupted with glee. Heath rarely let her watch so much telly, but it seemed like the perfect distraction so he could talk more freely with Aubrey.

"Let's see if she's on," he said, flipping through the channels.

By some miracle, Peppa was on, and within moments, Eugenie was focused on the telly so intently that Heath didn't think anything would draw her away from it.

Which was why he felt free enough to quietly say, "I joined an organization while at university, The Brotherhood, for queer men. And women, since the seventies. The man I was dating at the time, Reggie, was a member, and I thought that was going to be my life." He paused to blow his nose, surprised that Aubrey didn't interrupt. Once he was finished, he went on with, "Then I caught Reggie with someone else's cock down his throat, and that was the end of that. I have only dated women since. And then there was Gemma."

Aubrey's brow shot up. "You gave up the male gender entirely because one uni boyfriend cheated on you?"

Heath glowered at the implication of those words, but mostly at himself. He *had* given up men because of Reggie. That was how hurt he'd been. He'd decided that all men were just cruel and incapable of fidelity. And then Gemma had come along, and he hadn't thought he would ever have to worry about his wild youth again. At least, until she proved that women could be just as horrid as men.

Now Aubrey had swanned into his life, all joyful and ginger and caring. Who knew what sort of truth that might end up proving?

"It made sense at the time," he sighed, feeling like he needed a nap after his confession. "Everyone warned me that Gemma was only after my money and position, that she was more ambitious than she was in love. But did I listen to them?"

"Apparently not," Aubrey said.

And dammit, but he patted Heath's leg under the blanket and stroked him like he was trying to soothe away the monumental damage Gemma had caused. Heath did not need that sort of sweetness, what with the way his emotions were already in a complete mess.

"She was gorgeous," he sighed, watching cartoon pigs on the telly instead of looking at Aubrey as he spoke. "She was lively and funny as well. She insisted I accompany her to social events, where I ended up doing quite a bit of useful networking. I'm convinced that everything she taught me about networking is why I landed the position at Storm Productions that I have now."

"But then she ran off with another man and left you and Eugenie in the lurch," Aubrey said.

Hearing the truth stated so bluntly hurt.

"At least she gave up full custody of Eugenie," Heath sighed. He peeked at Eugenie, then lowered his voice as he went on with, "She didn't want to have her in the first place. The pregnancy was an accident. She…she wanted to terminate, but I talked her out of it."

A wealth of uncomfortable feelings followed that statement. Heath's life would have been so much worse without Eugenie, but his conscience still pricked him about whether he'd exerted too much pressure on Gemma and if he'd unintentionally bullied her into giving up her bodily autonomy.

Aubrey must have seen the conflict in his eyes. He rested his hand heavily on Heath's thigh and said, "It seems to me that a woman who would glibly leave her husband for another man wouldn't be the sort to have a baby unless she genuinely wanted to. If she genuinely hadn't wanted Eugenie, she would have gone behind your back to…you know."

Heath's heart stopped for a moment as the truth of that statement hit him. It was true. Gemma was exactly the sort who would have come home one night and announced that she was no longer pregnant in the same sentence as she announced she wanted to go to Greece for the weekend.

"Whenever we fought, she used to tell me that my insistence on having Eugenie ruined her career," Heath said.

"Oh, Heath, I'm sorry," Aubrey said, squeezing his thigh.

Heath felt awful, and it had nothing to do with the germs. It had taken him that long to understand just how viciously Gemma had manipulated him. Worse still, he'd fallen for it every time, caving in to whatever ridiculous and pricy demand had followed her insistence that Eugenie had been an impediment to her career.

"How about a nice bowl of homemade chicken soup?" Aubrey suggested, scooting to the end of the sofa, like he was going to stand. Of course, the move brought him closer to Heath as well. "Chicken soup makes everything better."

Heath's brow inched up. "Is that what you were doing in the kitchen all morning?" he asked. "Making chicken soup from scratch?"

Aubrey smiled. "I also cook," he said with false modesty. "It is yet another astounding talent I have."

Heath glanced up at him as he stood, a riot of emotions rolling through him. He should not set Aubrey up for more teasing. He should absolutely keep the leading thought that wanted to come out to himself. He should not give Aubrey the excuse to flirt with him.

"What other talents do you have?" he asked, losing his battle to rein himself in spectacularly.

Aubrey looked deliciously smug, cocked his hip to one side in an unusually fey gesture—Aubrey was definitely the masculine sort who most people wouldn't have pegged as gay—and said, "I think you've already worked out the answer to that, love."

He then turned to go, leaving Heath to stare at his shapely backside as he headed into the hall.

Heath let out a breath and sank into his blankets again. He was in serious trouble. Damn the virus that had robbed him of the walls he'd put up so he didn't have to deal with his feelings. He would have been perfectly happy to never fall in love, or lust, again after Gemma. Aubrey wasn't going to give him that option, though. The man was just too perfect, and Heath was deeply afraid that he would have to change everything he thought he knew about himself to adapt to it.

SIX

AUBREY WAS IN SERIOUS TROUBLE. It was nanny rule number one—don't fall in love with your boss.

Well, it was rule number two, after putting the child first in every situation, every day. But really, not falling for your charge's father was definitely a part of putting the child first, because children needed stability and continuity. And being sacked for inappropriate behavior with Daddy was a surefire way to upend a child's life.

And Aubrey was definitely falling for Heath.

"Everything changed last week, when he was sick," he explained to Ulrika and Lindsey, two of his nanny friends as they all took their kids on a walk through Hyde Park on a sunny, Thursday morning. "I don't know if it was the germs or if Heath was just blown away by having someone take care of him for a change, but we definitely turned a corner."

Ulrika and Lindsey hummed and nodded in sympathy as the three of them pushed their buggies along the gravel path. Eugenie didn't really need a buggy at her age—although she had fallen asleep in it, after running around, chasing after ducks, and playing with Ulrika's David, and Lindsey's twins, Daisy and Lawrence. Aubrey felt a certain sense of historical satisfaction as he pushed her along, though. As if he were part of the proud, Victorian tradition of nannies banding together to walk their little ones through the park while standing behind whichever one of them had a problem that needed solving.

"Not that anything more has happened," he told the other two, glancing to Lindsey on one side, then Ulrika on the other. "I would never cross that line."

"Never?" Ulrika asked, arching one eyebrow.

"No, never," Aubrey insisted.

"Not even if Heath made the first move?" Lindsey asked with a grin.

Aubrey let out a frustrated breath. "The thing is, I'm not sure if I would even know what the first move looked like with Heath. For all I know, he's been waving flashing neon signs at me for the past week, since going back to work, what with the kind smiles and abundance of thank yous I've been getting."

"So he's been flirting with you?" Ulrika asked, looking both shocked and delighted. She glanced across to Lindsey and said, "Mr. Everton always flirts with me. Sometimes when his wife is in the room." She let out a guilty laugh, then added, "To be fair, Mrs. Everton flirts with me too."

"And which one gets the prize?" Lindsey asked.

"We're talking about Aubrey right now, not me," Ulrika said with a coy smirk, blushing in a way that made Aubrey want to know more.

It was a sign of just how desperate his situation had made him that Aubrey didn't press for details of Ulrika's home life. "We will definitely circle back to that later," he said, giving Ulrika a frank stare. "But for now, the problem remains that I have a major crush on my employer, but I don't know if he's out as bi in any way. And even if he is, there are some lines that just cannot be crossed."

"He's at least a little bit out," Lindsey said. "When he

married Gemma Stone, it was all over the news and the tabloids. I remember seeing pictures of Heath with some guy in a pictorial spread of his and Gemma's past flames."

"That doesn't mean he's *officially* out," Ulrika argued.

"Well, Aubrey told us, so it can't be a complete secret," Lindsey pointed out.

Aubrey winced. "I probably shouldn't have said anything. But I trust the two of you with my life. Nanny's honor."

Lindsey and Ulrika laughed.

"What?" Aubrey asked with a smile. "It's a real thing. It's like, professional ethics. Nannies never disclose the things they learn about their employers."

"Unless someone offers them a million dollars to spill it," Ulrika said.

"Do James and Carly Everton know that?" Aubrey asked with a stern arch of one eyebrow.

Ulrika laughed. "I would never betray them," she said.

"And I would never do anything that would land Heath in hot water," Aubrey said with a nod.

"Because you're in love with him, not because you're Eugenie's nanny," Lindsey pointed out with a sly grin.

Aubrey sighed. "It's too early to be in love with him," he said. "But I fancy him to a truly embarrassing degree."

"And you can't tell if he fancies you in return?" Ulrika asked.

Aubrey shrugged. "Like I said, something changed when he was ill last week. I took care of him, and yes, I will admit that I was far more motivated to hover around him and see to his every need than I would have been with any of my past employers."

"I've no doubt about that," Lindsey said.

They reached a row of benches near Hyde Park Corner, and instead of calling an end to the walk and going their separate ways, they sat facing the traffic and tourists along Park Lane so they could continue their gossip.

"I can't help if I like him," Aubrey said, figuring it was well past time that he took some responsibility for his feelings. "He shared a lot with me while he was sick. I think he's wanted to get those things off his chest for a long time, and since I had him trapped in a vulnerable position, he spilled it all to me."

"Ooh! Vulnerable positions are delicious. Do tell," Lindsey said, pulling Daisy out of her buggy to sit on her lap, since she was awake.

Eugenie must have sensed that they'd stopped moving too. She fussed a little until Aubrey repositioned her buggy so he could get her out and let her rest on his lap. She was still drowsy and a little out of it, so she just leaned against him, watching people and clinging to Aubrey for a moment.

"I'm not revealing anything about what he said," Aubrey continued with the conversation. "I'll only say that his ex did a number on him. I was glad he had me to talk to about it, because those aren't the sorts of things someone should have gnawing away inside of them."

"And you think that him confessing his secrets to you brought the two of you closer together," Ulrika said with a nod of understanding. "Which, yeah, means you're in a unique situation now. You're his friend as much as his employee."

"Exactly," Aubrey said, letting out a heavy breath. He was so glad that someone had hit the nail on the head and that they understood that it felt like the sun had broken through the clouds.

"Gemma Stone is a selfish bitch," Lindsey said with surprising venom. When both Aubrey and Ulrika looked at her, she went on with, "Everyone knows she was trying to score her own reality show, and she only married Heath because he worked for a production company. Well, and because his father is a marquess and his brother is an earl, and they have at least two or three country properties, and probably a villa in the Mediterranean too."

Aubrey was pretty sure that was all true, but he'd never asked.

"That marriage was doomed from the beginning," Lindsey went on. "I'm not at all surprised to hear that she was cruel to him. What I still don't understand is why he bothered to marry her in the first place."

"She was his rebound relationship," Aubrey said before he could think better of it. Mostly because he was only really putting all the pieces together just then. Of course, that had been his first thought when Heath had told him how Gemma had used Eugenie as a way to guilt him into getting her own way, but there had been so much to chew on in that conversation that his jaw still hurt.

The information came as a surprise to Lindsey and Ulrika. The two of them stared at him, making Aubrey squirm.

"What dish is this?" Lindsey asked. "Who was Heath Manfred dating before Gemma who broke his heart?"

"I really can't talk about it," Aubrey said, wishing he hadn't already said so much.

Lindsey gasped and grabbed Aubrey's arm, upsetting Daisy a little in the process. "It was the guy in that picture," she said, drawing her own conclusions. "I bet that's why they had a photo of the two of them in that article to begin with. It all makes sense now." She let out a sad, vocal sigh and said, "Aww, poor Heath Manfred."

"Speaking of," Ulrika whispered, batting at Aubrey's arm. "Act natural."

Aubrey frowned at her, no idea what she was on about.

Until he happened to glance across the street only to find Heath stepping out of the huge, grey building that Aubrey had always assumed was part of the hotel next door. He had another man with him, and the two of them paused for a few more words once the door was shut behind them.

"Isn't that Oakley Manfred, Heath's brother, the earl?" Lindsey hissed, as if they were having their own celebrity sighting.

Of course, after being married to Gemma Stone, Heath sort of was a celebrity.

"I think so," Aubrey said. "I haven't met the man yet, but his picture is all over Heath's house, along with pictures of the rest of the family. They actually seem like a really nice, close family for a bunch of billionaires with a title that goes back to the Reformation."

"Ooh! I think he noticed you," Lindsey squealed.

Sure enough, as soon as Heath said goodbye to his brother, he glanced across the street and spotted Aubrey sitting there with his friends. There was no point in wondering how Heath had managed to pick him out from the rest of the tourists. Having flaming red hair tended to make a bloke noticeable. But the smile that touched Heath's face as soon as Aubrey raised a hand to wave to him did things to Aubrey's insides that were not morning-out-with-the-girls-and-their-kids appropriate.

"He's coming this way," Ulrika pointed out, oh-so helpfully.

"You have to introduce me," Lindsey said, sitting a bit straighter and giving herself and Daisy a once-over, as if they needed to be camera-ready.

"Of course I'll introduce you," Aubrey sighed, bracing for the awkwardness that was bound to happen.

He kissed Eugenie's sleepy head and thought about standing up as he watched Heath walk to the crossing, wait for the signal, then cross and head down the path their way. A wave of uncertainty made him squirm and then stand in an attempt to dispel the feeling. Seeing Heath at home, when it was just them, was one thing. Dealing with all the unspoken desire between the two of them was easy when there was no one else to see it. Facing the man he couldn't stop himself from having feelings for when two of his close friends were standing right there, analyzing every little thing between the two of them, was going to be something else entirely.

Eugenie saved the day as she noticed Heath walking toward her. "Daddy!" she exclaimed, holding up her arms and wriggling in the hope that Aubrey would put her down and allow her to run to him.

"Hello, sweetheart," Heath said, bursting into a genuine smile and reaching for her.

It was heartwarming how much Heath loved his daughter and was willing to show her affection, even in public. It was also heart-shivering how his arms brushed against Aubrey's and how close the two of them had to stand so that Eugenie could move from one of them to the other. Aubrey caught a strong whiff of Heath's cologne, and the warmth of his skin as their hands brushed. He might have leaned in closer than he needed to so that his lips came within centimeters of brushing Heath's earlobe too.

"Fancy seeing you here," Aubrey greeted him.

"Oh…er…I was just having a brunch meeting at my club," Heath said, glancing back across the street to the plain door in the grey, stone edifice.

And if that wasn't the most adorable, aristocratic nonsense that Aubrey had ever heard, he didn't know what was. The fact that it made him semi-hard to hear Heath talk about brunch at his club in that deep, posh accent of his was a sure sign that he was so pitifully in lust that Lindsey and Ulrika were probably sniggering behind their hands at him.

He checked.

They were absolutely sniggering.

"What are you two doing here?" Heath asked Eugenie in a kid-friendly version of his posh accent.

"We saw ducks, Daddy," Eugenie said, pulling at Heath's bright mauve tie and pulling it out of his suit jacket. "David threw rocks."

"Oh, I see," Heath said, as though ducks and rocks were the most interesting things in the world.

Aubrey wanted to jump the man right there and snog him senseless.

"Hello, I'm Lindsey," Lindsey introduced herself, thrusting her hand out to Heath, eyes as bright as flashing marquees. "I'm Aubrey's friend."

The excited look in Lindsey's eyes—Ulrika's too, for that matter—told Aubrey all he needed to know about what the two of them had observed between him and Heath already. As soon as it was just the three of them again, he was going to be mobbed with squeals and pokes and teasing.

"It's a pleasure to meet you," Heath said, shuffling Eugenie so that he could shake Lindsey's hand, then Ulrika's.

"This is Ulrika," Aubrey finished the introductions, since the fuss had woken David from his nap and she turned to scoop him out of his buggy. "As you might guess, they're also nannies. We've known each other for years, and we sometimes take all our kids on a walk together." A sudden jolt of worry smacked Aubrey. "I hope you don't mind," he rushed on. "I swear, I trust these two with my life, and I would never let Eugenie be around people I didn't trust."

"No! It's fine. I'm happy for Eugenie to have playmates," Heath said, smiling and nodding at Lindsey and Ulrika. He even smiled at David as Ulrika tried to settle him and said, "It is a pleasure to meet you."

That had Aubrey ready to swoon as well, like David was another gentleman he was meeting in the VIP area at Royal Ascot and not a bratty toddler who wanted to run after the dog someone had just walked past them.

Lawrence was awake now too and pointed at the big dog from the buggy. "Look!" he exclaimed to Lindsey.

Lindsey took that opening and ran with it. "If you'll excuse us, Mr. Manfred, sir. We'll just go take the kiddies to see the dog and let the two of you have a word alone."

Aubrey wanted to roll his eyes as Lindsey and Ulrika shuffled the kids off to a respectable distance so fast that he was surprised they didn't leave a trail of shoes, socks, and snacks in their wake.

"Is something the matter?" Heath asked. What his suddenly tight expression really asked was, "Did you say something to them about the two of us?"

Aubrey decided to go for a half-truth instead of pushing an issue the two of them hadn't talked about yet. "Lindsey reads the tabloids," he said with a small wince. "She knows the entire history of you and Gemma. I think she was a little star-struck."

Heath let out a long-suffering sigh, but that appeared to be the end of that.

Aubrey cleared his throat and looked for a change of subject. "So that's your club, eh?" he asked. "Is it the queer club you were telling me about last week?"

Heath's face flushed, but Aubrey couldn't tell if that was because he was ashamed of the club's queerness or if he hadn't remembered telling Aubrey about it.

Whatever had set him off, he recovered quickly enough to say, "Yes, that's The Chameleon Club. It's actually stood there since the eighteen-thirties, though no one seems to know it's there."

"I suppose that was on purpose for most of its history," Aubrey said.

"Yes, it was."

The two of them stood there staring at it for a moment, Eugenie hugging Heath's neck and resting her head on his shoulder.

Before things could get too awkward between them, Aubrey asked, "So you had a brunch meeting there? With your brother? That was your brother, wasn't it?"

"That was Oakley, yes," Heath answered quickly, like he was eager to prove everything was perfectly normal between the two of them by keeping the conversation going. "But the meeting was with Gerry, one of the producers from Storm Productions. We're working together on the *After the War* series. He's a member, and he's been trying to get me to spend more time there since…."

"Gemma," Aubrey said into the silence after Heath's explanation to spare Heath from having to say her name. He shrugged, and pushed the conversation in another direction. "It looks like a nice enough place. Good view of the park. I know those gentleman's clubs were all the rage in the nineteenth century."

"It's still really popular with our sort now," Heath said, still staring at the club.

Aubrey couldn't stop himself from grinning. It was beyond adorable that Heath considered the two of them the same sort. They most definitely were not the same sort. Aubrey wasn't even sure if there were "sorts" anymore. Although, he supposed there still were if your dad was a marquess and your brother was an earl.

"The Brotherhood is hosting a family picnic in Hampshire on Saturday," Heath said all in a rush, glancing back to Aubrey. "There's an old estate, Swanmore Glen, that was owned by the Brotherhood's founder. Since so many of the members are married and have children now, they've started hosting weekend events and things. I just found out about it, and I was thinking of taking Eugenie, and you're more than welcome to come with us, if you're interested."

Aubrey wanted to lean backwards and blink rapidly at the lightning-fast onslaught of words coming from Heath. Heath must have been nervous about something if he was talking that much, that fast, and in public.

Of course, he might have been nervous because everything he'd just said sounded very much like he was asking Aubrey out on a date. Maybe not a real date, since it was a family-friendly event and Eugenie would be there, but it definitely sounded like a kind of date.

He forced himself to play it cool by shrugging and saying, "Yeah, yeah, no problem, sounds fun," while shoving his hands in his jeans pockets and flushing red-hot. "My own country estate is closed for renovations at the moment, so it would be nice to hang around someone else's for a while."

Heath blew out a breath through his nose and sent Aubrey a flat look. Flat except for his eyes, which were sparkling. "No need for the nob jokes," he said.

Aubrey wanted to groan at the way Heath had set him up yet again for the perfect, inappropriate comeback. He couldn't be half as raunchy as he wanted to with Eugenie resting against Heath's shoulder, looking at him with those big, innocent eyes of hers, so he settled on, "Nobs are no joke."

It was Heath's turn to blush up a storm, and Aubrey loved it. "So you'll come?" he asked, as if pretending it didn't mean the world to him that Aubrey had said yes.

Aubrey smiled as genuinely as he could. "I would love to," he said.

Heath seemed to relax a little. He turned his attention to Eugenie and said, "Daddy has to go back to work now, darling, so it's time to go play with Nanny Aubrey and your friends."

Aubrey thought Eugenie would protest, but she slipped easily out of Heath's arms, stepped over to grab Aubrey's hands, then pointed at the dog—who was currently being mobbed by David, Daisy, and Lawrence—and said, "There's a dog, Nanny."

"I see," Aubrey said. "Would you like to go say hello?"

"Yes!"

Heath laughed. The unending love for Eugenie in his smile made Aubrey's knees weak. Gemma might have only had Eugenie so she could use her as a way to manipulate

Heath, but it was obvious that Heath loved and wanted the little girl more than enough for two parents.

"Go on then," Aubrey told Heath in a teasing tone, gesturing for him to be on his way. "Off to work with you. We'll see you at home later."

Heath chuckled and turned to go.

He paused before he'd fully turned around, like he had something he wanted to say. The look in his eyes sent a tingle down Aubrey's spine and straight into his balls. He held his breath, but whatever it was Heath had been about to say never materialized. "See you later," he said instead, blew Eugenie a kiss, then walked off.

"Come on, princess," Aubrey said, grabbing the buggy and leading Eugenie down the path to the others. "Let's go see the dog and listen to Nanny Lindsey and Nanny Ulrika tease me and say mean things to me."

His words went right over Eugenie's head, but the moment Lindsey and Ulrika looked his way, he knew they were true. And if things kept going the way they had been, Aubrey was sure his two friends would demand to know everything about his weekend come Monday.

SEVEN

IT HADN'T OCCURRED to Heath until he'd returned to his office that inviting Aubrey to go with him and Eugenie to Swanmore Glen for the picnic might have come off as asking Aubrey on a date. In his defense, he'd just learned about the picnic not half an hour before he'd encountered Aubrey and Eugenie in the park. Gerry had pointed out the announcement pinned to the club's message board as they finished up brunch. Then Oakley had argued with him to go, as a way to reconnect with The Brotherhood. So using it as a dating opportunity hadn't been on his radar.

Heath wasn't inclined to do anything remotely like a club picnic, especially on such short notice and with his trip to LA on Monday, but Oakley had insisted it would be a good way to network with other gay fathers, for Eugenie's sake, of course. While Heath wasn't exactly comfortable with being lumped in with what he imagined was a group of rainbow-wearing daddies, he'd thought it would be a good opportunity for Eugenie to begin to know other children.

Inviting Aubrey had come as a matter of course. Eugenie adored the man and couldn't do without him. Heath just wouldn't think about how Aubrey's face had shone with sentiment when he'd asked if he wanted to come along. He wouldn't dwell on the daydreams he'd had in the following days, of Aubrey looking fresh and happy in the sunshine on the lawn of a country estate. Perhaps wearing an old fashioned, striped, seersucker suit and a bowler hat with a matching band. He wouldn't lie in bed the night before the picnic fantasizing about getting Aubrey alone in some sort of moss-covered, Regency ruins, pressing his back up against the stones, and kissing him until the man turned into butter in his arms.

Nothing was going to happen.

"Are you certain you want to drive?" Aubrey asked the next day as they piled Eugenie and what felt like an unnecessary amount of stuff into his BMW on Saturday morning. "I looked at a map, and this Swanmore Glen place is near enough to a train station that we could go that way and walk."

Heath was in the middle of fastening Eugenie into her car seat and had his head ducked into the back of the car. Aubrey was loading things into the seat beside her and was also crouching. For some reason, the moment felt intimate when Heath glanced across to him in the confines of the car's back seat, like they were tucked into a space meant for confessions.

"It's no trouble to drive," he said, baffled by Aubrey's suggestion. "It will be easier coming home too, since Eugenie is likely to be exhausted and fussy."

"True," Aubrey said, pulling out of the car and standing. Heath finished with Eugenie's car seat and mirrored the movement. "I just thought you might want to save a few quid by taking the train," Aubrey finished over the top of the car.

Heath grinned slyly at him. "What have you learned in the last month that makes you think I need to save a few quid?"

Aubrey burst into one of those winning smiles of his that made ninety-five percent of Heath melt…and the other five percent harden. "Good point, guv'ner," he teased in a cockney accent.

Heath sent him a sideways look of amused non-amusement, then slipped into the driver's seat.

Only once he'd navigated their way to the main road did it occur to him that Aubrey might have been concerned about saving money because he didn't have any. Heath paid him well, of course, but the lightbulb that went off in his head was one of those uncomfortable reminders that class divides still existed, even in the twenty-first century, and he and Aubrey were on opposite sides of that divide.

London traffic was always horrible, but they managed to get to the M3 in a reasonable amount of time. From there, it was an easy drive through increasingly verdant countryside to Hampshire. It was lovely in its own way, but it also meant that Heath couldn't use the excuse of concentrating on busy roads to stay silent. Aubrey had finished his initial conversation with Eugenie in the back seat, and like Eugenie always did on long drives, the zoom of so much to see passing around them and the hum of movement ended up putting her to sleep.

"I wish I could fall asleep so easily," Aubrey said, settling to look out the windshield once Eugenie was out.

Heath sent him a minute look of concern. "Have you not been sleeping well?" he asked, his mind quickly filling with his own nights of tossing and turning and analyzing every creak that came from the ceiling above his bed.

"I sleep fine," Aubrey said with a tiny bit of alarm, like Heath had accused him of something. The reaction made him wonder if Aubrey was telling the truth. "That bed you've given me is one of the most comfortable I've ever had in my life."

"I bought the mattress new for you," Heath said, staring straight forward and feeling his neck and face heat. What a stupid thing to say.

"No wonder." Aubrey smiled and spread out a little in the passenger seat. Heath tried to keep his eyes on the road instead of on the muscles of Aubrey's thighs and the dusting of ginger hair on his forearm as he rested it against the window. "I should have guessed there'd never been a man in that bed before."

"Not since university," Heath said.

He instantly realized he'd heard Aubrey's question entirely wrong, and that his answer was a complete embarrassment. Lucky for him, he had to concentrate on the road for a moment to pass a slow-moving car without being squashed by a lorry at the same time.

Once the car was zipping steadily along again, Aubrey asked, "Does this Brotherhood organization usually throw parties like this?"

Heath peeked sideways at him, hoping that he'd gotten away with his slip. Aubrey was still watching the road in front of them, but his mouth had pulled up into a grin that was anything but innocent.

Heath cursed himself in words he would never utter aloud when Eugenie was around and said, "Honestly, I don't know. I haven't done anything with the Brotherhood for years. I don't even know why I maintained my membership for all these years."

He frowned at himself. He really hadn't analyzed why he'd kept his membership when being with Gemma had convinced him those days were behind him and he was now straight as an arrow.

"Sounds to me like someone's subconscious knew more than he did," Aubrey said, grinning sideways at Heath.

Heath sighed. "Sexuality has nothing to do with it," he

said, eyes firmly on the road. "You don't just suddenly stop being bi when you marry a woman."

He had the horrible feeling he was convincing himself instead of stating something to Aubrey, since he'd been contemplating the same thing himself of late.

"It's the whole social aspect of belonging to an organization that isn't really me," he rushed on before Aubrey could call him out for…something. "It's not really important to me. I've never needed to be all chummy with the group to feel happy or fulfilled."

Aubrey nodded. "You're an introvert. There's nothing wrong with that." He paused, and when Heath didn't have any comment, he went on with, "So why drive us all the way out to Hampshire for this picnic? Not that it isn't a lovely thing to do on a June Saturday, and I am extremely touched that you would include me."

There was something heavy and important in his otherwise general statement. Heath's heart sped up, and he sent Aubrey a sideways look before passing another car. Which was, of course, a delaying tactic. Was Aubrey subtly asking him if this was actually a date?

"Well, I'm leaving for LA on Monday," he said, trying to sound casual and sounding like a nutter instead. "I'll miss you—that is, Eugenie while I'm gone. I thought it would be nice for us to do something fun and unusual together before I go."

Aubrey hummed and nodded. "I see."

Heath couldn't tell whether he saw or not. He had no idea what the smile that wouldn't leave Aubrey's face, no matter how much of an arse the lorry driver who kept tailing him until they took the exit for Winchester was being.

He had to navigate through the interchanges to get onto the right road for Swanmore, which spared him from embarrassing himself further by blurting out things he didn't want to say. The problem was, he wanted Aubrey to say something, to press the issue so that they could get it out in the open and discuss it. He wanted a reason to tell Aubrey that they were just friends and he was sorry if there had been any misunderstanding about that.

The moment never came. Instead, the last fifteen minutes of the drive were taken up with maddening small talk about country estates and the time Aubrey had visited the estate where his parents had been attending some sort of artists' commune for the summer when he was eighteen, only to find that the entire place was inhabited by naturists.

"And I still haven't recovered from the sight of my parents standing there naked, with cocktails in their hands, chatting with the others as if they were at a garden party," Aubrey finished with one of his vibrant laughs as Heath turned onto the drive for Swanmore Glen.

There were discreet signs announcing the Brotherhood event and noting that the estate was closed to the public that weekend. Heath was surprised that a place with the storied history of Swanmore Glen opened to the public at all. Then again, he knew from his family's experience that estates needed to pay for themselves these days, and tourism was the way to go.

"I don't think I would survive seeing my parents like that," Heath commented as he pulled into a parking space at the foot of a gentle slope with the main house at its crest.

"I've met your mother," Aubrey said with mock seriousness as Heath cut the engine. "I don't think *anyone* would survive that."

Heath turned to him with what was supposed to be a casual grin. But the way Aubrey smiled at him, as if they were some sort of long-term couple who was so comfortable with each other that they could finish each other's thoughts had his heart catching in his throat.

For one, mad moment, Heath considered reaching across to Aubrey, hooking his hand behind the man's neck, and pulling him close for a kiss. It was reckless and ill-timed, and he jerked away from the thought and from Aubrey so fast that Aubrey probably thought he'd spotted a bee in the car or something.

"Let's get this over with," he sighed instead, exaggerating his uncertain feelings about the event so that he could put a wall between himself and Aubrey.

Aubrey's smile faltered for a second, and his face pinched with confusion. A beat later, he reached for the car door and got out as though nothing had happened, one way or the other.

"I have to admit, I'm looking forward to this whole thing," he said with perfect ease. "I Googled Swanmore Glen yesterday, and it really does seem like a fascinating place."

Heath made a non-verbal response to that as he got out of the car, then opened the back to wake Eugenie up and get her out of her seat. Once Eugenie was awake, there wasn't a spare second for him and Aubrey to talk about anything, much less have moments of near intimacy or ambiguous emotion.

Swanmore Glen was as beautiful as any estate Heath had ever visited. He hated to think how many country estates he'd visited in his days, and not as a tourist. Summer visits were expected and required in his mother's circles, even though the world had long since moved on from the house parties of the Victorians.

Swanmore Glen was a little different in that it was decorated with rainbow flags and stylish bunting for the occasion. Eugenie was immediately taken with everything, particularly when they rounded the corner of the house to find what amounted to an entire fun-faire spread out across the back garden. At one glance, Heath could see everything from a bouncy house to games where children were winning stuffed animals. There was even a pony giving rides at the far end of the garden, and a magician in drag performing a small show for a group of older kids.

"Wow," Aubrey said as they moved into the thick of it. "You people certainly know how to throw a party."

"And by 'you people', do you mean the gays or the aristocracy?" Heath asked flatly, instinctively on the defensive.

Aubrey laughed. "Well, since I'm the one here who wears the pride flag proudly while you stare at it gingerly from the corner…."

Heath flushed hot at all the implications of Aubrey's words. Mostly because, even though Aubrey was joking as usual, Heath thought he might have accidentally offended him.

"I'm sorry if you think I'm being a stuck-up arse," he said suddenly, before he could think too much about it and stop himself. "I'm out of my depth here, and I hate feeling this way. I haven't considered myself part of all this for so long that it's just…confusing now."

He wanted to groan and slap himself as soon as the far-too vulnerable words were out of his mouth. He did feel as if he owed Aubrey…something, but he didn't know if that was it.

Aubrey gazed back at him with a look that Heath couldn't read. There was a chance Aubrey thought he'd been talking about the social aspects of the event and how he was an introvert.

But one hand placed gently on Heath's arm to give it an encouraging squeeze was all Heath needed to know Aubrey was onto him, and that he was in serious trouble.

"Heath, you don't have to—"

"Is that Heath Manfred I see?"

They were interrupted, just at the moment Heath was about to clear his throat and get all fussy and tell Aubrey he had the wrong end of the stick and that he wasn't attracted to him, by a man Heath hadn't seen since his university days.

"Freddy," he said, turning to the attractive man with a

tight smile. "It's good to see you again." He used the excuse of shaking Freddy's hand to step away from Aubrey. Doing so made him realize how close the two of them had been standing before.

"Good to see you back with the Brotherhood as well," Freddy said, eyes alight with interest as he shook Heath's hand…and looked past him to Aubrey. "I heard about the divorce," he said, implying a thousand other things as he smiled at Aubrey.

"Yes, well," Heath said, then paused. What else could he say? "This is my darling Eugenie," he went on, resting a hand on Eugenie's head as she curled herself around his leg and simultaneously tried to hide from Freddy and smile shyly at him. "And this is Aubrey Kelly, Eugenie's nanny."

"Nanny," Freddy said, as if he were challenging Heath about what that meant, while shaking Aubrey's hand. "Pleased to meet you. Frederick Ingelsby."

"Likewise," Aubrey said with a smile.

"And how long have you been Heath's nanny?" Freddy asked, every sort of implication in the words as he glanced slyly to Heath.

"Only a month," Heath answered. He wondered how in God's name he'd ended up in an awkward conversation mere moments after arriving at the picnic. He'd known it was a bad idea. "Are you here with Oscar?" he asked, praying he could divert attention away from himself.

"Of course." Freddy took the bait. "Oscar's down at the bouncy house with the twins."

"Bouncy house," Eugenie whispered with reverence, tugging at Heath's trouser leg.

"I'll take her," Aubrey said, stepping in and reaching for Eugenie's hand. "Would you like to see the ponies, too?" he asked her in that bright, carefree voice that Heath loved.

"Ponies!" Eugenie exclaimed. She went to Aubrey as if it were the most natural thing in the world.

"I can take the bag," Heath offered, gesturing for the supplies they'd brought for Eugenie.

There were a few moments of shuffling things around and building up Eugenie's excitement for everything around her, but once it was all sorted, Aubrey and Eugenie headed off down the lawn as Freddy accompanied Heath up to the house so he could store the bag somewhere.

"He seems like a nice catch," Freddy said, his tone and expression full of implication.

"It's not what you think it is," Heath sighed. "Aubrey is just the nanny."

"Right," Freddy said. "And Oscar is just my roommate."

They reached a block of temporary storage cubbies near the porch at the back of the house, and Heath stashed the bag there before turning to face Freddy with a frown.

"If you heard about the divorce," he said, not wanting to be rude, but not wanting to let rumors fly around, "then you know how painful it was for me. And you would know that I am not interested in dating anyone new until the wounds heal."

"Understood," Freddy said with a conciliatory nod. Heath hoped for all of two seconds that Freddy would back off, but then he said, "Your new nanny looks like he's more than capable of helping the healing process along."

Heath clenched his jaw for a moment, wondering if that was how the entire event would go. "We've become friends," he said, then, in a flash of what he hoped was genius, added, "I wouldn't want to wreck that friendship by pushing for more."

Freddy looked like he was about to say something, but he stopped himself, apparently rethinking. "Of course," he nodded. "Sorry for jumping to conclusions. It's just that we've all been concerned about you these past few years. You might have moved on from the Brotherhood, but once we care about you, we're always going to care about you."

Heath was unexpectedly touched by that. "Thank you for that," he said, relaxing a little.

Freddy thumped his shoulder. "No worries. And as long as your nanny is keeping an eye on little Eugenie, why don't you come along and reintroduce yourself to some of your old acquaintances? A bunch of your old crowd is here, and I'm sure they would love to catch up."

Heath glanced down the hill to Aubrey, finding him right away in the increasing crowd of guests, and not just because the sunlight made his ginger hair shine like copper. Heath felt like he could pick Aubrey out of any crowd by the sheer force of how he felt about the man.

Those feelings turned into a jolt of…no, he refused to admit it was jealousy, when he spotted Aubrey already talking to a gorgeous, young, blond with a smile that Heath could feel across the lawn. That kind of smile was bait to hook a desirable catch like Aubrey.

"Nanny," Freddy said with a sympathetic laugh, proving he'd noticed where Heath's attention had gone, and that he'd noticed Heath's feelings. When Heath turned back to him, intending to tell him off, Freddy went on with, "You know, you are allowed to live again after a divorce. And as a father. There is no rule that says you have to be a monk for the rest of your life, just because you have a fresh, new soul to raise."

"I never thought any such thing," Heath protested.

But as he glanced across the lawn again, he wondered if he actually had been laboring under that assumption since Gemma. Aubrey had seemed very open to him from the beginning, after all. Especially after his cold. Why had he been walking around thinking that he couldn't do anything about it?

"Come on," Freddy said, nudging him. "Maybe you'll feel better when you reacquaint yourself with some of your old friends and see that people really do care about you."

Heath let out a sigh and forced himself to turn away from Aubrey. And to trust him.

Maybe that was what it was all about in the end. Maybe he needed to learn to trust that Aubrey wouldn't break him the way Gemma had so that they could all get what they needed.

EIGHT

AUBREY HAD no idea Heath had so many friends. He'd been out for supper a few times after work in the last month, which Aubrey had encouraged him to do, but he'd been under the impression those were work friends and networking drinks.

As Aubrey watched Eugenie in the bouncy house, then took her along to play some of the games that had been set up for the littlest kids, his attention kept drifting back up to the house. And nearly every time, Heath had been busy talking to some nicely dressed, posh-looking guy who seemed deeply interested in everything Heath had to say.

Once or twice, one of them touched Heath, and each time Aubrey noticed it, he was surprised that he didn't growl out loud.

His reaction startled him, really. He liked Heath. He definitely dreamed of getting in Heath's pants. But he hadn't felt truly possessive of Heath in the month that they'd known each other. Fantasizing about your boss as you rubbed one out in the shower was not grounds for being jealous when he talked to other guys at a country picnic.

Correction, when he talked to other guys of his class at a posh country estate.

That was the problem, really. From the moment they pulled up to the stately, perfectly manicured house and gardens of Swanmore Glen, Aubrey had felt as if he'd stepped into an issue of *Town and Country*. Him. An ordinary ginger from Cornwall. It was a recipe for disaster from the start, but to see Heath laughing at something a guy who was inexplicably dressed in a designer suit at a picnic while holding a crystal glass of something undoubtedly rare and expensive, made Aubrey feel like he should bow out quickly before he was discovered and horsewhipped off the property as a vagrant.

"Can I ride a pony, Nanny?" Eugenie asked, tugging on Aubrey's shorts and dragging his attention back from his uncomfortable musings about the haves and the have nots.

"Of course you can, princess," Aubrey said, sweeping Eugenie into his arms and swinging her around once before settling her on his hip.

Eugenie laughed, and that alone was enough to remind Aubrey that he was exactly where he needed to be. The precious little girl in his arms needed him something fierce. He'd decided that after being with her and Heath for three weeks. In all that time, Gemma hadn't called or done anything to indicate that she even remembered she had a child. Aubrey had asked Heath straight-out if Gemma had any intention of being a part of Eugenie's life. The answer had been an unequivocal no.

Maybe it was just sympathy and general affection for the broken family that pulled Aubrey toward Heath all the time. It could have been that sense that he was needed, perhaps more than at any of his previous placements. Or maybe it was the way that country sunlight did Heath a world of good, or the way his chest and arms were highlighted by the short-sleeve shirt he wore.

"You don't have to worry about him," the guy Aubrey had ended up standing next to in the line for pony rides said, jolting him from his thoughts. "He's not going anywhere."

Aubrey prayed that the guy, whoever he was, would think the heat that rushed to his face just then was from being in direct sunlight and not embarrassment at being caught looking where he shouldn't.

He smiled to cover his slip and said, "I just want to make sure I know where Daddy is at all times."

The guy laughed. "Is that what you call him?"

"What? No!" Aubrey exclaimed, his voice shooting up an octave and his face heating even more. "That's what this one calls him." He lifted Eugenie into his arms so he could use her as a shield against his embarrassment.

The guy continued to grin. "Trust me, you wouldn't be the only one here with a daddy. The estate and the Brotherhood have a long-standing tradition of accepting pretty much anything that its members want to get up to."

Aubrey was surprised at how mortified he felt by the man's implications. Although they would also give him a hell of a lot to think about later.

"I'm just the nanny," he explained. He shuffled Eugenie in his arms and moved her closer to the paddock fence so she could get a better view of the ponies as they waited.

"Ah, I see. My mistake," the man said. Aubrey wasn't sure if he really meant that or if he thought Aubrey was lying through his teeth. Either way, he thrust out his hand. "Casper Penhurst," he introduced himself.

"Aubrey Kelly," Aubrey introduced himself in return. He juggled Eugenie so that he could shake the man's hand, then tightened his grip on her, since she was getting squirmy. "And I really am the nanny."

"Oh, I believe you," Casper said. "It's just that you've been watching Heath like—" He stopped and pivoted back toward the house, then seemed to change his mind about whatever observation he'd been about to make. "People are a little excited to see Heath back at a Brotherhood event after so many years."

"Yeah, it's a shame that a guy can't just take his daughter to a nice picnic without everyone speculating who he's sleeping with," Aubrey blurted.

He immediately felt bad for snapping.

"I'm sorry," he said with a sigh. "I'm just a little protective of Heath and Eugenie after all they've been through."

"Perfectly understandable," Casper said, holding up his hands. "I'm sorry I got the wrong end of the stick."

"No worries."

Now that that was settled, Aubrey was surprised at how glad he was that Casper didn't just up and leave. He was cute, and there was nothing that said he couldn't chat up a cute guy while waiting for the ponies.

"So are you a member of the Brotherhood?" he asked, since that seemed as good a thing to ask at an event like that as any.

"I am," Casper answered with a solemn nod. "I'm actually the Brotherhood historian."

Aubrey's eyebrows flew up. "That's a thing?"

Casper laughed. "We're all a bunch of posh twats who spend our free time at a gentleman's club in London and a country estate in Hampshire," he said, making his voice and posture posher than they already were. "Of course we have an historian."

Aubrey grinned and said, "As one does."

"Yes, indubitably," Casper replied mock insufferably. He and Aubrey exchanged grins before he went on with, "The history of both the Brotherhood and Swanmore Glen are fascinating, though. I wrote my dissertation about the Brotherhood at Oxford."

Aubrey exaggerated his impressed expression, but mostly to cover the fact that he felt even more out of place faced with an Oxford scholar than he did just being around a bunch of blokes with money they inherited.

"I thought the Brotherhood was a big secret, what with it being all about queer men," he said.

"And women, since the nineteen seventies," Casper corrected him quickly.

Aubrey chuckled. "Heath was quick to make that same qualification too when he told me about it."

Just saying Heath's name made Aubrey check back up at the house to see if Heath was still there.

Not only was Heath still on the porch talking to the other nobs, he was staring down the entire length of the lawn, watching Aubrey. Probably watching Eugenie, actually, Aubrey told himself. Heath was a conscientious father. Although it also looked a bit like Heath was frowning at him, like he was some great, posh lord who didn't like his servants conversing with the guests.

Or maybe he just didn't want Aubrey talking to a cute guy who wasn't wearing a wedding ring.

"The Brotherhood was a secret organization up until the Sexual Offenses Act of 1967 decriminalized homosexuality," Casper said, starting to sound like an Oxford professor and not just a graduate. "It's not a secret anymore—although its existence still isn't widely known—but it was very much an underground organization throughout the nineteenth and early twentieth centuries, for obvious reasons."

"Yeah, I suppose it wouldn't have been the best idea to go around advertising the spot where all the queers hung out so that the Victorians could come round them up and hang them all," Aubrey said.

"It's a bit of a distortion of history to assume that all the gays were persecuted all the time throughout history," Casper said. "A lot of us got away with living pretty much as we pleased with whomever we loved, as long as we flew under the radar and kept our noses clean. Much depended on where you lived and who your neighbors were. And parties like this have taken place at Swanmore for nearly two hundred years."

"What, without the police coming in and raiding and dragging everyone off to the pillory or something?" Aubrey asked.

Casper laughed. "A lot of people got away with a lot of stuff before the internet," he said. "Back in its heyday, Swanmore Glen was far enough off the beaten path that most people had no idea who was here or for any length of time, let alone what they were doing. And the family has always hired servants for their absolute discretion, going all the way back to George, the third Marquess of Wilmore, and the man who started the Brotherhood.

"Well, good old George didn't start the Brotherhood personally," Casper said with a half shrug. "It was created as part of the bequest he left behind upon his death, though." He laughed. "The man was an absolute character. I mean, it was a far wickeder time than the folks who worship at the altar of Jane Austen would like you to believe. But George took wickedness to an extreme. He had a string of younger lovers a mile long. Apparently, several of them called him Daddy."

"You don't say," Aubrey laughed.

He also noticed that Heath had gone from just watching him to leaving his posh companions on the porch and heading down the sloping lawn toward them.

"George knew he wasn't long for this world," Casper went on, unaware that Heath was coming closer. "He decided to make a game out of his will. He gathered all of his favorite past lovers right here, at Swanmore Glen, in the summer of eighteen thirty-seven, and he had his solicitor hand them all riddles that would lead to whatever it was that he'd left for them in his will."

Aubrey was having an increasingly difficult time giving his full focus to Casper, what with Eugenie wriggling with impatience in his arms and wanting to get down, and Heath coming ever closer to them. But that bit of information was interesting.

"What, did he leave them all, like, a treasure hunt?" he asked.

"Very much like a treasure hunt, from the information I've been able to uncover from old diaries and letters," Casper said. "He charged two of the men, Lord Cecil Thurleigh and Mr. Austin Haythorne—who became lifelong partners, thanks to George's games—with creating The Chameleon Club in London in a house that he'd bought more than a decade before."

"It's next to Hyde Park," Aubrey said, glad that he knew something, at least. "I've seen the place."

"Oh?" Casper lit up a little. "Are you a member? I shouldn't have assumed you're not." He looked suddenly abashed at having assumed something about Aubrey.

Aubrey laughed. "No, not at all. I wouldn't know what to do with myself around a bunch of posh gentlemen." In fact, he didn't really know what to do with himself right there and then.

"You should join," Casper said, more interested than ever. "I would absolutely be willing to sponsor your membership. That is, if Heath didn't want to."

Aubrey smiled, but mostly because he was certain now that Casper was flirting with him.

And because Heath had gotten close enough that he would see Aubrey's smile and any show of interest in Casper that he made. Aubrey wasn't the sort to flirt with one man in order to make another jealous, but since Heath seemed so stuck and unable to make a move….

"Don't let any preconceived notions about class or wealth and gentlemen's clubs cloud your decision about whether or not to join the Brotherhood," Casper went on as Aubrey stood a little straighter and glanced past him to Heath. "The entire original purpose of the organization was to include gay men of all classes and backgrounds with the intent of helping one another, since the law couldn't always be relied on to help us. We've gotten away from that, which I consider a tragedy, and it's about damned time we got back to our roots. If you would like—"

Casper didn't get any further. Eugenie spotted her father and wriggled out of Aubrey's hold completely with an exuberant, "Daddy!"

Aubrey figured it was okay to let her go, but he stumbled after her with a quick, apologetic smile for Casper as she flung herself at Heath.

"There's my angel," Heath said, crouching to scoop Eugenie into his arms. "Are you going to ride the ponies?" He sent an irritated look Aubrey's way.

Aubrey's back was up in an instant. There was no call for Heath to look like that or to be angry with him for any reason whatsoever. "We were just waiting our turn," he said, trying and failing not to sound terse.

"Eugenie has trouble waiting for so long," Heath said, as if Aubrey didn't already know that and had done something wrong. Before Aubrey could defend himself, Heath nodded to Casper and said, "Hello, Cass."

"Hello, Heath," Casper greeted him with a smile that had suddenly gone a little too knowing. "It's nice to see you back in the fold."

"I thought it would be good for Eugenie to make some friends," he said, only paying attention to Casper for a moment before frowning at Aubrey. "It seems as though I brought her here to stand in lines instead."

"The ponies are very popular today," Aubrey said, crossing his arms.

"Yes, I can see that," Heath said, glancing from Aubrey to Casper.

Aubrey clenched his jaw for a moment. So Heath was

going to be like that? Did he even understand why he was suddenly so pissy?

"I hope you don't mind," Casper said, looking far too entertained for Aubrey's comfort. "I've just seen someone I've been meaning to talk to. Oh, but Heath, let's get together sometime. Gerry has been telling me about your *After the War* series, and I think I might have some insights that could help with the production."

"Yes, certainly," Heath said, suddenly in business mode.

Aubrey wondered if Casper had shifted that gear for him as he said his goodbyes and sped away, leaving the two of them alone. Well, as alone as two men could get at a crowded picnic with a line of parents waiting to get their kids a pony ride right beside them.

"I see you've met Casper," Heath said, looking like he was trying to concentrate on not dropping Eugenie, as she had apparently had enough of hugging her daddy and wanted down now.

"Yes, and he's nice," Aubrey said, debating just how much he wanted to make Heath jealous by implying they were getting a long well. It was so far beneath him, but after snapping at him the way he just did, it would serve Heath right to get a bit of a spanking. "He was telling me about the history of the Brotherhood and Swanmore Glen."

"Was he?" Heath said, as if that were a crime.

"Oh, come on, Heath." Aubrey dropped his arms and decided to dispense with the misery of jealousy so they could get things out in the open. "We were just talking."

Before Heath could have any sort of reaction, Eugenie broke free, and instead of dashing toward the ponies, she bolted off across the lawn to something else that had caught her eye.

She was three and had short legs, so Aubrey and Heath were able to catch up with her before she got far, but by then, her interest in ponies was over. She grabbed Heath's and

Aubrey's hands and pulled them toward a spot where some sort of ring toss game had been set up.

As soon as they reached the booth and were handed a few rings from the young woman with piercings and pink hair who was manning it so that Eugenie could throw them, Heath said, "You can talk to whomever you'd like, but you need to keep an eye on Eugenie while you do so."

Anger that bordered on ridiculous flared through Aubrey. He turned slowly toward Heath and just stared at him with utter incredulity for a moment. "You have no idea how snobbish you sound right now, do you?" he asked. "And where do you get off being jealous of me talking to other men?"

Heath—who had been bending close to Eugenie and helping her with the rings—straightened so fast Aubrey was surprised his back didn't snap. "I just told you that you can talk to whomever you like."

"Bull—puffies," Aubrey huffed, thinking fast enough to clean up what he'd been about to say. "We've been dancing around this all day, all week, so we might as well come right out and deal with it."

"Deal with what?" Heath asked, his face going pink. "The fact that you have friends? I like your friends. I don't mind if you have friends. You could even…you could even go out on a date now and then and I wouldn't mind," he added, flapping his hands around like he didn't know what to do with them and not meeting Aubrey's eyes. "You just have to make certain you're taking care of…of Eugenie first and foremost."

Aubrey was so tempted to snap back at him for using Eugenie as a front. The moment could have descended into an out-and-out brawl so easily, and Aubrey wasn't sure he would have been able to salvage the tender shoots of whatever was going on between them if they went down that path. Heath was clearly struggling. With a lot of things. With the divorce, with old feelings that had resurfaced because of him, and with people watching them and their every move with each other, like the booth woman was doing right then.

Mostly, he felt like it was his responsibility to take care of Heath in a moment when he was struggling to take care of himself. He'd done it when Heath had had his cold, and he needed to do it now while his emotions were all over the place.

"Fine," he said, nodding to the stack of rings that stood off to one side in the booth. "We'll settle our disagreements like men of old did."

"What are you talking about?" Heath sighed. Eugenie had lost interest in her rings and now leaned back against Heath's shins. She, too, glanced up at Aubrey, as if he could solve everything.

"Rings, please," he told the booth woman. When she handed him a fistful with a smirk, like she'd figured out what Aubrey was doing before Heath did, he handed half of them over to Heath. "I challenge you to a duel. If I win, you will stop acting like an arse and getting jealous over every conversation I have."

"I'm not je—" Heath started, then ended by breathing out heavily through his nose. "Fine." He snatched at the rings. "But if I win—" He paused, as if he hadn't considered what he might want from Aubrey. "If I win, then you have to do whatever I say."

"That's a really vague prize," Aubrey said with a grin. "I like it. You're on."

Heath flushed brighter, nodded, and repeated. "You're on."

NINE

SOMEWHERE IN THE back of his mind, in the part that was still thinking like an adult and feeling mature feelings, Heath knew that swiping the offered rings from Aubrey's hand and turning to face the array of bottles inside the booth was neither a good idea, nor his proudest moment. But watching Aubrey get along so readily with whatever man had approached him for the past half hour had set things off in Heath that were big and wild and ferocious. Seeing Aubrey laugh and treat other men to his breathtaking smile snagged onto other emotions he'd thought were over and done.

Gemma had smiled and laughed and flirted with just about everyone else whenever they'd gone to parties and events. The same, raw part of him that had stood back and watched as his wife had touched whatever man she pleased flared up in him now.

He could not lose another person he cared about and wanted to someone younger, handsomer, and more fun than him. Not again.

"Gentlemen, the game is simple," the woman manning the booth explained to them, a twinkle in her eyes, like she was already laughing at him for being a fool. "Get the ring around the neck of the bottle and you win a prize."

"We're not in it for the prizes," Aubrey said, all life and energy and fun. "We're in it for pride and glory."

Heath sent him a sideways look, smiling inwardly, but forcing himself to maintain his game face. His heart beat faster just standing next to Aubrey.

He'd lined up his stance and prepared to toss the ring when Eugenie tugged on his trousers. "Daddy, I want that one," Eugenie said, pointing to a stuffed pink bear.

"I'll win it for you, darling," Heath said, resting a hand on his daughter's head for a moment.

"And if Daddy doesn't manage it," Aubrey said, "Nanny Aubrey will win it for you instead." He sent Heath a smug smile that was full of teasing.

Heath narrowed his eyes competitively at Aubrey, his heart thumping so hard he could feel it in his cock, then tossed his ring.

And missed.

The clatter of plastic against glass brought a flush of humiliation to Heath's face that went far beyond what he should have felt at playing a child's game. It felt much more like the moment he'd opened his email only to find candid photos of Gemma in a corner at a party, sitting on the lap of an up and coming young star, his hand up her skirt.

"Too bad," Aubrey said with undignified gloating. He stepped up to the booth and said, "Nanny will be your hero, princess."

The wink he sent Eugenie went straight to Heath's pounding, withered heart.

Aubrey missed. He handled his failure far more gracefully than Heath did. Heath tried a second ring and missed again, flushing hotter. Aubrey missed on his second shot as well. Heath missed his third and final shot as well, but so did Aubrey.

"It's enough to make me think the game is rigged," he told the woman behind the booth with a strained grin.

The woman shrugged. "That or you're both just incompetent fools when it comes to throwing rings."

Heath frowned at her as he ran a hand through Eugenie's hair. He could have called it a draw and let it go, but his honor was at stake. And if there was one thing that dusty old aristocrats who still existed long past the days when anyone cared about those things could do, it was cling to their honor.

"Alright," he said, glancing around, then nodding at another booth. "How about the ball toss, then?"

Aubrey looked mildly surprised at the suggestion. "You want to keep going? I'm willing to let the whole thing drop."

"Coward," Heath huffed.

Aubrey flinched back, his expression cycling through half a dozen emotions, from amusement and affection to challenge and a slight bit of indignation. And perhaps more curiosity than Heath wanted him to have.

"Ball toss it is, then," he said, grabbing Eugenie's other hand as Heath walked her away from one booth and on to the other.

All of it was a terrible, humiliating idea. Heath tackled the ball toss with vicious enthusiasm, throwing the tennis balls with far more power than was necessary and knocking over the old, ceramic bottles that had been stacked in a pyramid with one satisfying crash after another. He could have thrown and smashed things all day.

Aubrey was just as talented at knocking things down as he was, which only fueled Heath's competitive fire.

"You thought you were going to master me, did you?" Aubrey teased him as the man behind the booth handed Eugenie not one, but two bright, cheap, stuffed bears.

"This isn't over," Heath said, still too hot and breathing too fast for his own good. "I'm not settling for a draw."

Aubrey's expression faltered. "Heath, it's all in fun, right? Don't take any of this too seriously."

The only thing worse than having Aubrey callously flirt with other men or beat him at children's games was having him notice just how desperately Heath was hurting.

"I hate losing," he said, hoping Aubrey would take it as an excuse. He glanced around, spotting another likely game. "I won't lose."

He pointed to the next booth—one that involved shooting golf balls off their tees using a water gun—and ushered Eugenie and her stuffed animals over to it.

"Is something wrong, Heath?" Aubrey asked, following behind as Heath made a bee-line for the game. "I didn't mean anything by any of this, I just thought it would be fun to play some games. And talk to some people. Casper is nice, but he isn't—"

He didn't finish his sentence, and Heath was grateful for it. Whatever now had him in its grip didn't want to listen to reason, and it didn't want to let go.

"Step right up, gentlemen," the young man at the water gun booth said, imitating a particularly grating American accent. "Win a prize and settle a grudge at the same time."

Heath wondered if the man had been watching the two of them compete or if he knew something about what Heath was feeling.

"We'll play," he said, moving over to sit on one of the stools by the table with water guns.

"Why don't you take this seat right here," the man behind the booth said, directing Aubrey to sit opposite Heath. "It'll make things a little more interesting."

He moved a stool and one of the stands with a golf ball so that Heath and Aubrey were seated directly across from each other. He then ushered Eugenie out of the way before saying, "On your mark, get set, go!"

Heath didn't think, he just acted, pulling the trigger on the large, powerful water gun he'd been handed. At first, he aimed for the golf ball, which was about two feet in front of Aubrey. But it became apparent in seconds, as he missed and soaked Aubrey's shirt, and as Aubrey did the same to him, dousing him in cool water, that the intention of the game wasn't really to knock down the golf ball and win a prize.

It was a free-for-all. Heath ignored the golf ball entirely, venting his anger and his hurt at being left, and his fear that it might all happen again, by spraying every last drop of water that he could all over Aubrey's chest and face. He was so caught up in imagining that if he could win this game, maybe he wasn't such a failure, maybe Gemma hadn't humiliated him into the dust, that he ignored the double entendre of spraying Aubrey's face.

He hardly even noticed that Aubrey was soaking his entire front as well, or that he'd handily knocked his golf ball off its stand while doing so. He didn't notice anything…until the sound of Eugenie roaring with laughter broke through the blind hurt that had consumed him.

Eugenie. She was all that mattered. She was the best thing in his life, and as big of a fool as he was for letting his emotions get the better of him, he'd made her laugh.

Everything would be alright.

He sighed and put his empty water gun down, sent Aubrey a brief, apologetic look, then swiveled on his stool to face Eugenie.

"Daddy, you look silly," Eugenie laughed, clutching a cheap, luridly colored bear in each arm.

The sight was pure joy and innocence, and when Eugenie dumped her new stuffed animals to run to him and throw herself into his wet and dripping arms, it made everything else in the entire world worthwhile.

"Careful, darling," he said, hugging her tightly, despite his warning. "Daddy's all wet."

"You squirted and squirted the water," she continued to

laugh, filling Heath's heart with a balm that nothing else could match for its healing power.

"Yes, and Daddy looked a right fool while doing it," he said, standing and lifting Eugenie with him.

"Nanny's all wet, too," she said, glancing over at Aubrey as he meandered toward them, squeezing water out of his shirt as he did.

"He is," Aubrey laughed, using a small dry patch on his sleeve to wipe his face. "Thanks to Daddy."

The grin Aubrey sent him was too knowing for Heath's comfort. He'd let Aubrey get to know him a little too well in the last month. There was so much the man didn't know, but they'd apparently grown close enough that Aubrey could see his wounds.

That wasn't the only thing being seen, though. Aubrey's shirt had lifted and bunched as he dried himself off, giving Heath a stunning view of his naked torso. He was all lean lines and muscle, with freckles on his pale skin and tawny hair that ran below the wet waistband of his shorts.

For three seconds, the hurt part of Heath tried to distance himself from it and shut out the feelings that looking at Aubrey gave him.

And then he let it go. He gave up, let himself embrace the attraction he'd been fighting for a month, and ogled the bits of Aubrey's body he could see.

Aubrey caught him at it.

"Well then," he said with a teasing grin. "Perhaps we should head up to the house and figure out how to dry off before we all catch our death of cold."

The teasing alone was a giveaway that Aubrey had his number. As they started up to the house, Heath just prayed that he wouldn't use it against him too humiliatingly.

They'd brought a change of clothes for Eugenie, in case of disasters, but neither of them had thought to bring anything for themselves. They were able to towel off in one of Swanmore's guest rooms—though not at the same time or in any way that would rile either of them up while they had Eugenie with them—but for the most part, they had to dry out the old-fashioned way, in the sun.

The rest of the day was surprisingly low-key. Perhaps it was the sense of resignation that Heath felt in the wake of humiliating himself in public. Or perhaps it was because Aubrey and Eugenie stayed with him for the rest of the afternoon as they had their picnic, watched the drag magic show, and got Eugenie the pony ride she'd wanted so badly. It was easier when everything was about Eugenie and when he could shelve his confusing wants and emotions for a while.

As soon as they tucked Eugenie into her car seat at the end of the day and started home, she dropped off to sleep like they'd kept her up for a month.

"Somebody's had a good time," Aubrey observed, twisting around to smile at the sleeping angel in the back-seat…and all the stuffed animals she'd won. "I think you might need to send her to Stuffies Anonymous to recover from a certain addiction, though."

Heath laughed. It was an open, relaxed laugh, too. "She'll forget about them in a day, and then we can throw them out."

Aubrey smiled and faced forward again. There was a bit of silence as he settled into his seat, and as Heath navigated the roads that would get them onto the highway.

And then came the moment Heath had been dreading.

"What was going on back there?" Aubrey asked. "Earlier, I mean. With the games."

"Nothing," Heath answered, a little too quickly.

Aubrey frowned at him. "Don't give me that, Heath. Just tell me what was going through your head." He paused, and when Heath didn't answer, he said, "Alright, tell me why you're so jealous of me talking to other guys, then."

Heath pressed his lips together and huffed out through his

nose. He thought about arguing the point, about telling Aubrey he wasn't jealous, but instead he just said, "No."

Aubrey's brow inched up. "Oh, so you *are* jealous, then."

Heath remained stalwartly silent, staring straight ahead at the road.

For a long time, Aubrey just watched him, as if waiting for him to confess to everything. The more he did that, the less inclined Heath was to say a word. He wouldn't have known what to say anyhow. He hadn't expected anything where Aubrey was concerned. He hadn't anticipated that he would have feelings for someone else after the devastation of Gemma, and he most certainly hadn't expected he'd have those feelings for a man.

Aubrey eventually gave up waiting for Heath to come around and shifted to sit more comfortably. He leaned his muscled, sun-pink arm against the window, like he had on the way down.

"My new friend Casper told me a lot of interesting things about the history of Swanmore Glen and the Brotherhood earlier," he said, staring out the windshield.

Heath darted a quick glance to him, then stared forward himself. "Did he?"

Aubrey hummed and nodded. "It sounds like a fascinating institution. I can imagine that it would have been a lifeline for the queer community back in the day."

"Yes, as I understand it, it was," Heath said. The tension started to drain from his body, and his shoulders unclenched. He could have this conversation. He could talk about something innocuous instead of the elephant in the…car.

"One thing he said did bother me, though," Aubrey went on with a slight frown.

"Oh?" Heath asked.

Aubrey peeked at him before saying, "He seems to think that the Brotherhood has become too hoity-toity for its own good, and that it's lost touch with its egalitarian roots."

Heath had never thought much about it. He hadn't thought about the Brotherhood at all in years now. "I suppose maybe it has," he said.

Aubrey paused for a brief moment before saying, "I'm thinking of joining."

Heath glanced to him in surprise before looking at the road again. "You're thinking of joining the Brotherhood?"

Aubrey laughed. "Is that such a strange thing?"

"Well, it's…."

There was nothing behind those initial words. At least, nothing that Heath felt proud of saying aloud. His immediate thought was that Aubrey couldn't afford the membership fees, but there were no membership fees. Not like other posh clubs. Donations were encouraged, but not required.

His second thought was that Aubrey wanted to use the club as a dating pool, which was somewhat against the club's rules, but inevitably happened all the same. The founders had wanted to stop the Brotherhood from becoming the Victorian Grindr, but hundreds of relationships had started among its members over the past two hundred years.

"You don't want me to join," Aubrey said, glancing to him with a grin.

"No! Quite the contrary," Heath rushed to say. "In fact, I think it would be a good idea for the Brotherhood to get back to its mission of including members of all classes."

"Are you saying that I'm lower-class scum, then?" Aubrey asked with mock offense.

"I'm not saying that at all," Heath rushed to defend himself a little too quickly, proving that he'd taken Aubrey's bait.

Aubrey laughed at him, and after a quick check in the rearview mirror to make certain Eugenie was sound asleep, Heath snapped, "Fuck you."

That only made Aubrey laugh more.

Which made Heath smile reluctantly and relax a bit more.

They spent the rest of the drive home talking about unimportant things—the food they'd been served for the picnic, the architecture of the house at Swanmore Glen, and a few things about Heath's upcoming trip to LA. By the time they arrived home, Heath was starting to feel a pleasant sense of happy drowsiness, like the day had been worthwhile after all.

It was a new and different feeling. One he'd never felt after spending a day in public with Gemma.

"Do you need help putting her to bed?" Aubrey asked as they headed up the stairs to Eugenie's room.

"I might need help unpacking her bag and putting everything away," Heath said with a nod.

They made it to Eugenie's room, and the two of them worked together like a well-oiled machine to get Eugenie out of her grass-stained and rumpled play clothes and into her pajamas, and to unpack the bag that was now filled with dirty socks, empty packets of snacks, and a bottle of sunscreen that had somehow popped open and leaked all over the spare clothes they'd brought for Eugenie.

It was peaceful and domestic. It was exactly the sort of cap that the day they'd just experienced should have had. It warmed Heath's soul and made him feel like he was a good father.

It made him feel other things too, knowing he hadn't gone through it alone, but with someone who was engaged and invested in being a part of his little family.

"Sunscreen comes out in the wash, doesn't it?" Aubrey asked as he inspected Eugenie's dirty clothes. He then tossed them into the hamper in the corner of her room. "I'm sure it'll be fine," he answered his own question. "And it doesn't look like the bag got any on it."

He was remarkable. Aubrey broke every rigid stereotype Heath had had drilled into him about how caring and affectionate a man should be. There was nothing artful or affected about him either. He didn't try to live up to the world's expectations of masculinity, but he didn't work to become what the world, or even the community, expected a gay man to be. He was just simply and unapologetically himself, take it or leave it.

Heath wanted to take it. He wanted to be a part of Aubrey's steadiness and his joy. He didn't want to fight to fit in or to be someone worthy of a magazine spread anymore. He didn't want to care what social media or his parents or… or Gemma would think anymore. He just wanted to embrace the joy right in front of him and soak in it.

"I can take these wretched stuffed animals down to—"

Heath cut off Aubrey's pedestrian rambling and fussing over Eugenie's things by stepping into him, pinning him against the tall bureau, resting a hand against Aubrey's face, and slanting his mouth over his in the kiss that he'd wanted to steal since the moment Aubrey showed up on his doorstep.

TEN

SHOCK AND AWE. Those were the two things that Aubrey felt as he found himself wedged up against Eugenie's bureau, Heath's warm hand cradling his cheek, Heath's lips plastered to his. The moment had come so quickly and unexpectedly that Aubrey could only exist and accept it for a second.

Fuck, when Heath came in, he came in hard. His other hand swept down Aubrey's chest, igniting every nerve-ending as it did, despite the t-shirt he wore. And Heath didn't stop with his chest. He swept his hand around to Aubrey's arse, squeezing and tugging him flush against him.

At the first touch of Heath's semi-hard cock against his own through the layers of their clothes, coupled with the asking brush of Heath's tongue against his lips, Aubrey was electrified back into action. He let out a deep, needy moan and wrapped his arms around Heath, kissing him in return. He didn't mess around or play cute any more than Heath was doing. He grabbed a handful of Heath's hair at the back of his head and opened his mouth to give back the frantic, hot energy that Heath was giving him and then some.

Heath moaned in concert with him and tilted his head just

so. Their tongues brushed together, then warred as they each tried to take the upper hand, tasting and claiming the other. Aubrey let his weight rest against the bureau and reached for Heath's arse with his free hand. He didn't settle for any over-the-trousers nonsense either. He shoved his hand straight down under Heath's waistband so that he could feel the hot flesh of Heath's body under his touch.

"Oh, God," Heath gasped, pulling back for a moment to gulp down air.

Aubrey tensed, certain Heath would chicken out and run.

Instead, Heath launched back into him, reaching for the hem of his shirt and pulling it up so that he could get his hands all over Aubrey's body. He rubbed with his palms, pressed with his fingertips, and even raked with his nails with such intensity that a whoosh of sensation hinted Aubrey would be done before they got started, if he wasn't careful.

He used the movement of shimmying out of his t-shirt and throwing it to the side to put enough space between him and Heath so that he could regain his control. The hunger in Heath's eyes as he drank in the sight of his naked chest wasn't helping that control at all, though.

The one thing that did snap both of them back to sense was the faintest of sounds and the slightest of movements from Eugenie.

They froze, panting and hot.

"She's really worn out," Aubrey whispered as they stood there, half-entwined, watching Eugenie to see if she would wake up or not. "She'll probably sleep for the rest of the night."

"Do you think?" Heath asked, glancing back to Aubrey.

The question was deceptive. It wasn't about a young child's sleeping habits. It was an indication that Heath was not going to chicken out. He wasn't going to use his daughter as a shield anymore. He'd stopped making excuses.

Aubrey melted into a smile, brushing his hands slowly

over Heath's clothed body. "Yeah. I think we've got all the time we need."

Heath let out a breath of relief that made Aubrey feel like he was letting go of a hell of a lot of baggage. "Your room is right down the hall," he said.

That was all the invitation Aubrey needed. He pushed away from the bureau, grabbed Heath's hand, and tugged him out of the room. He had just enough sense to shut Eugenie's door most of the way, while leaving it cracked so they could hear if she decided to get up after all. Once they reached his room at the other end of the hall, he did the same with his door. With any luck, if anything happened, they would hear it before anything was seen that shouldn't be seen.

"We should be good for—"

For the second time, Heath lunged at Aubrey before he could finish his sentence. He pushed Aubrey's back against the wall, planted one hand on the wall beside Aubrey's head, then leaned in and reached for his leg. Aubrey didn't hesitate for even a millisecond before lifting his leg over Heath's hip so he could trap their bodies together.

They both sighed and moaned hungrily as their mouths attacked each other again. So long. Aubrey had waited so long for this moment, and it did not disappoint. For a guy who hadn't kissed another guy in years, Heath absolutely knew how to do it right. He was hot and aggressive, claiming what he wanted when Aubrey might have expected him to be hesitant. He thrust his tongue into Aubrey's mouth like he wanted to thrust other things in other places, then drew Aubrey's tongue into his mouth so that he could suck it.

Aubrey let Heath have a slight, competitive edge while he put his attention into fumbling with the buttons of Heath's shirt. He did the best he could with the patience he had, but when that patience ended, he grabbed the two sides and yanked with his full strength.

Buttons popped and clicked as they scattered across the floor, and Heath tensed, then pulled back, laughing.

"Did you just actually tear my clothes off and send buttons flying?" he asked, a brilliant light shining in his eyes.

"Isn't that how they do it in the movies?" Aubrey asked, breathless.

"Yes," Heath said, looking like the devil himself as he shrugged out of his ruined shirt, then flew at Aubrey again.

Aubrey was helpless to do anything but stand there, giving and receiving wet, open-mouthed kisses and threading his fingers through Heath's hair so that he could grip it tightly. He gyrated his hips as much as he could with Heath trapping them against the wall, making himself and Heath hard with the friction of those movements. He could already feel a damp spot forming as his cock leaked in anticipation of where the night would go.

"I want you naked," Heath panted as he pulled away a few minutes later. "I want all of you."

"Likewise," Aubrey gasped, too aroused to feel stupid for the clumsy answer.

They pulled away from the wall, tugging and working at each other's clothes. Aubrey tried to toe out of his trainers as they neared the bed, but ended up losing his balance. He tumbled to the bed, taking Heath with him. That ultimately worked in their favor, as they were able to wriggle and pull each other out of the rest of their clothes, and yank the bedcovers down so that they could slide between the cool sheets together.

Nothing cooled about their groping and straining and rubbing, though. Aubrey couldn't remember the last time he'd engaged in anything so raw and so hot. Their mouths explored as eagerly as their hands. Aubrey didn't even care what he was tasting as they rolled this way and that on the bed—Heath's mouth, his neck, his shoulder. All of it was amazing and had his balls tight and his cock throbbing.

Heath muscled him to his back, and before Aubrey could turn the tables to prove his strength, Heath slipped down to close his mouth over Aubrey's nipple. The need to push and shove and get the upper hand died and sounds of pleasure ripped from his lungs as Heath nipped and licked and sucked at his nipple. He never would have imagined nipple-play could feel so good.

Or maybe that was the fact that Heath had also reached down to grip his balls and roll them at the same time, flooding him with sensation.

"Shit, Heath," he panted, digging his fingertips into Heath's muscled shoulders.

That was all he could manage, though. A moment later, Heath stroked his hand up the length of Aubrey's cock. Not only did that cause him to arch off the bed at the lightning-hot pleasure, it nearly made him come.

"Slow down, slow down," he managed to pant, pulling his thoughts together, but only barely.

Heath tensed and pushed himself above Aubrey so that they weren't touching. "Sorry, sorry," he gasped. "Are you close?"

"Yeah," Aubrey answered with an almost giddy need to laugh. "But that's not it. We've got some decisions to make."

For a moment, Heath looked terrified. Aubrey couldn't for the life of him figure out why, until he said, "I'm not ready for commitment."

That made Aubrey laugh out loud. He took advantage of Heath's moment of confusion to muscle him to his back and pin his hands above his head. Heath was too startled by the switch in power to fight back until it was too late. Even then, Aubrey dipped down and treated him to a deep, sloppy, open-mouthed kiss, and kept kissing him until he let go and relaxed.

"I'm not ready for commitment either," Aubrey panted once he had Heath how he wanted him. "I meant that if you want this sex sundae to come with a penetration cherry on top, one or both of us has some prepping to do. Unless you like mess."

Heath blinked up at him, going redder than he already was. "I don't want to stop," he panted. "I just want you. Are you...okay without *fucking* fucking?"

Aubrey grinned, affection pulsing through him. "I am absolutely okay with it," he said.

He then proved his words by stealing another deep kiss, then scooting down Heath's body and shoving his thighs apart. He gripped the base of Heath's cock, holding it up, then licked his way from where his hand held up to his tip. Heath gasped and shuddered, then reached up and grabbed hold of the headboard. The movement stretched his body, showing it off in absolute splendor, and spurred Aubrey on.

He pulled back Heath's foreskin, then lavished the flared, shining tip of his dick with kisses and licks, and eventually drew the whole thing into his mouth. Heath made a devastatingly sexy sound of surprise and flinched, which pushed him farther into Aubrey's mouth. Aubrey just went with it, challenging himself to see how deep he could take it.

The answer was not much. He choked and pulled back, swallowing a few times to clear the feeling, then laughing and saying, "Walk before running." He then resumed his adoration of the tip of Heath's cock. It wasn't that he was incapable of deep-throating, he just hadn't done it for a while.

He would brush up on those skills as soon as possible.

He wasn't the only one who evidently hadn't done things for a while. Heath's body practically rippled with pleasure as Aubrey resumed his sucking, holding Heath's balls for good measure. When he glanced up, Aubrey could see the intensity of the pleasure Heath was caught in, both in Heath's expression and in the swift rise and fall of his damp chest as he rushed closer to the edge.

Aubrey barely had to put any effort into bringing that

edge moments later. Without warning, Heath moaned and thrust as he released into Aubrey's mouth. Aubrey was taken a little by surprise, but didn't mind swallowing and milking Heath's cock for more as Heath began to shake. He was giddy, figuring he was probably giving Heath the best orgasm he'd had in a long, long time.

Heath flopped like a rag doll that had lost all its stuffing a moment later, as his orgasm subsided. Aubrey loved the satisfaction that seemed to wash over him and the smile that lit Heath's face. He let his cock go and kissed his way up Heath's abs to his chest, licking one of his nipples on the way for good measure, then made it all the way to his mouth for a sultry kiss.

He loved the juxtaposition of Heath's spent relaxation and his own, still-pulsing need. He definitely took the upper hand as he kissed Heath again, running his fingers through Heath's hair and keeping him from fully catching his breath.

Heath's relaxation only lasted for a moment. He gathered himself enough to push at Aubrey. Aubrey inched back, thinking Heath just needed to breathe. Instead, he was tackled, flung onto his back so that Heath could switch their positions and go down on him.

He laughed for a few seconds only until Heath devoured his dick, pulling it all the way to the back of his throat. Heath gagged, but instead of pulling back and reconfiguring, he stayed right where he was, letting his throat do half the work of bringing Aubrey to life. As if that wasn't enough, Heath pulled up, sucking hard, and sending even more pleasure racing through him.

For a guy who had been married to a woman for the last five years and hadn't been with a man in even longer than that, Heath sure knew how to suck cock. He took Aubrey deep again, swallowing with more control and using his tongue to tease and ignite. Aubrey propped himself up on his elbows, legs spread, and watched in amazement as Heath devoured him like a porn star. He was so surprised by Heath's talent that he forgot to try and hold off so he could feel more.

"Fuck, I'm coming," he gasped just in time, before tipping his head back and letting uncanny pleasure pour through him as Heath swallowed over and over.

It was bliss, made better by the sheer surprise of how good Heath was at blowing. As the last of Aubrey's pleasure slipped away, he flopped back onto the bed, arms and legs still spread, mind blown. He let himself stay there, lost in how good the whole thing had been for a few seconds.

"Come here," Heath panted a few moments later.

Aubrey opened his eyes to see Heath slouched back against the pillows at the top of the bed, wiping his mouth. That sexy little gesture alone had Aubrey wishing he could come a second time.

He moved like his limbs were made of lead, crawling around so that he and Heath could wrap themselves around each other and sag so that they were lying side by side, the right way around, heads on the pillow. Aubrey grinned at him, then pulled him close so he could kiss him as thanks. Heath kissed him back, losing his fingers in Aubrey's hair as Aubrey did the same with him.

It was a warm, cozy contrast to the blast furnace of the love that they'd just made. And Aubrey didn't care what anyone else might have said about it, that had definitely been some top-notch love-making.

"So, no more hiding from the feels, eh?" he asked some time later, when they were too worn out even for kissing.

They just lay with each other then, legs tangled, soft cocks resting against each other, hands stroking gently.

Heath huffed a tired breath and hid his face against the pillow for a second. Then he turned his head up to look at

Aubrey. "I got tired of hiding," he said, brushing his fingertips over Aubrey's forehead.

"Yes, hiding can get tiring," Aubrey said with a smile of sympathy. "What did it? The jealousy? The threat that I might look elsewhere for someone to suck my cock—which you do astoundingly well, I might add."

Heath laughed sleepily and snuggled against Aubrey. Aubrey found it adorable that he was so cuddly post-orgasm. "Just because I also like women doesn't mean I can't suck cock like a pro."

Aubrey laughed, snuggling down into the blankets with him. "So does this mean I have to adjust my expectations about you being a pillow princess who only considers himself bi because he doesn't mind topping men?"

"I'm vers," Heath smiled, then added a teasing, "Surprise!"

Feelings that ran so deep Aubrey didn't know what to do with them swirled through him as he laughed and hugged Heath closer. "Oh! So does this mean I get a go at your juicy arse one of these days?" he asked, grabbing a handful of the arse in question.

"If you'd like," Heath said with pretend casualness.

"Good," Aubrey said. "Because I, too, like it every which way, so you'd better be ready for anything."

Heath's smile faded a little. "Are you saying you don't want this to be just a one-time thing?"

Aubrey's grin disappeared as well. "Are *you* saying you don't want that?"

They just lay there blinking at each other for a moment.

Aubrey wasn't sure what to do. In that moment, he wanted to have Heath's babies. But would the feelings of closeness vanish in the morning? Had Heath just needed to blow off some steam, or were his walls coming down a sign that he wanted more?

"I liked this," Heath said at last, brushing his fingertips

through Aubrey's chest hair. "I really liked it. I was faithful to Gemma, even though she wasn't faithful to me, even when we were dating, so it's been years." His face pinched, as if he didn't like those thoughts, even if they confirmed what Aubrey had suspected about how long it had been for him. Heath looked him in the eyes, his smile returning, and said with a sigh , "That was like coming home again."

Aubrey smiled with him and stroked the side of his face. "It was pretty fucking good for our first time together. And we didn't even *fuck* fuck."

Heath let out one of those sweet, embarrassed laughs. "I hope you're not disappointed."

"Not at all," Aubrey said. "It gives us something to look forward to."

Heath hummed and closed his eyes, shifting a little into a position that would be comfortable for sleeping. "I am looking forward to it. I really had forgotten how much I like being with a man. I'd forgotten how much I like being with someone whom I like and who respects me."

Aubrey tensed a little, then forced himself to relax so that he didn't alarm Heath. He wondered how aware Heath was of what he'd just said or if he was already half asleep. And he wondered how the fuck Gemma could have used and abused someone as sweet and caring—not to mention hot and fucking amazing in bed—as Heath.

"We'll talk about it in the morning," he said, reaching for the covers so that he could tuck the two of them in together. "You need your rest now. It was a long and eventful day."

"Yes, Nanny," Heath mumbled sleepily.

Aubrey laughed, then rolled Heath so that he could spoon him, and the two of them settled in together. Aubrey liked it. He liked it a lot. Heath needed to be taken care of just then, and Aubrey was more than happy to do it. He smiled, kissed the back of Heath's neck, then closed his eyes, waiting for sleep.

The last thoughts that ran through his brain before he was out were that he would have to do whatever he could to keep Heath and nurture this amazing thing growing between them.

That, and if he ever met Gemma, that harpy would have to watch her step.

ELEVEN

ALL HEATH WANTED to do on Sunday morning was have a nice lie-in with Aubrey. What they'd shared the night before had been brilliant. Like he'd told Aubrey, it really had felt like coming home to Heath, which was the last thing he'd expected. It wasn't just remembering how much he really liked sex with another man either. It was the raw heat and the joy of having what he'd wanted for so long, but had intended to deny himself. It was real connection with his partner instead of skin-deep lust that was quickly sated.

Heath wanted to bask in that a while longer, feel the length of Aubrey's naked body along his, and maybe go for another round of cock-sucking before getting up and having a lazy day. But three-year-olds didn't do lazy days. Heath was grateful that he'd developed a parent's hearing and light sleeping habits, because he heard Eugenie as soon as she started to stir and was able to get up and dash downstairs for his robe and pajamas before she took it upon herself to get up and find them.

Sunday was a whirlwind after that. He and Aubrey hadn't done any tidying up after their day out at all, so the rest of the bag needed to be unpacked and put away, his car needed a going over, and Eugenie still expected to be entertained at the level she had been at Swanmore Glen. It didn't help matters that she was still tired from her big day, which made her cranky. On top of that, Heath had a business trip to pack for and final details of the presentations he would be making to Hollywood producers to iron out.

All of it meant that he and Aubrey didn't have time to talk about what had happened. It hung in the air between them, like faint music the origin of which Heath couldn't pin down. Was it a good thing or had their moment of impulsivity wrecked things? Did Aubrey want more, or was one night good enough. For that matter, did *he* want more, or was a taste of his wilder days all he needed?

Nothing was resolved. Nothing at all. And as Heath kissed Eugenie goodbye on Monday morning—then stood staring awkwardly at Aubrey, wondering if he should kiss Aubrey goodbye as well, and if he did, if that was a business trip kiss goodbye or a goodbye to any hope of having a relationship that might actually fulfill him—he already felt as if he was being tossed around by turbulence that he had no control over.

The flight was fine. The car that picked him up at the airport was fine. The hotel where Storm Productions had him staying in the heart of LA was fine. Heath couldn't fault any of it, but he knew it was more than jetlag that had him oblivious to most of it. The only thing that shook him out of the muddled stupor of questions and memories that he was stuck in was the text reply he got from Aubrey when he texted to say he'd made it safely to his destination.

"Miss you already. Best of luck with the presentation. You've got this. XXX."

Heath stared at that text, smiling like a fool, for so long it was embarrassing. No one had ever given him a pep talk before he had anything important to do. Not his parents, and certainly not Gemma.

He got another one just as he was going to bed on Monday night.

"Get a good night's sleep tonight so that you can slay in the morning. Everything is taken care of here, and we're cheering for you."

Heath's insides felt like they were in the plane, taking off again.

"What are you doing up right now?" he replied back. *"It must be insanely late for you."*

Almost instantly, Aubrey replied with, *"It's morning here, silly. Eugenie and I have been up for half an hour at least."*

Heath smiled at that as he stripped out of everything but his boxers and climbed into his chilly, lonely hotel bed.

A moment later, his phone pinged again, and when he looked, Aubrey had sent him a selfie of him and Eugenie sitting at the kitchen table. Eugenie's face was a mess of blueberry pancake and syrup. Aubrey's face was gorgeous with a smile. Heath could still feel Aubrey's stubble against his lips and smell his scent as if he were right there.

"Looks like you've got everything under control," he texted back, then added, *"Off to bed now."* He thought about it for a few seconds, then added *"XXX"* before hitting send.

A moment later, Aubrey replied with a sleepy-face emoji and a heart.

Heath caught his breath and stared at their exchange as he sank down into his bed. It felt so perfect, right, and warm. Aubrey was amazing with Eugenie, and honestly, he was amazing with him as well. Whatever was building between them, it was so different from what he'd had with Gemma that it was impossible to place them in the same category.

But was that what he wanted? So soon after being dragged through the wringer by the divorce? He'd be naïve to think there wouldn't be any public comment on it if he was found out to be dating a man after Gemma. The world had come a long, long way, but not that far.

Despite thinking it would be impossible to fall asleep with so much weighing on his mind, Heath was out within half an hour. He actually slept well too, which probably had more to do with all the travel than anything else. He wasn't exactly rested in the morning, but when he awoke to find several missed messages from Aubrey, then unlocked his phone to find various selfies of what he and Eugenie had done with their day while he'd been asleep, it gave him all the energy he needed to get up and prepare for a day of meetings.

Except, instead of focusing entirely on meeting prep, even after he met his counterparts in the LA office for a pre-meeting breakfast before heading off to make the final funding pitch, he couldn't help but stare at the photos Aubrey had sent him, over and over, to the point of ridiculousness.

"Who is she?" Dennis, his colleague from the LA office who would be making the pitch with him, asked once they were in the elevator heading up. The grin he wore as he watched Heath look at his phone was far too smug for Heath's liking.

"I beg your pardon?" he asked, in true British fashion.

Dennis's grin widened. "Everyone knows Gemma did a number on you, so I'm glad to see that someone has put that sparkle in your eyes again."

Heath flushed hot, but managed to hide his embarrassment at being caught with a flat look. He quickly swiped back to a pic that Aubrey had sent that was just Eugenie, then turned his phone to Dennis.

"The 'she' in question is my daughter, Eugenie," he said, trying to sound dismissive enough to end Dennis's smirking, but not so dismissive that the man would think he was an arse. "Her nanny sent me a few pictures, and I guess I'm just missing her."

He turned his phone back to look at it, and swiped to one of the pics Aubrey was in as well.

"Oh," Dennis said, a slightly surprised look on his face.

"Sorry. I could have sworn that those puppy-dog eyes were 'this woman rocked my world and I want more' eyes and not 'my daughter is an adorable jelly bean' eyes."

Heath smiled politely, even though a quick wave of panic over the way Dennis assumed it was a woman who had rocked his world—and how he might react when he found out the truth—hit him.

He was spared from having to say more as the elevator opened directly into the offices of the production company they were pitching to. From there, the next several hours were taken up entirely with negotiations over initial costs, casting input, residuals, and every other topic involved in green-lighting a television series that Heath could think of.

Luckily for everyone involved, not only was Heath devilishly good at his job, he was passionate enough about the project that he was able to fight for the things he wanted for it without letting anyone intimidate him. Blessedly, that impressed the team he was negotiating with.

"I know you have other companies you're meeting with this week," Steven, the executive in charge of the production company's team said as they all left the corner boardroom where they'd spent most of the day, "but I have a good feeling about our future of working together."

Heath breathed a huge, inward sigh of relief. *After the War* would be a reality now, he was sure of it. There was still work to do, and he and Dennis had two more days of meetings before he could go home, but he felt as if he'd done his job well.

"Hey, there's a party tonight out in Laurel Canyon," Dennis said as they headed out of the office. "You should really go. A lot of big names will be there, and it'll be a great opportunity to schmooze and put out some feelers for casting and crew."

Heath winced. Dennis was right, but the very last thing he wanted to do was attend a Hollywood party. What he really wanted to do was go back to his hotel and call Aubrey, hoping it wasn't too late and that he was still up. They had so many things they needed to talk about, and even though they would have to wait until they were in the same place again for most of it, Heath just wanted to hear his voice.

"Are you going?" he asked Dennis, wondering if he could get out of it if his colleague would be there.

"Yeah," Dennis said, touching Heath's arm as they stepped into the crowded elevator. "I can give you a ride. We'll just swing back to your hotel after we debrief everything at the office so you can change, then maybe grab some dinner, and be over there just as things really get started."

Heath wanted to sigh, but that would have been rude. He pulled out his phone, and as discreetly as possible, he texted Aubrey with, "*Would you be free to talk later?*"

Within seconds, Aubrey replied with, "*Yeah. What time?*"

Heath was a little too aware of Dennis watching him. He texted back, "*About two hours?*" hoping that would be enough time to wriggle away from work for a while.

"*I'll be here*," Aubrey replied. With a smiley face emoji.

Heath grinned stupidly at his phone for a few seconds before noticing that Dennis was watching him. "Eugenie," he said, gesturing to his phone, then put it back in his pocket.

He wasn't sure whether Dennis believed him.

Everything went well at the office. Gerry was still up in the London office, and he was thrilled that they were going to be able to get the production partners he wanted. Gerry also encouraged him to go to the party to network. There was no way Heath could wiggle out of it when Gerry wanted him to go.

And so, he went. Dennis drove him through the busy highways and winding, canyon roads, into the hills where the latest and greatest stars had their mansions. Beverly Hills was for the old, classic stars. The up and comers had snatched up their real estate a little farther out from the city. They were twice as extravagant as their old counterparts, though. Heath was amazed—and just a little bit appalled—by the ostentatious architecture of the mansion they found themselves at. They had to pass through two layers of security and show ID to get into the party, but once they were there, it was like something out of a reality competition show. The kind he hated.

"I just have to make a call," he made his excuse to Dennis before wandering off in the hopes of finding a quiet corner.

It took far too long for him to find a dark, relatively quiet spot in the garden, on the other side of an infinity pool that looked out over a stunning view of the sparkling, gaudy city at night. The view wasn't half as important to him as the sound of Aubrey's phone ringing as Heath placed the call.

"Well, hello," Aubrey answered the call in a smooth, sultry voice, making Heath smile and catch his breath.

"What time is it there?" he asked, instantly worried.

There was a pause and a small grunt, and Heath wondered if Aubrey was in bed, rolling over to look at his clock. "Do you really want to know?" he asked.

Heath did the math and winced. "Sorry. It's the middle of the night there."

"It's half four. That no longer qualifies as the middle of the night," Aubrey said.

"Sorry." Heath winced some more. "I...I just wanted to hear the sound of your voice."

God, he was awful. He'd turned into a soppy, ridiculous mess.

But Aubrey hummed warmly and said, "I miss the sound of your voice, too. And the sight of your grumpy face."

"I do not have a grumpy face," Heath grumbled, knowing full well he was making a grumpy face right then...as he was melting into a pile of sentiment under a palm tree decorated with fairy lights.

"And I miss the feel of your skin against mine, the taste of your lips and tongue. And the taste of your cum, for that matter." Aubrey's voice was a sensual purr.

Heath felt himself getting hard as he sat in his dark corner of someone else's garden, rich and famous people laughing and chattering all around him, throbbing, pulsing music playing off in the distance somewhere.

"Was it a one-time thing, or is it more?" he asked quietly, almost terrified of the answer.

"More," Aubrey said, putting more sensuality into that single word than Heath had ever heard from Gemma. "At least, I want more." Those words were tighter, more everyday Aubrey. "Is that what you want?" And those words were nervous, Aubrey's voice pitched slightly higher.

Heath glanced around, as if everyone at the party could hear the conversation he was having. "Yes," he said at last in almost a reverent whisper. "I absolutely want more."

He heard Aubrey let out a breath, and maybe flop back against his pillows. "Good," he said, his voice much more relaxed. "Then when you get home, we'll talk about things and see where we go from there."

"I…I want to do more than talk," Heath said, starting to shake a little with the importance of everything he felt, his heart racing and his head spinning. "I want…you."

He'd intended to say more, but he'd been noticed. A too-thin woman wearing a sparkling sheath dress that barely covered anything had spotted him and was wandering over.

"Oh, God," Heath sighed, the mood broken. "Heidi Allman is at this party, and she's just discovered me."

"You're at a party?" Aubrey asked, his voice changing to everyday excited Aubrey. "A fancy Hollywood party with celebrities and everything?"

"Yes," Heath said in a flat tone. "I'm here to *network*." He said the word as if it were sour.

Aubrey laughed. Heath got harder. "Go do your party,

then," Aubrey said. "I need an hour more sleep before Eugenie wakes up and demands I follow through on my promise to take her to the zoo so she can see her pony again. She's convinced the pony from Swanmore Glen lives at the London Zoo."

Heath smiled. He couldn't help it. The world Aubrey was in, with zoos and comfy beds at home and family, was the world he wanted to be in, not the one where Heidi slipped her way over to him and sat down on the garden bench beside him, staring at him with all the intensity of a falcon about to snatch its prey.

"You do that, then," he said. "I've got to go."

"Goodbye, Heath," Aubrey said, as if his name was an endearment.

Heath ended the call, too afraid to say goodbye in return lest he accidentally tell Aubrey he loved him.

"Who was that?" Heidi asked without even saying hello.

"Um, hello, Heidi," Heath told her in return, making it clear from his tone that she was being unforgivably rude to ask.

Of course, none of Gemma's model friends ever could take the hint. "Are you dating someone new?" she asked, playing her fingers through Heath's hair, as if they were an item or something.

"No," Heath said with a small frown, trying to scoot away from her.

"Are you sure? Because you were smiling," Heidi persisted.

Heath huffed. "It was the nanny," he said. "I was checking up on Eugenie."

Heidi looked delighted by that for some reason. "So you're fucking the nanny, are you? How very British."

If he could have stopped himself from flushing beet red, Heath absolutely would have. He could only pray that the darkness of the garden hid his reaction.

"Don't be ridiculous," he said, standing. He slipped his phone into his pocket

Heidi stood with him, her eyes aglow with avarice. "Oh, so you *aren't* dating anyone," she said. Apparently, she saw that as an invitation to slide an arm around his waist and to whisper in his ear, "I'm available, you know."

Heath glanced sideways at her. He had a feeling Heidi was as available as Gemma had always been whenever someone who could get her something was around.

"Good for you," Heath said.

He tried to step away, but Heidi wouldn't let him. "A little birdie told me you had a successful meeting with Charger Films today," she said. "Word on the street is that they're going to greenlight your historical series. I look amazing in a corset, you know," she said, thrusting her breasts against his arm.

It was everything Heath hated about Hollywood in one glittery package. Everything was pretend, from the interest Heidi showed in him to the carefully orchestrated party around him. Heidi wanted in on *After the War* to advance a career that she didn't have the talent to maintain. The fact that she seemed willing to use her body and sacrifice her dignity to do so turned Heath's stomach. Even more so, because seeing the intent behind Heidi's attention now felt entirely too much like the feeling he'd had when Gemma had set out to woo him.

"I'm sorry, Heidi," he said, extracting himself from her as carefully as he could. "I won't be in charge of making any casting decisions. You're wasting your efforts with me."

"Friendship is never a waste," she said, taking a different tactic and sending him an almost girlish smile. "Gemma was right about you being a stand-up guy."

Heath had absolutely no idea how to respond to that. He wasn't even sure what Heidi was getting at. Was she still in close contact with Gemma? Had she been sent to figure out if he was dating someone new for whatever reason Gemma wanted to know? Or was she truly trying to wheedle her way into his affections so she might be considered for a part.

Whatever the case, it was horrifically off-putting.

"I wish I could help you, Heidi," he lied with a smile, hating himself for it, "but those sorts of decisions aren't up to me."

"Aww," Heidi continued to flirt. "What a shame."

That was all Heath could take. "Excuse me," he said, nodding past her, as if he'd seen someone, when he'd done no such thing.

He walked away from her with a frown, intending to find a way to leave and get a ride back to his hotel. Everything around him was the antithesis of where he wanted to be and what he wanted to feel just then. He wanted to be at home, in a place with roots and history, that felt cozy and comfortable. He wanted to be with his daughter, who would love him even if he were a binman.

But most of all, he wanted to be with Aubrey. He wanted to be taken care of, the way Aubrey had done when he'd been sick. He wanted to take care of Aubrey as well, including but not limited to showing off just how good he was at blow jobs, on a regular basis. He wanted Aubrey's artlessness around him as he navigated a profession that was often without substance. He wanted a life of simple happiness, but if he was going to have that, he would have to work for it.

TWELVE

ONE NIGHT WASN'T NEARLY ENOUGH.

Of course, it hadn't really been just one night. It had been one month of living together, eating meals together, chatting about things like tidying the house together and putting Eugenie's best interests first together. It was nights of hanging out on the sofa, watching junk telly, or texts from Heath letting him know a meeting was running late and he would be home when he could be, or him texting Heath to ask if they needed tea, because it was on sale.

And yes, it was one night of sultry kisses and a blow job that Aubrey still got hard remembering on top of that. It was the promise of everything that was to come as well.

So much more waited just beyond Aubrey's reach that it took his breath away.

"I miss him so much!" he declared, far too loudly, as he and Eugenie walked through St. James's Park on Friday, Ulrika and Lindsey and their kiddos with him.

Ulrika and Lindsey paused in the middle of the conversation they were having about something Ulrika's bosses had done—he was so caught up in his feels that he couldn't even pay attention to juicy gossip from the other nannies anymore —and stared at him.

Then they burst into laughter.

"I knew it would come to this," Lindsey said, shaking her head at him as she laughed.

"What's funny, Nanny?" Lawrence asked her from his buggy.

Aubrey winced. He'd thought all the kids were asleep now, after they'd spent about an hour chasing after the ducks at the Buckingham Palace end of the park, then getting ice cream.

"Nanny Aubrey is being silly," Lindsey explained to him.

"Oh," Lawrence said, then laughed as if he got the joke.

Maybe it was being laughed at by a five-year-old, but that felt like the moment when Aubrey knew he had to stop avoiding things.

"It's hopeless," he said with a shrug and a sigh. "I'm in love with him. I have broken a nanny's first oath of office by falling in love with my employer."

Lindsey and Ulrika were still laughing at him as they all pushed their buggies through tourists and joggers and dozens of other people who paid them no mind, even though the conversation was about to get interesting.

"There is no nanny oath of office," Ulrika said, then added, "Thank God. We would all be in violation of it at every turn if there was."

"That's the truth," Lindsey said, slightly more sympathetic. "I had such a crush on the father at my last placement. He was a Greek shipping tycoon with an office here in London, and he looked like one of those sexy, ancient statues. The family took me with them to Corfu on holiday last spring, and you should have seen what he looked like, all oiled up with sunscreen, lying out in a tiny little swimsuit."

"As much as I would love to fantasize about Mr. Gabris

right now," Ulrika stopped her from going on, "we're listening to Aubrey getting all wet for Mr. Manfred right now."

Aubrey scowled at the cheeky look Ulrika sent him. "I am not getting all wet—"

He stopped. There was no point in lying, not to two of his closest friends.

"This would all be so much easier to navigate if Heath hadn't gone to LA just as things were getting interesting," he said.

"Ooh, and how is LA today?" Lindsey asked.

"I wouldn't know," Aubrey said, a tug of excitement in his gut. "Heath is flying home today. He's probably somewhere in the skies, making his final approach to Heathrow at the moment."

"Then why are you all worked up about missing him?" Ulrika laughed, having entirely too much fun with his misery. "You won't be missing him for long."

That was true. But not missing Heath meant that they'd have to deal with all the things that had been left unsaid between the two of them for the past week. As lovely as the text conversations they'd had over the last few days had been, and as sweet as the few phone calls they'd shared had been as well, they hadn't discussed anything serious.

Of course, it wouldn't have been right to tackle something so potentially important when eight time zones separated them. They'd mostly discussed how Heath's negotiations for his show had gone—very well, by the sound of things—and everything Eugenie had been up to. It had been a quiet week at home, but Aubrey had figured out within a day that Heath needed to hear about every tiny thing, no matter how mundane, to act as the antidote to the Hollywood lifestyle he had been thrust temporarily into.

"I guess I'm just worried about having *the talk* with him," he sighed and admitted at last.

"I hate *the talk*," Lindsey said, helping Lawrence out of the buggy so that he could crouch down and investigate a rock that was apparently fascinating. "It's that moment when you can't avoid the truth anymore. You're either on the same page or you're about to have your heart broken."

Aubrey winced, because his friend was all too right.

"I never have the talk," Ulrika said with a shrug. When both Aubrey and Lindsey glanced to her, she went on with, "I just assume we're casual until someone either hands me a ring or asks me to move in with them."

"Aubrey has already moved in with Heath," Lindsey pointed out.

"Oh, well, then you're fucked," Ulrika said with a smile.

"I would like to be," Aubrey said with mock solemnity. "Properly, that is."

Lindsey gasped. "I would never have pegged you as a bottom."

"That sentence could be taken in more than one way," Ulrika pointed out with a smirk.

That sent Lindsey into peals of laughter that woke Daisy. Once Daisy was awake and saw that her brother had been let out to roam free, she screamed until she could be let out too. Which woke Eugenie and David, which meant the conversation ended there.

Although Aubrey did get a last word in with, "I just want to know where things stand between the two of us right now so I can know whether to fan the flames of hope or to treat it all like nothing more than a good time."

That was the heart of it, after all. As far as Aubrey was concerned, things could go either way. Their conversations in the days since *that night* had been promising, but past experience had taught Aubrey that everything could change on a dime. Especially with a man who wasn't one hundred percent comfortable with his sexuality. He'd fallen down that rabbit hole before, and it wasn't pretty. He wanted to protect himself from feeling that shitty again.

The thing was, he liked Heath desperately, and he was certain that the feelings they both had could get bigger. But he wasn't so far gone yet that he couldn't pull back and readjust his expectations without suffering major heartache to the point where he would have to quit a job that was perfect for him.

Eugenie ended up being the one who saved him from himself. She kept him on his toes at the park, then as they took the Tube to get home in time for lunch.

"I think a nice jam sandwich and some reading time is just what we need after a lovely morning in the park," he told Eugenie as he carried her in one arm while pushing the buggy up the sidewalk to Heath's house.

"And Peppa?" Eugenie asked.

"If you mean one of the numerous books in your library, then yes," Aubrey told her. "If you're talking about the telly—"

He stopped as a flicker of movement behind one of the sheer curtains of Heath's house arrested him. It couldn't have been Heath. His flight had probably already landed, but he had to get through passport control, then collect his luggage and meet up with his driver. He'd mentioned that he might possibly stop by the office first as well.

Aubrey continued up to the front door, working to convince himself that he'd been imagining things and the movement was nothing. But when he reached for the handle, he found the front door unlocked. More than that, there were sounds coming from inside.

A moment of almost panic froze Aubrey. Very few break-ins happened in the middle of the day, but if someone out there knew Heath was away on business and that he and Eugenie had gone out, they might try anyhow.

A moment later, Aubrey dismissed that idea. The house had more security than a palace. If someone had broken in, alarms would be going off. He would probably have gotten a call from the police as well, since Heath had added him to the house contacts. It was far more likely that Heath had arrived early, and that he was puttering around, putting his things away.

Leaving the buggy on the front steps, Aubrey shifted Eugenie in his arms so he could shelter her if whoever was inside turned out to be anyone other than Heath, then pushed open the door.

"Hello?" he called into the house, standing just inside the doorway with the door still open, so he could rush Eugenie to safety if he needed to. "Heath? Are you home?"

A loud tapping sound came from down the hall, and a moment later, Gemma Stone appeared at the far end. She burst into a smile, then hurried toward them, her three-inch heels clacking on the hardwood.

"Eugenie! Baby!" she called out, greeting her daughter with a bright smile.

She stretched out her hands with their perfectly manicured nails, like she would take Eugenie from Aubrey's arms. But instead of going to her, like Aubrey would have assumed all little girls wanted to do with their mothers, Eugenie squirmed to bury her face against his shoulder and made a panicked, fussing sound.

"Sweetie, I've missed you so much," Gemma went on in an over the top, sing-song voice, her enormous hoop earrings swinging wildly as she leaned forward. "Mummy has missed her little angel."

She ignored Aubrey entirely and went so far as to grab Eugenie in an attempt to wrench her from Aubrey's arms.

Eugenie shrieked and scrambled to get away from her.

"What are you doing?" Aubrey sidestepped Gemma, coming all the way into the house, grabbing the buggy with one hand and pulling it in with him so he could use it as a blockade.

"Who are you?" Gemma demanded, as if she were really asking what right Aubrey had to withhold her daughter from her.

"I'm the nanny," Aubrey replied, deadpan. "Heath said he sent you my CV and that you signed off on me."

"Oh, yes." Gemma frowned at Aubrey for a moment—or at least tried to, the immobility of her brow hinting she'd had a recent Botox treatment—then went right back to trying to coax a now wriggling Eugenie away from Aubrey. "Come and give Mummy a hug, Genie. I've missed you so much! You should see what I brought you from Paris."

Aubrey tried to hold Eugenie back, even though Gemma kept reaching for her. In the end, neither of them got her. Aubrey was forced to put Eugenie down, and as soon as he did, she bolted for her playroom.

"Is that any way to greet your mummy?" Gemma scolded her, starting after her, heels clicking. "When I've dropped everything and come all the way from Paris?"

Aubrey frowned. "What are you doing here anyhow?" he asked, following her. "And how did you get into the house?"

Gemma stopped halfway down the hall and sent Aubrey a scathing look. "This is *my* house," she snapped. "Eugenie is *my* daughter, and Heath is *my* husband."

Aubrey's brow went up. "That's not what the divorce papers say."

Gemma scrutinized him even more, somehow without moving her perfectly made-up face too much. "You don't know anything about it. You don't know what my relationship is like at all. You're just the hired help."

The argument was so ridiculous that Aubrey couldn't even be angry about it. He just gaped at Gemma as she continued down the hall and into the playroom.

He followed her, amused when Gemma just stood there,

looking around dumbfounded. She evidently couldn't see Eugenie hiding in the middle of her stuffed animal mountain, watching them.

"Heath isn't here," Aubrey said, trying another approach. "You should leave, then call him later to sort whatever it is you're here about."

"His plane landed an hour ago," she said, still searching the room. "He'll be home in time for lunch. I've brought Nando's, which I know he loves."

Aubrey blinked. Heath didn't like fast food of any sort. More importantly, how did Gemma know he was on his way home?

"What are you doing here?" he asked, crossing his arms.

Gemma didn't answer. She'd just spotted Eugenie, and all of her focus went into her daughter.

"There you are, baby," she said, back to using the treacly-sweet voice again. "Why are you hiding from Mummy? I've missed you, yes I have."

Aubrey's eyes went wide. "She's a child, not a chihuahua," he said, stepping over to the stuffed animal pile.

Gemma snapped straight from where she'd bent over in an attempt to get Eugenie to come out of hiding. "Don't you tell me how to be a mother," she said. "And who in their right mind hires a man to be a nanny anyhow?"

"In the first place, how very sexist of you," Aubrey said, trying extraordinarily hard not to raise his voice or use a tone that would upset Eugenie. His little princess was upset enough already. "Secondly, something tells me I'm more qualified to care for a child than you will ever be."

"There's no such thing as qualifications to take care of a child," Gemma said, definitely talking down to him now. "But you wouldn't know that, since you're a man." She ignored Aubrey's indignation and crouched down to be on Eugenie's level. "Mummy has brought you some lovely chocolate from Paris, and Nando's for lunch. Would you like lunch or chocolate first, baby?"

"Chocolate?" Eugenie showed a hint of interest in her mother.

"Not before lunch, princess," Aubrey said.

It proved to be the wrong thing to say.

"I want chocolate," Eugenie wailed, reaching out for Gemma.

Gemma turned to give Aubrey a smug look before standing and pulling Eugenie into her arms. "I knew you would pick Mummy in the end," she said, then clicked her way past Aubrey and on to the kitchen.

Aubrey took a second to breathe and marshal his defenses. Gemma was after something. She wouldn't have been there if she wasn't. And it wasn't Eugenie, that much was certain. At the same time, she was using Eugenie as a tool to get what she wanted. Just like she always had, if the few stories Heath had told about the harpy were any indication.

Aubrey refused to let his princess be used that way. Heath wasn't the only one he'd grown serious feelings for in a short amount of time.

By the time he made it into the kitchen, Gemma had plunked Eugenie in her booster seat at the table, but she hadn't strapped her in. She'd opened a bar of what looked like fancy French chocolate, but she hadn't broken it into bite-sized pieces. She had the Nando's bag open and was unloading takeaway containers onto the table. The only drinks in sight appeared to be soda, and one entirely too large cup had been set at Eugenie's place along with the chocolate.

"Eugenie isn't allowed soda," Aubrey said, figuring that was as good a place as any to start taking back control of the situation. "She's too young."

"Nonsense," Gemma said, popping open a container of chicken that was probably far too spicy for a three-year-old. "There's no such thing as being too young for soda."

"Heath doesn't like Eugenie drinking sugary drinks," Aubrey went on. He stood on the opposite side of Eugenie's chair from Gemma, reaching for the soda to move it away.

Gemma made a derisive noise and moved the cup closer to Eugenie again. "Heath always was an annoying stick in the mud."

Since he didn't want Eugenie to become the center of an actual tug-o-war, Aubrey opted to fasten the buckle of her booster seat instead. At least that way, Eugenie wouldn't fall out of her chair if Gemma snatched at her again.

"If you dislike him so much, why are you here?" Aubrey challenged Gemma.

Gemma ignored the question. "What do you think of the nummy, nummy chocolate, baby?" she asked, crouching to be closer to Eugenie's eye level.

Eugenie had dived into the chocolate with gusto, but after just a few bites, she had made a face and was trying to spit it out again. "Yucky," she said, using her hands to get it out of her mouth and getting chocolate and spit everywhere.

Aubrey spotted the label on the table. "You bought dark chocolate with lavender for a three-year-old?"

"It's my favorite," Gemma said with a pouty shrug. She stood and broke off a piece for herself. "I would offer you a piece, but seeing as you aren't going to be here long enough to enjoy it…."

That was it. Aubrey wasn't going to put up with any sort of insinuation like that from Gemma.

"I'm the nanny," he said. "I'm not going anywhere. And you had better believe that I am going to look out for Eugenie's best interests, no matter who I have to protect her from."

"I'm her mother," Gemma said. Aubrey couldn't tell if she was startled by his statement or if it was just the Botox preventing her from wearing the expression that fit her emotions. "The moment Heath comes home, I will have you sacked so fast that you won't know what hit you."

"The moment Heath comes home," Aubrey countered her, stepping slightly closer to Eugenie, "he will throw you out of his house and prevent you from coming anywhere near his daughter."

"She's *my* daughter," Gemma said. "And you're a nobody. You mean nothing to Heath, but I'm his wife. All I have to do is crook my finger, and he'll take me back."

"You really believe that?" Aubrey demanded.

His tone was too much, and Eugenie burst into wailing cries. Aubrey didn't blame her one bit.

"It's alright, baby," Gemma said, trying to scoop Eugenie out of her seat. She didn't get very far, what with the strap holding her in. "Mummy's got you."

Eugenie screamed louder, turning away from Gemma and reaching for Aubrey.

"Hold on, sweetheart," Aubrey said, trying to soothe her and get around Gemma's grabby hands to undo the buckle of her seat.

As soon as it was loose, Gemma tried to take advantage of the moment to pick Eugenie up. Eugenie wanted nothing to do with her, though, and scrambled to get to Aubrey. The result was that she was in serious danger of falling.

"Let her go," Aubrey snapped, no longer concerned with keeping his voice calm. Eugenie was already upset. "She's going to fall."

"Then you need to give her to me," Gemma snarled back. "She's my daughter."

"You're putting her in danger. Stop now," Aubrey said.

"She's my daughter. This is my house. Get out now before I call the police."

"You're hurting her," Aubrey snapped, roiling with frustration as his need to get Eugenie away from danger warred with his instinct to let Gemma have her to avoid a bigger accident. "You need to let her go."

"She's mine!" Gemma shouted.

"What's going on here?" Heath's voice boomed through the kitchen, drowning out even Eugenie's crying.

They both let go, and Aubrey twisted to see Heath in his rumpled business suit, travel stubble and anger making him look sexy as hell, as he marched up to the table and plucked Eugenie out of her seat and into his arms. Aubrey had never been so relieved to see anyone in his life.

THIRTEEN

HEATH HAD NEVER BEEN SO DESPERATELY happy to end a business trip and go home in his life. If he could have gotten out and pushed the plane to make it go faster, he would have. Even a first-class seat couldn't stop him from squirming and checking the flight track map every half hour to see if he was that much closer to the love of his life.

Which was Eugenie, of course. He missed his darling girl more than he'd ever thought he would. But he'd been confident in Aubrey's ability to take perfect care of her while he was gone.

If he were honest with himself, it was really Aubrey that he was itching to see again. He'd had more than enough time to think about Aubrey, what had happened between them, and what he wanted to do about it, in between meetings in LA. After everything for the series had been settled and he'd had time to drive up the coast a little to go for a walk on the beach, he'd thought about it some more.

He'd come to a few conclusions on that walk—that life was short and there was no reason he shouldn't enjoy it, whether anything more would come of his relationship with Aubrey or not—and he'd spent most of the flight rehearsing the speech he would deliver to Aubrey as soon as he was home and settled. He was going to tell him how they should just go for it.

Settled. That was what he wanted to be. He was part of an industry that was all about glitz and glamor and stars, but Heath wanted nothing more than a cozy, peaceful nest where he could unwind from the stresses of the film business and be with someone who would appreciate him, and whom he could appreciate.

He was warm with the anticipation of calm, domestic things as he climbed out of the car he'd hired to take him home from Heathrow and as he rushed up the steps and into his nest…and was immediately assaulted with the sound of arguing coming from the back of the house.

Worse still, he knew both of the voices that were raised against each other and mingled with Eugenie's miserable crying.

Gemma was back.

A dozen conflicting emotions tore through Heath as he set his suitcase down and headed down the hall to the kitchen, none of them good. What the devil was Gemma doing back in his home, and what did she want now? What had she done to upset Aubrey the way he clearly was? And what was going on with Eugenie that had her wailing?

"What's going on here?" he demanded as soon as he stepped into the scene in the kitchen.

Gemma was trying to yank a red and squalling Eugenie out of her booster seat at the table. She was obviously hurting Eugenie in the process, which wasn't surprising. Aubrey seemed to be trying to get Eugenie away from Gemma without hurting her, but his face was flushed and the anger in his eyes would have been a complete turn-on, if the situation wasn't so utterly mad.

Both Aubrey and Gemma turned to Heath as soon as he made his demand. Gemma immediately let go of Eugenie and straightened up to smile at him. Aubrey let go as well, but guided Eugenie to sit safely in her booster seat.

"Heath, love. You're home," Gemma said in her sing-song "I want something" voice and moved around the table as if she would embrace him.

Heath wanted absolutely nothing to do with that. He turned his body away from her and to Aubrey. But instead of embracing the person he really wanted, he scooped Eugenie out of her booster seat and hugged her close.

Aubrey watched him and Eugenie carefully, and actually answered Heath's question with, "We came home from a walk and Gemma was here. Eugenie wasn't pleased to see her, so I tried my best to ask her to leave."

Heath nodded to show he understood, but his focus was on Eugenie. She seemed to cry harder, now that her papa had her, and threw her arms around Heath's neck tight enough to choke him.

"I know, darling, I know," Heath did his best to soothe her with words and touches. He rested a kiss against her forehead, but Eugenie shifted away from that to lay her head against Heath's shoulder. "Daddy is here now."

His soothing might have worked if Gemma hadn't turned on Aubrey and shouted, "How dare you try to keep my daughter away from me? I should have you sued for child endangerment for turning her against me."

Heath rolled his eyes at Gemma's ignorant theatrics. He opened his mouth to sort things, but Aubrey jumped in with, "You were upsetting Eugenie. She wanted nothing to do with you."

"She's my daughter. Of course she wants me around, don't you baby," Gemma snapped. She tried to shift her way around the table to get closer to Eugenie. The way she stretched out her arms indicated she would try to take her from Heath.

Heath pulled away, glaring at Gemma as he rested a

protective hand on Eugenie's head. "You are obviously not here out of any concern for our daughter or you would let her be with her nanny, whom she adores."

Gemma pulled up short and looked at Heath mutinously. She huffed and said, "Who hires a male nanny to care for a little girl? Are you certain he isn't, you know, *hurting her*?"

"I would never—" Aubrey started, his voice a low hiss. He stopped himself, turning away and pushing a hand through his hair, like he knew he needed to calm down or things would get out of hand.

"Gemma," Heath said, trying to be firm, but without flying off the handle, since Eugenie was just starting to calm down. "Why. Are. You. Here?"

Gemma went tense, studying Heath with her mouth slightly open for a moment. Then she gave up with a sigh and slumped into what felt to Heath like an affected and very practiced pose of contrition and regret. "I've had an awful time these last few weeks, Heath," she said, pouting a little and making sad eyes at him. "Simply awful. I nearly tripped on the runway in Milan, and then there was this awful reporter who continually hounded me about it, and about our divorce."

She lowered her eyes slightly, then peeked up at him through her fake lashes, like she was trying to seduce him. The worst thing about that was that the tactic had worked in the past. Heath had swallowed Gemma's sob stories so many times in the past and rushed to make her feel better—not unlike what he was doing for Eugenie now—because he'd always liked the feeling that he could do something to make the people around him happy.

He didn't feel that way now. At least, not about Gemma.

"Might I remind you that we are divorced, Gemma," Heath said, shifting Eugenie in his arms as she calmed down and went limp and heavy. "You no longer have the right to come running to me when things don't go your way."

Gemma stared flatly at him for half a second before turning on the water works. "He's left me, Heath," she said, letting her lower lip wobble and tears artfully fill her eyes. Gemma always was good at crying on demand. "Maurice has left me. He said that his mother doesn't approve of me, of all things. Can you believe it? And he tossed me out of his flat as well."

Heath narrowed his eyes. While he believed it was entirely possible that Gemma's new flame had left her—or she had left him when she saw a better opportunity—the story was full of red flags.

Aubrey seemed to think so as well. He looked incredulous as he tried to stay still and keep calm at the other end of the kitchen. His body was as tight as a bow-string, though, and his skin was still flushed with anger. He shot Heath a look as if to say, "You aren't really buying this shite, are you?"

He was hot as hell. Heath had imagined his homecoming in so many different ways, most of them ending with the two of them in bed, but those fantasies had always played out with him on top. The way Aubrey was now, Heath's fantasies took an entirely different turn. He wouldn't mind Aubrey working out some of those emotions on his arse.

Now, however, was not the time.

He turned back to Gemma and took a deep breath. "We are no longer together, Gemma," he said as coldly as he could when his blood was running hot. "You must call before you visit, and I think it would be a good idea if I were here when you visited going forward." He sent Aubrey a glance, worried that he was still furious enough to cause a greater scene with Gemma.

It was never fruitful to cause any sort of a scene with Gemma. She thrived on drama too much.

"I don't need permission to enter my own home," Gemma said in the most derisive tones possible.

"This is my home," Heath explained, growing calmer the

more indignant Gemma was—because that felt more familiar than anything. "The divorce settlement gave no part of it to you." Gemma opened her mouth to say more, her gaze slipping to Eugenie. "The settlement also gave full custody of our daughter to me. You gave up those rights willingly. I would ask that you respect the authority of Eugenie's nanny, who is more than competent and of impeccable character, and ask first before waltzing into our lives."

"This is insufferable," Gemma complained, her back going straight. "You cannot do this to me. I have rights. I'll call my lawyer about this."

Heath was tempted to smile. Right on cue, Gemma had switched tactics from victim to Valkyrie. It was her usual routine.

"Gemma, get out," Heath sighed. He rubbed his forehead with his free hand, truly starting to feel the jetlag as the scene wound down. "I just got home from a business trip in LA. I'm exhausted, dehydrated, and all I want to do is take a nap and be with my daughter. We'll discuss whatever it is we need to discuss later, but for now, just…leave."

Gemma crossed her arms and swayed slightly on her spot as she studied Heath. Heath could see she was thinking about things, planning her strategy, and likely looking for weaknesses. She glanced to Aubrey for a moment, but Aubrey wisely stayed silent.

Finally, Gemma said, "Fine. I'll leave." She marched across the kitchen to where her designer bag sat on the counter, grabbed it, then kept going for the door. "But I will be back, Heath. We have so much catching up to do."

Her demeanor changed at the last moment to be flirtatious. The smile she left him with was as good as a formal announcement that she would try to wheedle her way back into his life. Heath wondered what the hell she wanted now.

"I'm sorry about that," he told Aubrey, shifting Eugenie in his arms again so he could kiss her hot little face.

"You've nothing to be sorry for," Aubrey said, letting some of his anger out, now that Gemma was gone. He paced away from the counter he'd been leaning against and gripping, heading for the table to clean up the food Heath was just now noticing. "I had no idea you were married to such a —witch." He looked at Eugenie—who was too out of it to hear him swear, one way or another.

"Leave the food," Heath said with a sigh. "I'm hungry anyhow after that flight."

"Are you sure you want this?" Aubrey said, looking at the takeaway cartons and sodas. "I could make you something healthier."

Heath grinned. If that wasn't a summation of the tangle between him and Aubrey and Gemma in a nutshell, he didn't know what was.

"I'll eat this. I haven't had Nando's for ages, and even though I'm against fast food in general, God, I love this and I miss it," Heath said. He sent Aubrey a look that invited him to find a double meaning in those words.

"I guess I wouldn't say no to a bit of spicy chicken myself," Aubrey said, smiling.

That smile signaled the end of the ordeal. The three of them sat down at the table to eat what Gemma had brought. Eugenie refused to let go of Heath, but that was perfectly alright, as far as Heath was concerned.

Heath was so drained by the time they finished eating that he could hardly see straight. "I truly am sorry about Gemma," he said as he took Eugenie up to her bedroom for a much-needed nap. "She's conniving and manipulative, and she obviously wants something from me. Probably having to do with *After the War*, since I encountered one of her friends at a party in LA who seemed to know the project was about to be greenlighted."

Aubrey followed them up the stairs, graciously carrying

Heath's suitcase. He set it inside Heath's bedroom before continuing up to the second floor with them.

"That makes sense," he said. "I wish we'd been here when she first showed up. I wouldn't have let her through the door."

Heath grunted as he headed into Eugenie's room at the top of the stairs. "She would have found a way in anyhow. She might have even called the police. It wouldn't have been the first time she did that."

"She's called the police before?" Aubrey asked, eyes wide with shock and anger.

"It didn't amount to anything," Heath sighed, taking Eugenie to her bed. "She thought she could threaten me with a domestic violence charge because I refused to let her come along on a business trip to New York."

Aubrey gaped, but Heath didn't really want to think about it any more than he had to. He focused instead on taking off Eugenie's shoes and settling her in for a nap, surrounded by some of her army of stuffed animals. He noticed that the two cheap, ugly ones she'd gotten at the Swanmore Glen picnic seemed to have the place of honor near her head.

"She hasn't grown tired of these yet?" Heath asked, picking up one of them as Eugenie closed her eyes and fell instantly to sleep. He wished he had that talent.

Aubrey grinned. "She loves them. She calls them 'Daddy' and 'Nanny'." He paused, then added, "I'm the chartreuse one and you're the magenta."

"Oh, God," Heath said, rolling his eyes as he stood.

He liked the names, though. He liked the implication behind them. Children were far cleverer than some people gave them credit for. He wondered if Eugenie had picked up on the currents flying around the house in the past month. He wondered how she would react if he and Aubrey got into an actual relationship and Aubrey stuck around as more than her nanny.

"You look knackered," Aubrey said, his warm smile drawing Heath out of Eugenie's room and into the hall.

"I am seriously jetlagged," Heath sighed, rubbing his face. "And I haven't slept well this past week, away from…home."

He raised his eyes to Aubrey. All the feelings he'd had before Gemma had ruined his homecoming were back. The longing he'd felt the whole time he was away swirled around him, and his heart sped up.

"You'll sleep well now that you're *home*," Aubrey said, his smile turning seductive. "I'll make certain of it."

A shiver of longing shot through Heath. It would feel so wonderful to let everything slip and to allow Aubrey to take care of him. To take care of all of him.

As if he could sense Heath's thoughts, Aubrey stepped into him, circled his arms around Heath's waist, and pulled him close for a kiss. It was the kiss Heath had waited all week for, and he didn't waste any time before melting into it. Never had strong arms enclosing him felt so peaceful and perfect. Aubrey kissed him with passion, but also with tenderness instead of the raw demand of their one night together. He teased and coaxed, making Heath close his eyes and hum with delight at the arousal that washed over him.

"I know the perfect cure for jetlag," Aubrey told him in a teasing purr. He lowered one hand to squeeze Heath's arse. "Guaranteed to make everything better."

Heath smiled as he leaned back in Aubrey's embrace. "Let me shower first," he said. "I'm gross from traveling, and… and I need to clean up first." He met Aubrey's eyes intently to communicate what he actually meant.

Aubrey's whole face lit up. "Yes, sir," he said with a saucy lilt. "I'll get everything ready."

That was all Heath needed from him. The two of them hurried downstairs. Heath stripped out of his travel suit as Aubrey opened up his suitcase and started unpacking and sorting Heath's things. It was the most unexpectedly sexy thing Heath could imagine. It made him hot and horny to think about Aubrey sorting his laundry and putting everything in order as he showered and prepped for what they were about to do.

As if things couldn't get any better, as soon as Heath stepped out of his en suite, still a little damp from the shower, a towel wrapped around his waist, Aubrey had pulled back the bedcovers and lay waiting for him, naked and hard, a sultry grin on his lips.

"Did you miss me?" he asked with cheeky charm.

Heath let out a breath, and with it, the tension he'd been holding inside for a week. He dropped his towel and practically lunged for the bed.

"More than you can ever imagine," he said as he covered Aubrey's body with his own.

He went straight for the kiss, slanting his mouth over Aubrey's as Aubrey pulled his body close and swept his hands over Heath's back and arse. Few things in the world felt as good as Aubrey's kiss. The man kissed with abandon, wet and demanding. Heath's head spun with the pleasure of it as their tongues explored each other and their bodies heated.

Just kissing wasn't nearly enough, though. Heath broke away from Aubrey's mouth to kiss his way to his neck. Aubrey hadn't showered, which Heath was glad for. He was treated to the full scent and taste of him as he nuzzled his neck, then kissed his shoulder and worked his way down to tease and lick one of Aubrey's nipples.

He would have been happy to keep the pace slow and tender, but his energy really was depleted. Aubrey seemed to sense that and flipped their positions. As soon as Heath was on his back, Aubrey kissed him again with fervor. It was so good that Heath let go and sagged into the mattress, letting his body be used for whatever Aubrey wanted.

Heath had never considered himself even remotely kinky,

but he could definitely see the appeal of bottoming to the point where he had no control at all. It was bliss to let Aubrey kiss and touch him, to give up that control and just feel. Aubrey's mouth on his neck and chest was heavenly, and when he scooted lower, leaving a wet trail as he did, Heath thought he might have died and gone to heaven.

"Let me know if you want more from me," he gasped as Aubrey scooted down and nudged his thighs apart. "I'm tired, but I can give, too."

"Don't you dare," Aubrey said in a deep, intensely aroused voice. "You're doing everything for me just the way you are."

He must have been. Aubrey was very much into the moment as he kissed and worshiped Heath's stomach, and then his inner thighs. Heath sucked in a breath and nearly bucked off the mattress as Aubrey stroked his wet tongue across the crease between his groin and his thigh. And he had only barely touched his balls or cock so far.

He did that a moment later, causing Heath to moan and grip the pillow on either side of his head to keep himself from coming too soon. It was almost like Aubrey had practiced while he was gone and was intent on showing off as he sucked Heath deep, then pulled back and lavished the head of his cock with his tongue. Heath closed his eyes and bathed in the pleasure of it for a moment.

"Oh, God, I'm close," he gasped a moment later, eyes popping wide. He hadn't realized how close until he nearly lost it.

"Me too," Aubrey panted, shifting over him and reaching for the bedside table. Heath had been too caught up to see the condom and lube there earlier. "Ready?" he asked as he fetched them.

Heath held his breath for a moment, then nodded. He was more than ready. He'd waited for and wanted Aubrey for so long that time seemed irrelevant.

All the same, as Aubrey opened the condom and rolled it on, Heath shifted to his stomach and offered up his arse that way. Part of him wanted to fuck face to face, so that the two of them could look at each other while lost in their pleasure. But for some reason, that contact felt too intense for the moment. They still had things to work out, and silly as it was, he wanted to feel fucked in that particular moment, not loved and adored.

Aubrey was absolutely up to the challenge of giving him what he wanted. He was conscientious about prepping him with his lubed fingers, even commenting, "God, you're tight. Are you sure you want this?"

"I'm sure," Heath sighed into the pillow, willing his body to unclench.

That was what he needed and wanted, after all. He wanted to let go of everything and give it all to Aubrey.

That didn't stop the sting and burn as Aubrey pushed into him. Heath grunted and winced for a moment, then let out a long, sexy sound as Aubrey worked his way in deeper. Aubrey wasn't quiet either, which Heath liked. As overexaggerated as porn was when it came to sounds, Heath did like to let it all out and to show his partner he was enjoying himself. He let Aubrey know that with sound and by moving to meet his tentative thrusts.

And then Aubrey found Heath's prostate. Heath cried out with genuine surprise and pleasure.

"That's it," Aubrey said, wicked pride and a grin in his voice.

That *was* it. As soon as Aubrey knew he'd found Heath's prostate, he went for broke. It was so good that Heath could only hold onto the pillow and go along for the ride. And as the buzz of orgasm built in him, he wondered why the actual fuck he'd let Gemma convince him that he didn't really like this and that it had just been a phase.

Aubrey was clearly getting close, judging by the sounds

he was making. That prompted Heath to reach for his cock so he could push himself over the edge. He came with a deeply satisfied moan, hoping Aubrey could feel it instead of just hearing it.

"Fuck, Heath," he gasped after a few more thrusts. The intensity of his movements increased for a moment, then he collapsed over Heath's back, panting and spent.

Heath loved it. He loved every second of it. Even the fact that Aubrey stayed inside him for a second while pinning him to the mattress with his weight. He was sore and out of practice, but he loved that feeling of something lodged in him, filling and stretching him. It wasn't just something, it was Aubrey, his lover.

"Welcome home," Aubrey whispered into his ear, then nipped his earlobe.

Heath smiled and tried to come up with a witty reply, but he was too sated and happy to do anything but fall asleep.

FOURTEEN

AUBREY WANTED to wrap Heath up in cotton-wool and keep him safe from everything in his life that stressed him out. His already low opinion of Gemma had sunk even lower after witnessing the way she treated Heath. Aubrey was certain that the exhaustion Heath had given into after their afternoon delight had as much to do with her bullying ways as jetlag.

It had been amazing to top the hell out of Heath, though. And while part of Aubrey was convinced Heath had simply given in to bone-deep tiredness and the need to forget about his problems for a while, it had felt like fucking him had brought them closer on a deeper level. He never would have imagined someone like Heath would enjoy having his arse reamed so much, but Heath had most definitely enjoyed it.

But Aubrey's duty of care extended far beyond giving his boss an orgasm and then letting him sleep. He shouldn't have been sleeping at all, not when he needed to adjust back to London time. So when Eugenie showed the first signs of stirring from her nap forty-five minutes later, Aubrey woke Heath up with a playful slap on his deliciously used arse and told him to get back in the shower and prepare to be distracted with a toddler for the rest of the day.

It had worked, to a point. Heath made it to the end of the day on the sheer force of Eugenie's bliss at seeing him again. She kept him busy with stories and playing all afternoon, while Aubrey did laundry—both Heath's clothes from traveling and his sheets—then made them all a proper supper.

Without being asked or asking, Aubrey tucked himself into bed with Heath that night after the two of them had put Eugenie to bed. No comment was made about the gesture, and they did not have *the talk*. Aubrey was relatively certain they'd had *the fuck* instead of *the talk*. And as Saturday morning dawned, they had *the fuck* again, with Heath topping this time. It was the perfect way to greet the first day of the next chapter of their lives.

Aubrey had every intention of coddling Heath through the weekend with a lavish breakfast, a lazy morning, and maybe a walk in the park, since it started out as a lovely day. But Eugenie was overstimulated from having Heath home and threw a temper tantrum every half hour, the skies decided to give Heath a proper British welcome home by clouding over and pouring down rain halfway through the day, and Gemma kept ringing Heath until Aubrey was ready to throw his phone out the window.

"I'd turn it off, but I'm also getting calls from Gerry and the rest of the team about *After the War*," Heath sighed, tapping his phone to reject yet another call from Gemma halfway through the afternoon.

"She doesn't know when to give up, does she," Aubrey said with a frown as he brought Eugenie down to the living room after her nap.

Heath sent him a flat look. "She showed up at my house after divorcing me, knowing I would just be getting home from an international business trip, and she tried to woo me. Of course she doesn't know when to give up."

Aubrey hummed in frustration as he handed Eugenie over to Heath and looked for the remote to change the channel to something Eugenie would like. "It's the part about her knowing you would get back from a business trip yesterday that bothers me," he said.

Eugenie scrambled down from Heath's lap and flopped on the floor so she could watch the cartoon Aubrey had found. She wouldn't normally have been allowed to watch so much telly, but it was convenient with so many other things going on.

"I can guarantee that Gemma found out about *After the War* from Heidi, or one of her other LA friends," Heath said, moving closer to the center of the couch so that he and Aubrey could sit with their sides pressed together, watching Eugenie watching cartoons. "Hollywood is the land of gossip."

"I don't doubt it," Aubrey said with a humorless laugh. He took Heath's hand and threaded his fingers casually through it. "How did you get involved in such a weird industry anyhow?" he asked.

Heath shrugged. "The same way most things happen. By accident. I studied business at university, graduated with honors, and took the most interesting, highest-paying job that was offered."

Aubrey smiled, leaning his head against Heath's shoulder. "I bet every company in London head-hunted you the second you stepped off the graduation stage."

Heath cleared his throat, blushed a little, and mumbled, "Not *every* company."

Aubrey's heart swelled, and he twisted to kiss Heath's neck. He was so modest and just a tad grumbly. The entertainment industry might have been fun, but Heath wasn't really suited to it. He wasn't suited to be caught up in Gemma's games.

Speaking of which, just as Aubrey started to get comfortable, Heath's phone rang again. Heath picked it up and sighed heavily, then answered it with, "What?"

Aubrey couldn't hear what was said on the other side of the call. He wasn't certain he wanted to.

"No, that won't work at all," Heath said, frowning. "I just got back from a trip. I want a quiet, peaceful weekend. Maybe we can talk sometime during the week."

Aubrey frowned, but also squeezed Heath's hand in his and brushed his thumb over Heath's knuckles.

"I don't believe you, Gemma," Heath went on, then with just a hint of Gemma's voice being raised on the other end of the call said, "We'll talk about this later. Don't call me anymore this weekend. Goodbye."

He hung up, then sent Aubrey an apologetic look.

Aubrey returned that look with a sympathetic smile, then leaned in to kiss Heath's lips gently. That was all Heath needed right then.

Aubrey gave him the other kind of kiss he needed later that night. He gave him kisses and far more. More than once. Heath's energy had come back, and with it, the expressed desire to remember and revisit all the things he'd once loved. Sucking cock wasn't the only thing Heath was good at. Nailing prostates was another skill he picked up again, like riding a bike, after years.

Sunday was a much better day. The sun came out and stayed out, Aubrey impressed Heath with his breakfast sandwiches, and Eugenie was in a much better place after a good night's sleep. The three of them decided to go out and make a day of it. They ventured all over London, popping into the Museum of Natural History, and catching a musical show in St. James's Park.

It was exactly the sort of thing Aubrey wanted for his life, not just a weekend. Heath was relaxed and engaged with Eugenie. He had that healthy glow that came with being fucked and fucking well. The two of them were in perfect accord without being over-the-top clingy and obvious. They were easy with each other, which was exactly where Aubrey wanted to be.

"Are you certain you want to cook tonight?" Heath asked as they returned home as the sun started to think about setting. "We've been out all day, and you're looking like you caught some sun. I can order in, if you'd like."

"I wouldn't think of it," Aubrey said in mock horror. "It's my job to take care of you and Eugenie, so the least I could do is put together a Sunday roast. And I catch the sun when I so much as look out a window. It's the curse of gingers."

Heath smiled at him and laughed with easy grace. "You're not some nineteen-fifties housewife, you know," he said. "You don't have to do everything domestic for me. And I like your ginger."

"You'll pay me back later tonight," Aubrey said with a saucy wink as they lifted Eugenie's buggy through the front door, Eugenie asleep in it. "I wouldn't say no to that thing you did last night with your—"

He stopped at the sound of clattering coming from the kitchen.

Neither he nor Heath had to wonder for more than a half second what the noise was all about. Aubrey was furious in an instant and Heath rolled his eyes and sighed a few seconds before Gemma's falsely cheerful voice sounded from the other end of the hall with, "Honey, I'm home." She stepped out to where Aubrey and Heath could see her, then laughed and said, "That's what you're supposed to say."

The comment about being a fifties housewife seemed bitter now as Aubrey narrowed his eyes at Gemma. She was anything but a traditional housewife. She wore an apron, but that was about it. Her hair and make-up were camera-ready, and she wore heels with one of those designer outfits that was meant to look like it came from Asda when it actually cost thousands of pounds.

"Gemma, what are you doing here?" Heath sighed, moving around the buggy so he could take Eugenie out. She was waking up anyhow.

"I feel badly for the scene on Friday," she said, pretending to be all sweetness, but giving Aubrey the evil eye as she came down the hall. "So I figured I would just pop 'round and make a Sunday roast for you."

Aubrey exchanged a look with Heath. He was happy to see that Heath apparently didn't trust Gemma anymore than he did.

But there were delicious smells coming from the kitchen. Smells that were much better than he would have imagined Gemma to be capable of. He could smell lamb and something garlicky, as well as fresh-baked bread.

"Consider it a peace offering," Gemma said, clasping her hands together in front of her in the perfect picture of innocent contrition. "I've got the table set and everything." She paused, then added, "Even Nanny has a place. Come along, and you can have everything fresh from the oven."

She turned and walked back down the hall. Aubrey hadn't ever been interested in female mating displays, but the way Gemma's arse moved as she walked, not to mention the tightness of her jeans, seemed like a deliberate siren's song.

He turned to Heath with an unimpressed look. "I'm not sure what we just walked into."

Heath sighed and shook his head. "She still wants something. And I have no idea where the food I smell came from, but she most definitely did not cook it. I'm starving, though, and if she's paying, I'll eat."

The decision made, Aubrey and Heath headed into the kitchen. Aubrey was surprised Gemma hadn't set the formal dining room or brought out the good china. The table was set, though, and even Eugenie's booster seat had been placed to make her part of the scene.

On top of that, the food was exquisite. Even if Gemma wouldn't own up to where she purchased it.

"I made it all myself," she insisted when Heath asked her.

"You despise cooking, or any sort of domestic chore," Heath told her as he ate the last of his lamb. He breathed out through his nose as he chewed, then said, "Alright, the time has come for you to tell me what you're after."

"Why would you think I'm after anything?" Gemma asked, batting her eyelashes. She inched her hand along the corner of the table, as if she could take Heath's hand.

"You know this has become ridiculously tiresome," Aubrey said, rolling his eyes.

"You need to stay out of things that are between me and my husband, *Nanny*," Gemma snapped.

"We are no longer married, Gemma," Heath said, putting down his cutlery and leaning back from the table. "What do you want?"

Gemma did not, in any way, take the hint. "I'm beginning to think that I was a little hasty in signing those divorce papers," she said, her eyes downcast. The smile she wore when she peeked up at Heath made Aubrey want to laugh just as much as it made his blood run cold.

"You left me for a French actor," Heath pointed out to Gemma with a frown. "You humiliated me in the press."

Gemma shrugged. "The press always exaggerates things. And Heidi says you're lonely."

That was the answer to that. Heath had been right to suspect that Heidi, whoever she was, had given Gemma all the gossip about Heath and *After the War*.

Gemma tried to reach for Heath's hand again, but he pulled it away. "I'm not lonely, Gemma," he said with a serious look.

"I'm right here," Aubrey added. He wanted so desperately to just tell Gemma he and Heath were together, but that was Heath's information to share.

Gemma curled her lip in a sneer and pulled away from her pursuit of Heath enough to stare at Aubrey. "Yes, why *are* you still here?" she asked, reaching for her wine glass.

"Because you invited me to supper?" Aubrey countered.

Gemma waved her hand like she was dismissing him as she drank a large gulp of her wine. "Well, you're free to go now," she said once she'd swallowed. "And take Eugenie with you. Heath and I have a lot of catching up to do."

Aubrey stayed right where he was, despite the fact that Eugenie was quickly getting to the point where she would be over the whole meal.

Heath seemed to catch that they had a limited amount of time left before toddler chaos broke out. "We're not getting back together," he said. "Furthermore, I will neither be offering you a part in *After the War*, nor will I be recommending you be brought in to audition. There are no parts for you in any project I am associated with."

Gemma's back snapped straight so fast Aubrey thought she would knock something over. "What makes you think I want a part in your show?" she asked in a breathless voice, blinking rapidly.

"That's what you're after, isn't it?" Heath asked. "It's what you've always wanted me for. I'm just a way for you to advance your career."

"Nonsense," she said with an airy laugh. "I care about you, Heath," she went on, overdoing her sympathetic look as she reached for Heath's hand again. "I don't want you to be unhappy."

"I'm not unhappy," Heath said, rubbing a hand over his face. "I'm happier than I've ever been in my life right now, actually," he went on, glancing to Aubrey.

His smile was a dead giveaway. Even if Gemma hadn't suspected a single thing moments before, there was no way she could miss the heat in Heath's gaze as he looked at Aubrey now. But just in case she wasn't seeing what was right in front of her, Heath reached out and took Aubrey's hand.

Aubrey waited, practically doing a countdown in his head until Gemma put two and two together.

"But Heidi said you weren't interested in her," she started, "and I thought that meant you hadn't gotten over—"

Aubrey broke into a smug grin the moment she figured it out.

"No!" she shouted, staring bullets at Heath. "No, you don't do that sort of thing anymore Heath. You aren't gay."

"No, Gemma, I'm not," Heath said, sounding calmer than he had since the meal started. "I'm bi. I always have been. You knew that when we met."

"I thought you were just saying that to be on trend," Gemma said, her voice turning shriller by the second. "You don't *actually* like men."

"He *actually* does," Aubrey said. He was sorely tempted to add that Heath had a sore hole to prove it, but this was Heath's fight to win, not his to mess up.

"Aubrey isn't just the nanny," Heath said. "We're together."

The moment felt charged and alive. There was just something about saying the words aloud that made if all official in a way that even wet, messy fucking didn't.

Aubrey smiled at Gemma, trying to mirror Heath's relieved calm. He ended up showing her smug satisfaction instead.

"You can't do this," Gemma said, glaring between the two of them. "It isn't fair. Heath is my husband, and I'm not finished with him yet."

Aubrey sighed, feeling a headache coming on. They were back on this roundabout again.

Heath let go of Aubrey's hand, pushed back his chair, and stood. "Now that you know the truth, I think it would be best if you left, Gemma. Thank you very much for providing a lovely supper, but in future, please contact me in advance before you enter my house, or if you wish to spend time with Eugenie. Please note that I will be changing the locks and security codes immediately. I should have done it ages ago."

Gemma stood angrily. She glanced at Eugenie for the first time since the meal had started, but that was all it was, a glance. She glared at Aubrey, and if looks could kill, Aubrey would have been dead several times over.

"No one steals a man from me," she said in a low, threatening hiss. "I'm not done with him yet. But you are more than done."

"Gemma, there's no need for theatrics," Heath said, shutting his eyes for a moment. "This sort of behavior is beneath you."

"Unless you're aiming for your own reality show," Aubrey added in a mumble.

Heath's mouth twitched with amusement, but Gemma seemed madder than ever.

"You had better watch yourself, Nanny," she said, stepping away from the table. "I don't know what kind of game you're playing, but you're not going to win. You have no idea who you're up against."

Heath sighed. "Enough of this. Gemma, goodbye."

"I'll leave," she said, clacking her way around the table to the hallway. "But you haven't seen the last of me."

Aubrey burst into laughter as she marched down the hall, grabbed her handbag, and left. "Is she for real?" he asked. "Because I feel like I've just been threatened by one of Eugenie's cartoon villains."

Heath sat again, looking across the table at Eugenie, as if making sure she was unaffected by the dramatics. "She's existed on a steady diet of celebrity for the past five or six years," he said, shaking his head. "She's come to think staged moments like that one are normal and actual, normal life is boring."

"How long does she expect to maintain that?" Aubrey asked, picking up his cutlery again. The very best sort of revenge he could think of for the threats Gemma had made was to continue on with the meal she'd provided as if nothing at all had happened. "It must be exhausting to live that way."

Heath got up and switched his place with Gemma's so that he could sit next to Eugenie and help her. "She probably is exhausted," he said. "Which is why she's looking for the easy way into a career instead of doing the necessary hard work."

"You're not going to help her at all, are you?" Aubrey asked, pausing with a fork full of mashed potatoes halfway to his mouth.

"Don't be absurd," Heath said, grinning temptingly at Aubrey across the table. "I am quite happy just as I am right now."

Aubrey met that smile with a heated one of his own. "So, we're together, then?" he asked, immediately forgetting about Gemma and her drama.

"If you'd like," Heath said, blushing.

"I would definitely like that," Aubrey said, flirting back at him with a dreamy look.

"Then we're together," Heath said, then turned his smiling, pink-faced attention to Eugenie.

Aubrey's heart danced a jig against his ribs. He'd never felt so giddy or so excited at the beginning of a relationship before. Nothing had ever felt so right before either. Not even Gemma could stop the joy he felt, even though she was bound to try.

FIFTEEN

MONDAY MORNING WAS PERFECT. Heath woke up with Aubrey in his bed. His lover wasn't touching him or trying to get him hard or start something. He wasn't even awake when Heath's alarm started to ping. He was just there, comfortable and steady, as if he'd been there all along.

Heath slipped out of bed with a smile and headed to the bathroom for his morning routine. The routine nature of washing, shaving, and brushing his teeth was settling, and he couldn't wipe the smile from his face. Aubrey wasn't in his bed when he came back into the room to dress, but the bed had been made, and he could hear the sounds of Aubrey's and Eugenie's voices from upstairs as he dressed for work.

He headed downstairs and started the coffee, then turned on the news while puttering around, getting breakfast ready. Aubrey and Eugenie were downstairs a few minutes later, and as soon as Aubrey had Eugenie settled in her booster seat with some juice, he set to work making a proper breakfast. The three of them ate it at the table together, he and Aubrey grinning at each other the whole time and playing footsies under the table.

It was absolute, pure domestic bliss. Heath couldn't remember a nicer morning in his entire life.

"If every morning was like this for the rest of my life," he commented when breakfast was almost finished and Eugenie was starting to get bored of her fruit slices, "I would be the happiest man on earth."

Aubrey grinned at him with just a hint of a blush. "It is pretty nice," he said as he leaned back in his chair and sipped his coffee. "I could get used to it." He slipped his socked foot up the cuff of Heath's trousers, caressing his calf.

Heath's cock stirred with interest, but not enough to do anything about it. It was as if his body was just waking up and saying, "Oh, hello! This is nice. Yes, let's keep doing this."

"It's going to be a busy day at work today," Heath said with a sigh, letting the cozy moment go as he stood to take his dishes to the sink. "Now that *After the War* is officially greenlighted, we'll be shifting into the next phase of the production."

"Casting and filming?" Aubrey asked, getting up to help with the dishes.

Heath laughed ironically. "Hardly. More like getting the finances in order, setting up production accounts, and sending out feelers to distributors."

"So, in other words," Aubrey said, leaning back against the counter beside Heath, "all the boring things that make the fun things happen."

Heath smiled. "Yes, pretty much."

It felt like Aubrey's description fit the two of them perfectly. He was the boring half that made the fun half, Aubrey, work. Not literally, of course, although the whole thing had started out with him employing Aubrey. Heath liked the idea that he would go out there and fill his days with boring, high-powered work so that he could bring home enough money to keep Eugenie and Aubrey happy and stress-free. He didn't want the two of them to have to worry about things ever again. And if that made him a slave to heteronormative domestic roles, then he was willing to deal with that.

"Do the two of you have anything fun planned for today?" he asked once his dishes were taken care of. He wasn't quite ready to leave his happy place.

"Oh, a few things." Aubrey shrugged, then moved to stand in front of Heath, straightening his tie and brushing his hands over Heath's suit. It was a surprisingly dominant gesture, like Aubrey was reminding Heath of who really pulled the strings, and that Heath was a good boy. So much for heteronormative gender roles. "Eugenie and I are going to watch a little Peppa, play with some toys, maybe go for a walk and pick up something for supper, since it looks like it'll be a passably nice day. All of it is terribly important, of course."

In other words, perfection.

"Sounds lovely," Heath said, dipping in to kiss Aubrey's lips. That didn't feel like enough, so he grinned and moved in for a longer kiss. "I will do my level best to be home at the ordinary hour tonight," he said, stepping back and smiling at his lover. Those words felt so good. But he had to get to work, so he stepped past Aubrey and heading for the door.

"You'd better be," Aubrey said, swatting his backside as he passed.

Heath giggled. Actually, fucking giggled. He'd been asking himself for months what was wrong with him, but that question took on an entirely different feeling now. And now it had an answer. What was wrong with him was that he was in love.

"Goodbye darling," he said, veering close to Eugenie once he had his wallet and keys. He kissed Eugenie goodbye, then kissed Aubrey one more time for good measure. "Goodbye…." He let out a half laugh. "I feel like I should come up with some sort of pet name for you now."

Aubrey laughed, the sound pure joy. "How about sexy beast?"

Heath smiled broadly, but peeked at Eugenie. "I'm not sure about that one. You might get a few comments from your nanny friends if Eugenie started calling you that in the park."

"Because children repeat everything," Aubrey finished his thought with a smile. He kissed Heath quickly, then said, "We'll come up with child-friendly names later."

"I'm looking forward to it," Heath said with a smile. And he most definitely was.

He kissed Aubrey and Eugenie again, then headed out the door.

It didn't take him long to get to work, but as soon as he was there, he hit the ground running.

"Richard wants this thing to move fast," Gerry came into his office to say nearly as soon as Heath sat down. "We've got a meeting in fifteen minutes."

"I'll be ready," Heath said.

He expected Gerry to rush on, but he seemed to do a double-take in the doorway, then sent Heath a broad smile. "Something's different about you," he said.

Heath immediately blushed, then tried to overcompensate with a frown. "Nothing's different," he insisted.

Gerry stepped all the way into the room, nodded at Heath, then said, "Tell that to the hickey you're sporting."

Heath slapped a hand to his neck, but that only made Gerry laugh harder.

"I don't have any hickeys," Heath insisted, moving his hand back to his desk. He didn't. He'd checked while he was shaving. But it didn't matter if he had one or not. Gerry had found him out.

"Can I assume it's that gorgeous nanny of yours?" Gerry asked.

Heath blushed harder, which was probably all the answer Gerry needed. "You can assume no such thing."

"I don't need to assume," Gerry continued to grin like a cat with a canary. "It's written all over your face."

"Fuck you, Gerry," Heath sighed.

"If I'd known you were coming back over to our side, I might have actually tried for a fuck," Gerry laughed on.

Heath sighed and shook his head. Gerry was a good friend as well as a colleague, so there was no point in holding things back from him.

"I'm very happy," he said in clipped tones. "That's all you need to know, really. Things are new, and I'd rather not talk about it at work, because we have an important television show to produce now."

"Right you are," Gerry said with a cheery nod. "But I am happy for you, Heath. You deserve love after what Gemma put you through."

Heath managed a grateful smile, but was even more grateful when Gerry left him alone to do his work. He would have enough on his plate explaining Aubrey to people once their relationship became public. For the time being, he just wanted to focus on work.

The morning pretty much went by in a whirlwind. The first meeting turned into a second. Heath was fully engaged in work before ten. But he did pause when Aubrey sent him an adorable text message filled with heart emojis—and eggplants and peaches as well—that made him smile and blush right before he had to meet with Richard, the CEO of Storm Productions.

He sent Aubrey a rude text in return, then lost himself in the meeting.

At one point during the meeting, his phone pinged and he cursed himself for forgetting to put it on silent mode. Part of him was convinced that had been a subconscious decision so that he could be reminded of how in love he was.

As soon as the meeting let out, he checked his phone.

The message he'd gotten wasn't from Aubrey. It was from a number he didn't recognize.

Heath waited until he was back in his office to check the message. He was unsettled to find that someone had texted him a photograph. At first, he wasn't sure what it was. A bunch of guys with their shirts off at some sort of party, he figured. But when he looked closer, he realized one of the guys was Aubrey, and Aubrey was in a compromised position with the others.

Heath frowned and put his phone aside, almost like it contained a virus. There wasn't anything inherently wrong with the photo. Aubrey looked a little younger, so Heath didn't think it was recent. The fact that it was sent from an unknown number unnerved him.

He went back to work, but a few minutes later, his phone pinged again. Heath warily checked it, only to find another embarrassing picture of Aubrey with what might have been an old boyfriend. Still, there was nothing terribly wrong with the photo.

Half an hour later, an email came through from an undisclosed address. Heath was on his computer, dealing with work, and at first, he thought it had something to do with the production. Like a fool, he clicked on the link in the email. It led him to a police records site in Cornwall. At first, Heath was just confused...until he realized the link showed an arrest record for Aubrey.

Heath sucked in a breath, alarmed for about three seconds, until he started to read the record. Apparently, when he was seventeen, Aubrey and some friends had been arrested for stealing someone's boat and taking it out to sea, where it was damaged. It was juvenile criminal mischief, as far as Heath was concerned, but again, the fact that someone had sent it to him was disturbing.

No, not someone. Gemma was clearly behind it. She had

to be behind the texted pictures too. It was exactly the sort of thing she would pull.

Heath sighed and deleted the email, then reached for his phone, intending to call Gemma. Just as he picked his phone up, another text came through. Heath opened it with a clenched jaw, his anger rising, and found another embarrassing photo of Aubrey doing some sort of drinking challenge. As Heath stared at his phone, a video of that same challenge came through that showed Aubrey having a good time with friends, then puking up a lot of alcohol. It definitely looked like the sort of thing people did at university, even though Aubrey had never gone.

With a slight growl, Heath started typing back, telling Gemma to stop. He thought better of it and deleted his message, just calling Gemma instead.

He intended to give her a piece of his mind, but his call went directly to voicemail. Heath huffed out an irritated breath, then slammed his phone down on his desk. He refused to engage in the sort of immature games Gemma wanted to play with him.

Except, just because he was determined not to play, that didn't mean Gemma would just stop. Heath tried to ignore the increasingly steady barrage of embarrassing images and videos of Aubrey that she sent to him throughout the day. There were a few more emails as well with minor, barely-offensive things Aubrey had done over the years. Gemma sent him Aubrey's school files as well, and although Aubrey's grades had been surprisingly low for how intelligent Heath had found him to be, nothing Gemma sent him was damning. Not really.

Until the email that came through as Heath was getting ready to leave for the day.

Heath almost ignored that email and the link it contained to something having to do with London South Bank University. He let his hand hover over his mouse for a moment, then gave in and clicked it.

Immediately, he wished he hadn't. The link took him to a report that Heath was certain should have been private and inaccessible to the public. It was a disciplinary warning issued to an admissions officer from several years ago, condemning him for attempting to trade sexual favors for admission. Heath broke out in a cold sweat as he read bare details about how Aubrey had met with the admissions officer at a hotel in exchange for being accepted to the university. They'd been caught, Aubrey had been denied admission, and the officer had been placed on administrative leave for a term.

Heath swallowed the sick feeling the report gave him. So that was the reason Aubrey had never gone to uni. He'd done something despicable. The very idea of trading sex for gain made Heath's skin crawl.

He started reading the report again, but was jolted when his phone rang. He actually found himself hoping it wasn't Aubrey.

It wasn't. It was Gemma.

"What the hell game do you think you're playing?" Heath demanded as he answered the call.

Gemma got right to the point. "I just thought you should see what kind of person you have taking care of our daughter," she said in her pouty voice. "Is that really someone you want around Eugenie?"

"You had no right to go poking around in Aubrey's business like this," Heath answered. His anger was tinged with more hurt than he wanted to admit to. How could Aubrey have held back something so important from him?

Because it was none of his business, the sensible voice at the back of Heath's head answered. Because it had happened years before the two of them met.

"Those were only the things I was able to find this weekend," Gemma went on, too much self-satisfaction in her voice. "There's no telling what other dirt is out there."

"How did you discover any of this?" Heath demanded. "It's all personal, private information." There was no way any of it should have been accessible.

"I called in a few favors," Gemma said. Heath could practically hear her shrug. "I'm willing to call in a few more to dig deeper."

Heath let out a heavy sigh. "Stop this at once, Gemma," he said. "Despite what you may have found, Aubrey is a good person. Most of these things happened years ago, when he was barely more than a kid."

Except the admissions thing. That felt far more recent and immediate, even though it was years ago. The sordid nature of the whole thing stuck in Heath's throat, like something sour he couldn't swallow.

"I don't want a criminal taking care of my baby," Gemma went on. "You shouldn't either."

"Aubrey is hardly a criminal," Heath snapped. "Depending on how you accessed this information, I think that title belongs to you."

"I'm just looking out for my—"

"You haven't cared about Eugenie for a single day of her life," Heath cut her off. "I don't for one moment believe that you care now. You're just trying to wheedle your way back into my life for your own gain, but it's not going to happen."

"How dare you accuse me of—"

"It's not going to happen, Gemma," Heath insisted. "So stop this childishness at once."

"Heath, be reasonable," Gemma started to say.

Heath cut her off by ending the call. He put his phone down and shoved it across the desk for good measure, then took a moment to plant his elbows on the desk and just breathe. Aubrey had done some things wrong. Everyone had done *something* wrong in their life. The sensible thing to do would be to let it go.

But now that it was there, Heath couldn't shake the image of a younger Aubrey on his knees for some tweedy, balding, paunchy admissions officer. Who would be stupid enough to sleep their way into being admitted to university anyhow?

It didn't seem right. Gemma was likely just making things up to get her way.

But as Heath rose and grabbed his suit jacket and headed out of the office, the lingering feeling of disgust stayed with him. The link had directed him to the university's website, not something Gemma had made up. All of the other, petty things she'd sent him had been from official sources as well. It was possible that Gemma had invented a bunch of lies, but Heath had the horrible feeling that all she'd done was uncovered the truth.

The only way he could find out for certain was to go home and confront Aubrey.

SIXTEEN

"*YOU'LL BE SORRY.*"

Aubrey didn't recognize the number that the threatening text was sent from, but he knew immediately who had sent it.

"*No, I won't, Gemma,*" he texted back, then tucked his phone away and continued the game of helping Eugenie build her stuffed animal mountain. It was the best trick he'd thought of so far to teach Eugenie that tidying up was a good thing.

Fifteen minutes later, he got another text.

"*Heath is mine. He's straight, and I won't let you corrupt him.*"

Aubrey laughed at the message and shook his head as he typed, "*Based on how deep he swallowed my cock last night, I'm pretty sure he's not straight.*"

He thought twice about the message, then deleted it and slipped his phone into his back pocket again. It was better not to engage Gemma in whatever drama she was trying to create. He had better things to think about anyhow.

A soon as the playroom was cleaned up, he put together a few snacks, then bundled Eugenie into her buggy to take her out for a walk. The sun was out, or at least trying to be out, and Ulrika had texted their WhatsApp group that she was taking David out to a kiddie concert in Hyde Park. Aubrey had so much to catch his friends up on anyhow, so he and Eugenie headed out into the early afternoon full of smiles.

Those smiles died as he reached the park when Gemma texted him, "*Does Heath know that you're a criminal?*"

Aubrey glared at his phone and typed back, "*STOP,*" as if Gemma were some sort of text subscription service and he could end her messages with a one-word reply.

"*You'll be sorry,*" Gemma texted him again.

Aubrey thought about calling Heath to tell him what was going on. He might have some insight on how to deal with Gemma. But as soon as his finger was hovering over his phone to make the call, he changed his mind and blew out a breath. Heath was back in the office for the first time since his trip to LA. He'd said it would be a busy day, and Aubrey doubted he would want to be interrupted by something as petty as Gemma's jealousy.

He shoved his phone into his back pocket again, just as he spotted Ulrika and Lindsey over by the Serpentine.

"A friend in need is a friend indeed," he said to no one in particular and picked up his pace as he pushed Eugenie over to join their little nanny club.

"What's gotten into you?" Lindsey asked as soon as Aubrey met up with them.

"Not Heath, obviously," Ulrika teased him with a smirk.

"Actually, we're officially together now," he said, rushing through the revelation far too quickly. Before Ulrika or Lindsey could react, he went on with, "Gemma is causing trouble."

Aubrey's friends made sounds of sympathy.

"There's nothing worse than a jealous ex," Ulrika said as the three of them helped their kids out of their buggies so they could run around and play on the grass. "Ask me how I know."

"Gemma does have a vicious streak," Lindsey said, as if Gemma were her personal friend from way back.

"She found out about me and Heath last night, and she was brassed off, to put it mildly," Aubrey said with a humorless laugh.

"What did she do?" Ulrika asked.

"Nothing yet," Aubrey said with a shrug. "She's been texting me with threats since about nine this morning."

"That sounds juvenile," Lindsey said.

"At least it's not something worse," Ulrika said.

She'd spoken too soon. Aubrey's phone buzzed again. He thought about leaving it, but on the off chance that it was Heath, he pulled his phone out to take a look.

What met his eyes when he opened the text was a photo of an obvious minor that was so graphic and so mind-numbingly horrific that he felt his face drain of all its color. Gemma had sent him child porn.

Aubrey raced to delete the image as Lindsey and Ulrika looked on in confusion, but as he managed to get rid of the vile thing, another one appeared. Then another one.

"What is it?" Lindsey asked. "What's going on?"

The offensive—no, the *illegal* images that flashed into his texts started to arrive faster than he could delete them. Aubrey's initial anger at Gemma and abhorrence of the images that he absolutely did not want branded into his brain turned into bone-deep fear that made him start to tremble.

"Is it Gemma?" Ulrika asked, moving closer to his side. "What is she sending you?" Ulrika peeked over his shoulder and gasped at the images she saw. "Oh my God. Turn your phone off! Turn it off now!"

"I need to get rid of them," Aubrey said, starting to sweat.

"Get rid of what?" Lindsey said, then looked over his other shoulder. "Oh my God!" she gasped too. "Ulrika is right. Turn it off."

"Do you know what would happen to me if these images

are found on my phone?" Aubrey asked in a panic.

"Yes!" Lindsey and Ulrika shouted at the same time.

Ulrika yanked the phone out of his hand. "That's why you have to turn it off. Turn it off and take it right to the police." She turned the phone off for him.

"I can't let her get away with this," Aubrey said, taking his phone back once it was off. "Pestering me with texts is one thing, but landing me in prison is entirely different."

"You have to go to the police," Lindsey said, agreeing with Ulrika. "This isn't just some sort of game anymore. Not with those images on your phone."

Aubrey sighed and glanced off to where Eugenie and the other kids were playing some sort of game of tag. The worst feeling he could possibly have was not knowing what to do, but that was exactly how he felt. Gemma had backed him into a corner so fast and so efficiently that his head was spinning.

He should call Heath and let him know what was going on immediately. The trouble was, Heath's number was on his phone, and if he turned his phone back on before handing it over to the police, it could open up a can of worms that he wouldn't be able to close. And stupid wanker that he was, he didn't have Heath's number memorized. He could get it from home, of course, or get Heath's office number, but then he would have to find a phone to call from.

That wasn't the most difficult problem to solve, though. Not being prosecuted for having child porn on his phone was definitely a worse problem. Who was to say that Gemma hadn't sent images to his email or social media accounts either. If she had the ability to load his phone with pics like that so quickly, she could probably hack him into oblivion.

"I have to go to the police," he said with a helpless shrug.

"We'll come with you," Lindsey said with a stalwart tilt of her chin.

Aubrey smiled at her, and at Ulrika. "You're good friends," he told them.

They gathered up the kids—who were none too happy to have their play cut short so soon—and headed out of the park toward the nearest police station, as figured out by Ulrika's porn-free phone. As they crossed over Park Lane, Aubrey glanced fleetingly to the building Heath had pointed out as The Chameleon Club. He wondered if the Brotherhood that Heath had described to him would be able to handle something as tricky and damaging as being phone-bombed with porn. Maybe he should take Casper up on his suggestion of joining after all.

The rest of the morning and the early afternoon turned into a nightmare of hassle and police procedure. It took forever for someone to see them, even once he explained the situation. From there, all that happened immediately was an interview with a detective, who confiscated his phone. Aubrey wasn't at all encouraged when the officer turned his phone on again, only to have his eyes go wide and his expression turn shocked. But the worst was that a quick investigation showed that the images had been sent from a dummy account on an untraceable computer. Same with the images that had been sent to his email.

While all of that was happening, Eugenie decided to throw fit after fit as she was stuck in the police station with Aubrey, without lunch. Lindsey and Ulrika stayed as long as they could, but they had their own kids to look after. They prevented Eugenie—and Aubrey, too—from going nuclear by getting lunch, but they had to leave before the whole thing was done.

Aubrey considered it a small miracle that he was allowed to leave the police station after an official report was filed, and that Heath hadn't shown up to take Eugenie and blast him out for taking her along with him for the ordeal. He was unclear on whether someone at the station had even called Heath.

His head was a mess, and he was frazzled beyond

comprehension by the time he and Eugenie made it home close to six in the evening. Eugenie was bawling in his arms as he dragged her and the buggy over the threshold and into the front hall, but that wasn't the end of his troubles. Not by far.

"Where have you been?" Heath shouted at him as he came marching down the hall, face red with fury. "Why haven't you been answering your phone?"

Aubrey flinched at the level of anger Heath was sending his way. His eyes went wide, and he had to bite back the nasty retort that wanted to escape from him, exhausted as he was.

And then everything got ten times worse when Gemma stepped out into the hallway from the same room Heath had been in moments before. "See?" she said with a smug smile. "I told you he was nothing but trouble."

"This is all your fault," Aubrey shouted—too loud, as it happened, because Eugenie burst into another round of wailing sobs.

Heath had come in close to reach for Eugenie anyhow, so Aubrey carefully handed her over before storming down the hall to Gemma.

"I've just spent most of the day at the police, turning over my phone—which has been loaded with child porn," he added as he turned back to Heath to inform him, then faced Gemma again, "and having them question and investigate me for all the shite you sent to me," he blasted her.

"Me?" Gemma blinked innocently, placing a manicured hand on her chest. "I don't know what you're talking about."

"What are you talking about?" Heath asked. He looked like he was caught between trying to calm Eugenie and being furious over everything that was going on.

Aubrey turned to Heath. "Gemma spent the morning texting me threats," he said. "And then she sent all sort of vile child pornography to my phone." He turned back to Gemma.

"And my email accounts, and all the other things you hacked as well."

"I have no idea what you're talking about," Gemma said in a high, too-excited voice. Her eyes glittered with victory and with malice. "I'm sure Heath will be the first to tell you I'm not tech savvy at all."

"You spent the day texting me, too," Heath said. "Things that you and I need to talk about."

It took Aubrey a second to realize those words were meant for him, and that Heath was furious with him as well.

"What are you on about?" he asked.

"She sent me records," Heath said with a scowl. "Of past arrests. Other things, too." He looked upset.

Aubrey's first reaction was utter indignation. He was the one who had just spent most of the day at a stuffy, noisy police station with a toddler, terrified that the law would decide he was a criminal for something that someone else had done to him. It might have been the twenty-first century, but the insidious belief that all gay men were pedophiles was still out there, ready to turn deadly. Heath should be on his side, not glaring at him like he was actually guilty.

But first things first.

Aubrey whipped back to Gemma and said, "You need to leave. Now."

Gemma's mouth dropped open as if she were the victim. "This isn't your house. You don't have any say in whether—"

"Gemma, get out!" Heath shouted so loudly that Eugenie screamed.

Apparently, that was enough to put the fear of God in Gemma at last. Her mouth snapped shut, and for a moment, she dropped all pretense and just looked worried. It didn't last, though.

"Why don't I take Eugenie up to bed," she said, moving past Aubrey to get to Heath, her arms outstretched. "Come to Mummy, baby."

"You will leave right now," Heath said, stepping to the side so Gemma couldn't take Eugenie. "Get your purse and go."

Gemma stood there, mouth slightly open, looking like she was trying to figure out her next move. Aubrey was three seconds away from chasing her physically out of the house before she made a small huffing sound, then fetched her handbag from the corner near the door and headed out.

"Just remember everything I said," she told Heath before she left. "I don't want a criminal caring for my baby."

"Gemma," Heath said once more, threateningly.

Gemma dashed out and shut the door behind her without a backward glance.

Aubrey wished he could be relieved, now that she was gone, but everything that had happened that day still hung over him. It didn't help matters when Heath turned to him, his eyes wide with anger and upset.

"Where have you been?" Heath asked. His voice was quieter, but his tone was still seething.

"I told you, I've been at the police, terrified that my life was about to be turned upside down because your ex can't handle you moving on," Aubrey said, also trying to be quiet for Eugenie's sake, but too upset to manage it well.

"Why didn't you call me? You had Eugenie with you. I could have taken her," Heath said.

"Because the police had my phone," Aubrey nearly shouted, throwing his arms out to his sides. "I turned it off completely the second the porn started flooding it."

"You could have called me from another phone," Heath argued.

"I don't have your number memorized." Aubrey moved closer to him, but with every second that ticked past, he felt like he was moving farther away. Why wasn't Heath on his side?

"You could have come back to the house and found it. You

could have called my assistant or my mother," Heath said, seemingly colder and angrier.

Aubrey was so confused that he said something he knew would backfire on him. "What's wrong with you? You should have my back on this one. You know I would never, ever look at that kind of porn."

"I don't know what sort of things you might do," he said, trying to settle Eugenie when it was clear he wasn't settled either. He walked past Aubrey and into the playroom.

"What's that supposed to mean?" Aubrey demanded, following him.

"It means that you're capable of all sorts of things that I never would have imagined you'd be capable of," Heath said in a dark, sharp tone.

Dread swooped down into Aubrey's stomach as he followed Heath and Eugenie into the playroom. "What did Gemma tell you?" he asked. "Did she send you something?" It made sense that she wouldn't just try to ruin his life. She would definitely have sent something to Heath as well, and there were only a handful of things that he'd done in his life that were bad enough to turn Heath against him, like he was turning now.

"Why weren't you accepted into university, Aubrey?" Heath asked in short tones, trying to put Eugenie down. She kept clinging to him, though. Her wailing felt like a fitting backdrop to the argument he and Aubrey were having.

Aubrey let out a breath and lowered his head. That was the one thing that came close to being bad enough to come between him and Heath. There was no point in trying to bury that truth. Heath probably knew the entire story anyhow. He'd said Gemma had sent him records.

"I slept with the admissions officer and got found out," he said in a firm voice, not trying to hide, but refusing to be humiliated any more than he had been all those years ago.

Heath's expression pinched with distaste, but Aubrey wasn't about to let the story end there.

"He flirted with me through the entire interview," he said. "He was new to the job, only a few years older than me, and hot as hell. I was a kid, just out of secondary school. I thought I was cool because an older guy was interested in me. I was of legal age, and so was he. And yes, I was stupid enough to stuff up my one chance to go to university and become a teacher, like I'd always wanted, because I let the contents of my pants take precedent over the contents of my head."

"I—" Heath started to answer, but didn't have anything beyond that one word. He turned his attention to Eugenie instead and sat down on the sofa with Eugenie in his arms, still clinging to him.

"That doesn't make me a criminal," Aubrey went on, remembering the things Gemma had said. "Neither does whatever else she told you I did. I stole a boat once when I was a kid. Did she tell you that?"

Heath kept his focus on Eugenie as he nodded sullenly. "You could have told me those things yourself," he grumbled, like he was fighting to keep hold of his anger.

"I could have," Aubrey said, nowhere near being done with his anger yet, "and I probably would have after a while. And there are probably a heap of things I don't know about you yet either. Gemma forced things, and from the look of it, you let those things get to you."

"How was I supposed to react?" Heath glanced up at him. "To me, it looked like you'd done something sordid."

"That's the entire point of what Gemma was trying to do," Aubrey said, beyond frustrated.

"Gemma is a nuisance," Heath grumbled.

"Yes, well, she's your nuisance to deal with at the moment." Aubrey hadn't realized what he was going to do until the words came out of his mouth. "I need a few days to breathe and to deal with this bomb she's just tossed into my life before I have the spoons to deal with her again," he said.

Heath's eyes went wide. "What are you saying?"

"I'm saying that I need a few days off," Aubrey said. "I have to step away from this for a second to think. Gemma could have seriously ruined my life today, and until that threat is neutralized, I need to protect myself and stay out of her way."

"Are you leaving?" Heath asked pushing himself to stand and bringing Eugenie with him.

Aubrey let out a heavy sigh and rubbed a hand over his face. "Just for a few days," he said, suddenly feeling bereft. "Just until this blows over. And it's not about you, it's about Gemma. I don't want you to think I'm leaving because of you."

"But you are leaving," Heath said, looking forlorn.

The last thing Aubrey wanted to do was leave. That intrinsic feeling that Heath needed him was still there, tight in his gut. But he was hurt, right or wrong. Heath should have had his back and dismissed whatever trifling nonsense Gemma had tried to dredge up against him. None of it mattered. It was all in the past. But as long as Gemma had her sights set on destroying Aubrey's future, he couldn't risk staying where he was.

At least that was what he told himself.

"I just need to breathe," he repeated his reasoning. He glanced to Eugenie and said, "I'm sorry, princess."

Heath let him move forward and kiss Eugenie's hot, weepy face. Aubrey glanced up into Heath's eyes, debating whether he should kiss Heath goodbye as well. If he did, would it be the last time they ever kissed?

Instead, he took a step back and sent Heath an apologetic look. Then he turned and marched out of the room, intending to go upstairs and pack an overnight bag. He wasn't sure where he'd go, he just knew he needed to protect himself.

SEVENTEEN

EMOTIONS WERE STUPID, ridiculous things. Heath wished he didn't have them. He didn't want the anger and frustration that came with Gemma's horrible persistence, and he didn't want the anguish and longing that Aubrey left in his wake when he took his time out. He didn't want the misery and self-pity that he had to fight hard for the rest of the evening, as he calmed Eugenie down, found supper for them both, and took her up for an early bedtime that involved three stories, then him falling asleep in her bed for a while before she did.

When he got up, groggy as hell, after a short doze, made certain Eugenie had fallen asleep, and headed downstairs to put himself to bed properly, he regretted everything that had happened earlier. As he walked through the house, turning off lights, locking doors, and setting the security system—which he really would have to change or reset soon so that Gemma couldn't get in—regret started to take over as his primary emotion.

He should have worked harder to support Aubrey. He shouldn't have let his lover walk out, feeling like he wasn't wanted or as if Heath were angry with him. He should have changed the locks on his house already and barred Gemma from entering. He should have called the police when she'd started harassing him that morning.

The shoulds were all pointless, of course. He hadn't done any of those things, and now he would have to live with it. He took a quick shower before climbing into his big, empty, lonely bed at an obscenely early hour, then instinctively reached for his phone on the bedside table. Without thinking, he sent Aubrey a text.

"*I'm so sorry for everything that happened today. I should have done better. I miss you already, and I—*" He paused with his fingers over his phone, heart racing, wondering if he was ready. But of course he was ready. He had been ready for a long time, and Aubrey had helped him to see that. He finished the sentence with, "*I love you,*" then hit send.

Then he remembered that Aubrey didn't have his phone with him. It was tucked away at a police station somewhere, serving as evidence.

"Shit," he hissed, smacking his phone onto the bedside table, then flopping to his side, facing away from it. The entire thing was one bloody awful mess, and Heath couldn't help but feel responsible for it, even though it was Gemma's doing.

Anger and the hollow feeling of missing Aubrey kept Heath tossing and turning for most of the night. He managed to fall asleep closer to morning, only to be awakened by Eugenie calling out for Aubrey and getting more upset by the second.

Feeling like his body had been filled with cold, sad lead, Heath dragged himself out of bed and went to fetch Eugenie. His poor darling was as sad as he was that Aubrey wasn't there to get her up, like he had every morning for more than a month. And Heath was given an entirely new appreciation of everything Aubrey did as he went through Eugenie's morning routine and his own, trying to do right by them both.

Somehow, he managed to get Eugenie down to the kitchen for breakfast, but he had to call Gerry to tell him he'd be a little late to work.

"Is everything alright?" Gerry asked as Heath used his shoulder to hold his phone to his head while preparing cereal and juice for Eugenie. "You sound ill or something. Is that nanny-lover of yours taking good care of you?"

"Aubrey has taken a short leave of absence," Heath mumbled into the phone.

Gerry's tone changed entirely as he said, "Did you have a fight?"

"Of sorts," Heath sighed. "Gemma was involved."

"Say no more," Gerry said in a low voice. "Get here whenever you can, and if you need help, let me know."

"I will."

Heath ended the call, saw to Eugenie, poured himself some coffee, then sat at the table. He tried to fight off the feeling of hopelessness as he called the only person he truly trusted to help him in his current situation.

"Hello, darling," his mother answered the phone after only one ring. "You never call so early. Is something wrong?"

"Yes," Heath said on a heavy breath. "Gemma is back, and she's already driven Aubrey away."

Heath thanked God he'd been able to sum things up so succinctly, and that his mother was a woman of action. "Say no more," she said in her stiff upper lip voice. "I'll be over in a trice."

Heath smiled, ignoring the way his eyes stung and threatened to get watery. He put his phone down, looked at Eugenie, and said, "Grandmama is coming to the rescue."

Heath was lucky that his mother and father were in London just then. They had a townhouse in Mayfair as well, another acquisition of the family from over two hundred years ago. When his mother said she'd be over in a trice, she truly meant it. She was sweeping into the house less than twenty minutes later, dressed as if she'd been on her way to some country club.

"You've no idea how grateful I am for you, Mother," Heath said, greeting her with a kiss to her cheek as she walked into the kitchen.

His mother surprised him by actually hugging and kissing him in return. "Have you called him to apologize?" she said, her grin a little too cheeky as she let him go.

Heath sighed, feeling as if things were on their way back to being alright. "His phone is currently with the police."

"The police? Whatever for?" His mother blinked rapidly at him.

"Because he's a horrible, disgusting pornographer," the very last voice he wanted to hear right then answered from down the hall.

Heath's blood pressure shot up so fast he was afraid his heart would stop entirely as he and his mother both turned to find Gemma swanning into the kitchen.

"You sent him those vile pictures," Heath accused her, in no mood to go another round with his ex.

Gemma shrugged noncommittally. "Either way, he's in possession of child pornography and will most likely end up in prison." She smiled gleefully at that.

"If anyone is going to end up in prison, it will be you," Heath said, working up a head of steam.

Eugenie started to fuss just then, and Gemma ignored him in an attempt to rush to her.

"My poor baby," she said. "Mummy's here."

Heath's mother stepped straight into Gemma's path, blocking her with a frosty stare of the sort that could have stopped the Blitz. "Heath, go to work. You are needed there, and I will handle this little matter."

Heath was tempted to grin at everything Gemma had coming. "Yes, Mother," he said, shifting to pick Eugenie up so he could give her a goodbye kiss. "You be good for Grandmama, darling," he said, exchanging a knowing look with his mother.

There was a bit more fuss, as Eugenie didn't want him to go. But Heath's mother was able to console her, keeping Gemma at a distance as she did. Heath was convinced his mother was some sort of supernatural being. He would have loved to stay and watch her take Gemma down, but he genuinely needed to get to work. Production of a major series did not stop just because one man was having domestic problems.

But it felt like so much more than that, and as he sat through meetings and worked on proposals and budgets in his office, Heath had a devil of a time concentrating. His mind kept wandering, and his heart ached and raced with every thought of Aubrey.

Where had Aubrey gone? Was he still in London somewhere, thinking about him and wanting to come home, or had he left the city entirely? Was he so disgusted by Heath's unsupportive behavior the day before that their relationship was over? That thought turned Heath's stomach. He and Aubrey were just at the beginning of their story, he was certain. He'd meant what he texted to Aubrey the night before. He loved him. Love had snuck up on him from the most unexpected quarter, but Heath felt it as certainly as he felt the sun's rays.

He loved Aubrey, but he had no way to find him and tell him.

"You need to get out and breath the fresh air," Gerry jolted him out of his thoughts late in the morning. "It's obvious this whole thing has you tied in knots."

Heath heated and avoided his friend's eyes as he finished the sentence he'd been typing. Except he couldn't remember what he'd been saying, or even who he'd been sending the email to. "I have too much work to do," he said, almost by rote.

"Yes, that's my point," Gerry said, coming all the way into the office. "You have too much work to do to let this distract you. Come on."

Heath glanced questioningly up at him.

"It's lunchtime," Gerry went on. "Like Victorian gentlemen of old, we're heading to the club for a bite and, if we're lucky, a little help and advice."

Heath hesitated for a moment, then got up and silently followed Gerry. There was no need to ask which club they were going to. There was only one for the two of them. And the mad idea grabbed hold of Heath that the Brotherhood might be exactly what he needed just then. The entire point of the organization was for men and women like him to help each other in the tightest of situations.

They took a cab to Park Lane, which Heath saw as an unnecessary expense, both in terms of time and money, but the moment he walked into The Chameleon Club, hope began to seep into the spots that had held nothing but despair and heartache.

Perhaps better still, Oakley was already seated at one of the tables in the dining room, talking to Casper Penhurst. On the one hand, the two men were among the last Heath wanted to spill his heart out to, especially about Aubrey—he was willing to admit now that he'd been green with jealousy at the way Aubrey had chatted with Casper so easily at the picnic when he'd had yet to recognize his true feelings—but then again, if ever two men would understand the situation, it might be those two.

"Heath, what are you doing here?" Oakley asked, standing up to greet him with a thumping hug. "Mother called me to say she was taking care of Eugenie today because Gemma showed up and chased Aubrey away."

Heath let go of his brother with a sigh and sank into the chair beside him. "That saves me the trouble of having to spell out the shit-heap I'm in right now," he said.

Their conversation paused for a moment as one of the servers came over to take their order. Heath barely paid attention to what he was ordering, to eat or to drink. Part of him wanted to order a large, stiff drink, but he still had the rest of his work day, and then God only knew what else to deal with.

"This is your ex-wife we're talking about?" Casper asked with a sympathetic frown once the server left.

Heath sighed. "Yes, and she's only back because she heard that *After the War* was greenlighted, and she wants a part."

"God forbid," Oakley said, sipping his drink. As he put it down, he went on with, "Mother says she's been threatening you and Aubrey, and that she should be arrested and thrown in jail for child pornography? Which makes no sense at all."

Heath laughed humorlessly. "She used some sort of dummy account to load Aubrey's phone and email up with illegal images, thinking it would get him arrested and put away."

"Has Aubrey gone to the police?" Casper asked, alarmed.

"Immediately," Heath said with a nod. "They have his phone, which is why I can't contact him right now. I don't know where he is."

Oakley and Gerry both looked sympathetic, but Casper seemed interested in something else. He caught the attention of a man at the other side of the room, then waved him over. Heath winced and was about to tell Casper he didn't need any more company, but something about the middle-aged gentleman who came over to stand beside their table seemed familiar to him.

"Geoffrey, you know Heath Manfred, right?" Casper asked.

"By name and reputation at least," Geoffrey said, reaching to shake Heath's hand.

Confused, Heath shook it.

"Detective Chief Inspector Geoffrey Bolton might just be

able to help Aubrey with his phone problem," Casper extended his introduction with a sly grin.

Heath's brow shot up. "You're from Scotland Yard?"

"I am," Geoffrey said, taking the empty seat beside Heath. "What seems to be the problem?"

Heath was stunned by how swiftly a potential solution to Aubrey's phone problems had been found. For the next fifteen minutes, as their food arrived and they ate, he explained Aubrey's entire situation and Gemma's mischief to Geoffrey. What was even more remarkable was that Geoffrey had more than just insight and suggestions about the situation. Before Heath had even finished his sandwich, the man was on the phone to his office, finding more details of the case and apparently talking to people at the top.

"Your friend did the right thing by taking the phone directly to the police," Geoffrey said as he ended his call. "It'll be a thousand times easier to prove he's not at fault in the situation."

"Thank God," Heath said.

"It'll be trickier pinning anything on Gemma, though," he explained. "It sounds like she had someone do the dirty work for her, and unless they left a paper trail, which they almost never do, it won't be traced back to her."

Heath frowned. "Would this be grounds for a restraining order?" he asked.

"Very possibly." Geoffrey nodded. "I'll handle everything for you, one way or another."

Heath gaped at the man. His emotions were already raw because of the situation, Aubrey's absence, and lack of sleep, so he felt as though he were in serious danger of embarrassing himself over finding so much ready help.

"Thank you," he said. "And if I can ever repay the favor in any way, just ask."

Geoffrey smiled as he stood and clapped a hand on

Heath's shoulder. "We're brothers," he said with a nod. "We look out for each other. Always have, always will."

The sentiment took Heath's breath away. He watched Geoffrey leave the table, in awe of how easy it had been to get help for a horrifically difficult situation.

"And to think," Gerry said with a grin. "You've been a member of the Brotherhood for all these years without taking advantage of its most important amenities."

"This is why the Brotherhood has gone out of its way to court members of law enforcement and get them to join, isn't it," Oakley said with a sly grin, finishing his drink.

"Actually," Casper chimed in, "Right from the very start of the Brotherhood, it has naturally drawn law enforcement agents. Why, one of the original members, an Officer Derrek Talboys, made it a special point to assist queer men with the legal troubles they often had back then. He set the bar, so to speak, for queer officers joining the Brotherhood specifically so that they could help with legal matters. You're just part of a long and noble tradition."

Heath laughed lightly at the short history lesson, not because there was anything funny about it, but because he was so bloody grateful that he'd fallen back into the Brotherhood when he had.

But a few minutes later, as conversation swung back around to Aubrey, Heath's heart sank again.

"It kills me that I can't get in touch with him right now," he said, pushing his plate back as the last of his appetite left him. "All I want to do is apologize for everything that's happened to him and make it up to him."

"Do you have any idea where he's gone?" Oakley asked, looking surprisingly sympathetic, for a rotten older brother.

Heath shrugged. "He has several friends in London. He could be staying with them. His parents live in Cornwall, so he could be out there."

"Why not give his friends a call and see what they know?" Casper suggested.

Heath's heart leapt at the idea and urged him to seek the other nannies out immediately. His head had a different reaction. He winced and said, "Aubrey said he needed space. I...I have to give him that space."

The other three men hummed in agreement.

"If that's specifically what he said, then you're right, you have to wait for him to come back," Gerry said.

Heath blew out a heavy breath. "This is ridiculous. I never ate my heart out like this for Gemma, and she was my wife."

"She was also a conniving bitch who married you for the sake of her career," Gerry pointed out.

Heath sent him a flat look. That wasn't what he wanted to hear just then.

"I think our parents messed us up," Oakley said.

Heath turned to him with a wry smile. "Don't tell Mother that."

Oakley laughed. "Everyone's parents mess them up. Our mother and father are part of a different century. They taught us that we had traditions to maintain, and that we had to do that with dignity. There was no time or place for love or tenderness."

"Mother and Father aren't that bad," Heath argued. "Not like other parents in their set. Mother actually hugged me this morning."

Oakley made an exaggerated shocked face, then broke into a smile. "I'm glad to hear it, but that's not what I meant." When Heath stared at him, he went on with, "Who we were and what we owed to our ancestors and the country always came first with them. It was never about self-fulfillment or allowing ourselves to really feel loved and accepted for who we were."

"How so?" Heath asked, suddenly fascinated with his brother's take.

Oakley shrugged. "I don't think any of us were ever taught that it's alright for us to be loved. It was all about duty and what we owed, never about what was owed to us. We were never taught that we were worthy of love."

Gerry burst into a wide smile. "You're in therapy, aren't you."

Oakley smiled. "Of course. I wouldn't be so wise and in touch with my feelings if I weren't."

"You? In touch with your feelings?" Heath laughed, though his insides were warm with affection at everything his brother had to say.

Oakley sent him a smarmy look, then went on with, "It's even worse with you, little brother. Gemma did a number on you, but you let her. You let her because Mama and Papa taught you that you came last, and that your responsibility to your immediate family, however shitty it might have been, was more important than your own self-preservation."

Heath sucked in a breath. Oakley was right.

"But it sounds like Aubrey has been teaching you something different," Oakley went on. "It sounds like he was showing you just how much your happiness matters. Not to him, but to you."

"Fuck, you're right," Heath said, breathing out like someone had punched him in the stomach.

"So why are you sitting here when you should be out scouring London for your beloved?" Gerry asked.

Heath turned to him with a snort. "Because this is not a romcom. It's real life. I have a job to do, Aubrey asked for space, and there will be no swell of music once we finally see each other across a crowded Tube station, right before we run into each other's arms for a kiss that makes bystanders applaud."

"But wouldn't it be fabulous if that happened?" Gerry asked, grinning.

It would be at first, Heath was convinced. Now more than

ever, all he wanted was to have Aubrey in his arms again so he could kiss him and apologize and more. But once the movie-like reunion was over, there would be things to sort. No matter how badly he wanted things with Aubrey to work and last, they would have to deal with Gemma and her antics first.

EIGHTEEN

THE ONE THING that had always calmed Aubrey when he was at his most upset, even when he was a boy, was the sea. He supposed that was stereotypically Cornish of him. There was just something timeless and deep and unchanging about the sea. The sea was always there. It didn't care about your petty problems, your bad decisions, or your temporary frustrations. It just existed, moving in and out, crashing against rocks and beating them down over long, patient eons.

So it was only natural that Aubrey took the first train heading west when he walked out of Heath's house, going all the way to Penzance before taking the bus to Porthleven, then walking to his parent's cliffside cottage. He'd scared the everloving shit out of them, arriving just after dawn and cupping his hands over the kitchen window to look in, because the door had been locked. His mother had screamed, something in the kitchen had broken, and moments later, his father had arrived at the door, cricket bat in hand, naked as the day he was born, ready to murder the intruder.

Everything had changed as soon as his parents got a look at him, with his dark-rimmed, exhausted eyes and his admittedly hang-dog expression. They'd whisked him into the house, fed him tea and sausages, and after Aubrey had told them the short version of what had happened, they'd whisked him off to bed in his old room, telling him to sleep first, then fill them in on the details later.

Aubrey didn't wake up until after noon, and only then because he could swear that he heard Eugenie calling for him from the other room. He rolled over and blinked blearily at his old bedroom door, held his breath for a second as he tried to remember where he was and what was going on, then let out a heavy sigh when he realized the sound he'd thought was Eugenie was actually a sheep somewhere nearby.

He flopped all the way to his back and stared up at the cracked ceiling. What the actual fuck was going on that had landed him back in his childhood bed—which still had the hand-made quilt composed entirely of sailboat fabric on it— on a Tuesday in the middle of July? Nothing around him felt right, from the sound of the ocean instead of London traffic to the narrow bed he lay in. Alone. It had only been days, but he'd gotten far too used to sleeping in a bed with Heath.

Heath.

Aubrey blew out another breath and rubbed his eyes. He supposed there was no point in denying the fact that he was in love with the man. A wry laugh escaped him. He was a nanny who had fallen in love with his boss. How perfectly cliché of him.

But Heath was so much more than just his boss. He was a good man who had been put through shit by the person who should have loved him the hardest. And who knows what Heath's family had subjected him to? He'd only met Heath's mother a handful of times and his brother, Oakley, once. He didn't want to judge people he didn't know. All he was willing to say was that Heath's parents weren't anything like his own.

Aubrey let out a moan and rolled back to his side, curling up in bed and trying to go back to sleep to fight off the gnawing feeling in his stomach. He shouldn't have run out on Heath like that. If anything, Heath needed him to stand by his side and be strong as they dealt with Gemma. She'd gone from being a nuisance to a serious problem, and instead of keeping a cool head and helping Heath, he'd bailed.

Aubrey moaned again and pulled the quilt over his head. Just thinking about what he'd left behind in London made him feel a little sick. He still didn't think he was out of the woods where the mess with his phone and email accounts were concerned. There was no telling whether the cops who had dealt with his case the day before would come down on his side or cart him off to prison the second he stepped back into London. What if he'd already committed some kind of crime by fleeing the city before the matter was resolved.

That thought was terrifying enough to spur him out of bed. He headed straight for the bathroom to pee and shower, then returned to his room, still feeling blurry and out of sorts, to dress and make himself pseudo-presentable for the day. Not that he really cared what he looked like. He was home, and caring about appearances was not something his family did at home.

That point was underscored when he grabbed himself a glass of water from the kitchen, then headed out to the garden, where his mum and dad were working in the garden. The garden was their pride and joy, and it extended from the back of the house to near the edge of the cliff. The work they'd put in to plant flowers and veg and everything else made the already spectacular view look like something that belonged in a magazine or on a tourism poster for Cornwall. A lot of the work had been put in after Aubrey had left home for the big, bad world of London, but he still appreciated it and felt like it was his own every time he came back.

The garden was beautiful and kept up appearances. *His parents* were another thing entirely.

His dad wore only an old, ratty pair of shorts that had a hole in the seat, giving anyone standing behind him more of a view than they needed of his pasty arse. That arse was a sharp contrast to the deep tan of his skin and the white hair that covered his head and part of his body. And as much as his father's appearance was within the bounds of normal, the problem was that his mum was dressed entirely too similarly, including the fact that she was topless as she worked.

"Ugh, Mum," Aubrey complained as he dragged himself over to one of the chairs in the shade of the back porch. "Please put something on." He held up his hand as if he were hungover and his mother's tanned, pendulous breasts were the sun.

His mother made a tutting sound and straightened, turning toward him, which only made the vision worse. "What do you care about the female body?" she asked him, though she headed to the wicker table to fetch a shirt that had been abandoned there all the same. "I thought you weren't interested."

"You'll turn me gay again with those," Aubrey joked, starting to feel a little better, though he kept his revolted look in place just to annoy her.

His mother huffed. "I have it on good authority that I did nothing to turn you, son. You were born that way."

"Why?" Aubrey asked, sinking into his seat as the comforts of home and his mad parents started to chip away at his misery. "Did Lady Gaga tell you?"

"No," his mother said, slipping into her shirt. "You did. When you were eight and took it upon yourself to tell me and your father what we'd already known since you were three."

Aubrey grinned, but that grin faded quickly. Three. Like Eugenie was.

Oh, God. He missed Eugenie as much as he missed Heath.

She was the sweetest, funniest, cleverest little girl. He'd bonded with her far beyond any bond he'd had with previous children in his care. Eugenie really was his princess, despite the failings of her mother.

His thoughts swung around full circle, hitting him in the back of the head like the boom of a sailboat swinging around and clocking him when he wasn't paying attention.

"Oh," his mother said, managing to fit about five syllables and four different emotions into the single word. "So you're ready to tell us more about why you ended up here with the dawn chorus this morning, are you?"

"I've got to hear this," his dad said, leaving his work to join his mother at the table.

"Dad, you need a new pair of garden shorts," Aubrey said, holding up his hand again. "Those ones leave nothing to the imagination."

"Your mother likes them," he said, winking at Aubrey's mom with a dirty old man laugh.

His mom laughed and blushed, then hit his father's arm hard enough to make him wince.

It was embarrassing and wrong on so many levels. No one to look at them would have imagined that both his parents were teachers at the local primary school. Well, not the state school. They worked for a progressive school with views on things that were just as odd as their own, so anyone who happened to spot them out in the back garden, acting like naturists, would hardly blink at them.

"Come on now, Bernie. This isn't about us. It's about Aubrey and his pitiful love life," his mother said, pouring a glass of what looked like lemonade, but was probably spiked, from the pitcher on the table and handing it to Aubrey's dad. "You said something about Heath's ex showing up and meddling?" she prompted him.

Aubrey sighed, figuring it was best to get the story-telling portion of the visit over with. "Gemma is a model who wants to be an actress. She married Heath thinking it could advance her career. But Heath is far too good for her, or that entire industry, if you ask me, although he does like it." Aubrey pondered that oddity for a moment before going on. "Their divorce was recently final, but she showed up again, acting like it had never happened, and all because Heath is involved with a project that Hollywood just green-lighted."

"My, son. You do live quite the interesting life these days," his father said, coming over to sit in the chair next to Aubrey's. "Very chic."

"There's nothing chic at all about taking care of an adorable three-year-old girl while her father works on the periphery of the movie business," Aubrey said, watching his mum as she came to sit on his other side. "It's downright unnerving to have your boss-turned-lover's crazy ex-wife show up and dredge up your past while simultaneously sending illegal images to your phone and email with the intent of having you arrested."

"You shouldn't go around calling the mentally-ill 'crazy', Aubrey," his mother said. "We've raised you better than that."

Aubrey stared flatly at his mum. "She bombed my phone with child pornography, Mother," he said. "She dredged up records of everything bad that I've ever done and sent them to Heath."

"What sort of bad things have you done?" his dad asked with a small smile. He sounded more curious than anything else.

Aubrey suddenly wished the day wasn't so sunny and that lightning would strike him or the entire cliffside would fall into the ocean. "Well, there was that time Charlie and I stole Mr. Hayle's skiff and wrecked it," he sighed.

His dad snorted and laughed. "Is that the best she could do?" Before Aubrey could say anything, he glanced across at Aubrey's mum and said, "Remember how mad Gavin was?"

His mom laughed. "You'd've though Aubrey had stolen a bucket of gold and rowed out to dump it in the Channel."

"Gavin Hayle always was an arse," his dad went on.

Aubrey could feel a trip down memory lane coming, and he needed to stop it.

"There was more than just that," he said sinking into his chair a little more. "She sent him the reason why I wasn't accepted at university."

"Not everyone is meant for a life of academia, dear," his mum said, patting Aubrey's arm. "You did well enough to get into the childcare program, and you've done splendidly since then."

"There's nothing wrong with being a nanny, son," his father added with a nod, gesturing with his lemonade.

"No, stop, listen," Aubrey said with a huff, feeling as though he'd regressed to being an irritated teenager again. He squirmed in his seat, grimaced, and looked straight out at the sea instead of at either of his parents. "The reason I didn't get into university, other than the fact that only the one place even agreed to interview me before rejecting my application, was because…." He sighed. He'd gone eight years without saying a word to his parents, but now his time was up. "I slept with the admissions officer, and we were found out."

His parents were silent. They exchanged stunned looks across him.

Then they burst into laughter.

"Is that the worst you've done?" his dad asked, still rolling with humor.

"Dad. I was nineteen. He was…not nineteen," Aubrey said. "I only did it because I thought it might improve my chances of getting into university." He paused, then added, "And because he was hot and had been flirting with me through the interview."

That only made his parents laugh harder. "That's what you're worried about?" his mum asked. "That's what has driven a wedge between you and Heath? Because he found out you were a horny teenager who thought sleeping with an older man would get you something you wanted?"

"God, Mother," Aubrey said, slumping down in his chair. "Please don't ever use the word 'horny' in my presence again."

His parents laughed on. "Sleeping with an older man is tame compared to some of the stuff we did, eh, Essie?" Aubrey's father asked, winking.

"Oh, oh, remember the time we were caught smuggling weed onto the boat for that summer camp trip the summer you turned eighteen?" his mum laughed.

"That old rat, Cunningham, smoked the entire bag instead of turning us in," his father roared with the memory. He then felt the need to top that story. "Or how about the time we were caught with our pants down, so to speak, in the bell tower in Falmouth?"

His mum whooped and then covered her mouth to hide the sound. Her eyes shone with love and joy, though, so despite the mortification of his parents recounting their wild, younger days, Aubrey was actually happy for them.

"You think you're bad for getting caught with an admissions officer?" his mum went on. She and his dad looked absolutely wicked as they looked at each other for a moment, then she blurted, "Your father and I got out of a speeding ticket by having a threesome with the policeman."

"In the back of the van," his father finished the story.

The two of them burst into uproarious laughter again. Aubrey was shocked and let that shock show on his face. He also felt as though a weight had been lifted from his shoulders. He'd spent so many years feeling awful for doing something stupid that had cost him the future he'd wanted to have, but his parents had done something arguably worse. More than once.

"Why do I have the feeling that I don't want to know

when this van ménage à trois happened?" he asked, sitting up a little straighter and actually managing to smile a bit.

"Because it was about five years ago?" his dad suggested.

Aubrey squeezed his eyes shut and shook his head with exaggerated indignation.

As soon as he made the gesture, he realized he was subconsciously imitating Heath.

That only made his insides hurt and his heart long to get on the next train and head back to London.

"I've made a terrible mistake," he sighed, standing up and taking his empty water glass to the table so he could pour some lemonade.

"Have we not just established that your mother and I have made worse mistakes?" his dad asked with exaggerated politeness.

"No," Aubrey said, "I mean, I shouldn't have left London. I shouldn't have walked out on Heath at the very moment when he needed me to stay by his side the most. He shouldn't have to deal with Gemma alone, and I shouldn't have gotten upset the way I did."

His parents were suddenly more sympathetic.

"Ah, darling one," his mother said, getting up and joining him at the table. She kissed his cheek, then said, "Lovers argue all the time. Especially when they're in a stressful situation. I'm sure Heath feels like he should have done more to stop you from leaving."

"And besides, sometimes a time out is good for the soul," his dad added. "You're a nanny. You should know all about time outs."

For a moment, Aubrey thought his father was teasing him. But the more he thought about it, the more he saw the point. Children were given time outs when their emotions got the better of them and began to affect their actions. They needed to remove themselves from whatever it was that had set them off so that they could approach life like the good kids they were again.

That felt very much like what Aubrey had done, what he and Heath were experiencing. He'd needed a break. He'd needed to sit on the naughty stair for a moment to think about what he'd done.

The only problem with that was that he didn't like thinking about Heath sitting on his own naughty stair all alone.

"None of this is Heath's fault," he spoke his thoughts aloud. "We're both just targets of Gemma's thwarted ambition. She's being an absolute bitch, and the two of us are letting her get away with it."

"That does sound like the case," his mother said.

Aubrey took a long drink of his lemonade. Its tart sweetness invigorated him. So did his parents' silly and embarrassing method of supporting him. But mostly, it was his faith in Heath to be a good person, even if they'd both made stupid mistakes, that made him feel as though he was ready to tackle the challenge of Gemma again.

"Sorry," he said, putting his glass down and taking a step toward the house. "I know I've just arrived and you'd probably like me to visit for longer, but I need to go back to London."

"That's the spirit," his dad said.

"Heath needs me to stand by his side right now, not to run off and pout. I have to get back to him and help him tell Gemma what's what," he went on.

"Don't be too hard on yourself," his mom said, following him into the house. "There's nothing wrong with taking a moment to breathe. And if you hadn't come all the way down here, you never would have been showered with the excellent advice of your indomitable mother and father."

Aubrey twisted to glance over his shoulder at her with a smirk as he headed into his room to repack his things. "Mum, you are a constant embarrassment and thorn in my side," he said with all the love in the world, then stopped to throw his arms around her and hug her tightly. He kissed her cheek, then said, "I love you more than words can express."

"I know, my boy," his mum said, patting the side of his face. "Now go catch the next train to London, race to the rescue, and go save your man from that horrid witch before it's too late."

NINETEEN

IF HEATH HAD EVER DOUBTED the power of the Brotherhood to actually help in the lives of its members, those doubts were proven wrong when a small package arrived at his office just as he was preparing to pack up and head home to see if his mother had survived the day with Eugenie.

"It was delivered by special courier," Sara said with a frown as she handed the padded envelope to him.

"Thank you, Sara."

Heath looked at the envelope, no idea what it could be. If Gemma was attempting to hurt or ruin him again, he wasn't that impressed. Unless the envelope held some sort of new horror.

But that wasn't what it held at all. Heath opened it gingerly, half expecting some sort of glitter bomb to go off in his face, but instead, the envelope contained a cell phone. Not just any cell phone, Aubrey's cell phone.

Heath stared at it for a moment, debating the ethics of opening it and searching through, maybe to look at Aubrey's pictures. Before he could do more than see that the phone was password protected, as he set the envelope down, a note slipped from the envelope to the floor. Heath set the phone aside with a frown in order to retrieve the note.

"Dear Mr. Manfred," the note read. *"Your friend's phone has been thoroughly checked and the offending images removed. A few additional security measures have been added to prevent this from happening again. Unfortunately, all of your friend's stored photos and media needed to be wiped by my team, and we recommend he purchase an entirely new phone immediately. But his contact list is intact and should be able to be transferred without a problem."*

The note was signed by Detective Chief Inspector Geoffrey Bolton.

Heath blew out a heavy breath and sank to his office chair to read the note again. He stared at the phone as well, a little afraid to touch it. There was no possible way it was legal for him to have someone else's phone returned to him when it was the subject of an investigation. Not that Gemma's mischief constituted a national crisis or anything. But there the phone was, sitting there on his desk, as innocent as a babe. All because he was a member of the Brotherhood, and the Brotherhood protected its own.

Heath stared at the phone for a while longer, letting the impact of being part of such a powerful group sink in. Those thoughts blended into thoughts of Aubrey, which made his chest hurt with longing for his lover to come home so that they could sort everything and make it right.

With those thoughts in mind, Heath stood and snatched up Aubrey's phone, pocketing it. He moved the envelope to the bin, then briefly considered that he should burn or even eat Geoffrey's note, as if it were all part of some spy drama and needed to be destroyed.

He pocketed that as well in the end, then gathered up the rest of his things and headed out of the office.

He barely registered his trip home. It had only been a few days, but he felt like so many things had happened. He was bolstered by the help Geoffrey had given him, and as furious as he was with Gemma still, he felt, maybe for the first time since he'd met her, that he could confidently face the challenge she presented and hold his own long enough to rid her from his life. Well, as much as he could, considering she still had some rights to Eugenie. But Oakley had been right as well. It was about damn time he looked out for himself and his own happiness.

Aubrey was part of that happiness. A major part. By the time he pulled into his parking spot behind his house, Heath was determined to turn London upside down in order to find his lover. He might not have had the ability to call Aubrey at the moment, but there had to be other ways to find out where he'd gone. If he had to, he would enlist Geoffrey's help again, or the help of someone else in the Brotherhood.

Those thoughts were still rattling around his brain as he stepped into the house and headed straight for the kitchen. He was so caught up in strategizing how he would find Aubrey that when Aubrey stepped out from the living room just as Heath approached it, Heath nearly jumped out of his skin with fright.

"God, you scared me," he gasped, reeling back a step. He didn't know what his expression was doing, but his heart suddenly beat furiously and his mind felt like it short-circuited with joy and relief.

"First, I just want to say that I'm sorry for running out the way I did," Aubrey said, holding up his hands as if Heath were still angry with him. His back was tense and his shoulders slightly hunched, but there was a bright, excited, hopeful look in his eyes. "It was the coward's way out, and I did not react well in the moment. Secondly, I just want you to know that—"

"I love you," Heath interrupted, unable to hold it inside any longer. "I love you more than I thought I would ever let myself love another person, besides Eugenie. And I don't care whether you ran away to the other side of the planet or to Mars, you came back, and I love you."

He stepped into a stunned Aubrey, clasping the back of his neck and pulling him in for a kiss that conveyed so much more than words ever could. He slipped his arm around Aubrey as well to hold his body close as their mouths melded together.

For a moment, Aubrey was too stunned to react. Heath just kissed him without getting anything in return.

Within a few seconds, though, Aubrey let out a breath and grasped the sides of Heath's face. "I love you, too," he said, with so much emotion that Heath swore he could feel it in his own heart.

Neither of them said another word. They didn't really need to. Words wouldn't have been enough anyhow. Heath made a sound of need and relief as he pulled Aubrey back to him, kissing him from the bottom of his heart.

Aubrey gave back everything and then some as their mouths met and their tongues sought each other out. It was wild and feverish, each of them trying for the upper hand. Heath was able to push Aubrey up against the wall and slide his hand under Aubrey's t-shirt so that he could touch skin. He couldn't get enough of Aubrey's skin. He wanted to see it and feel it. He pushed his hand up Aubrey's chest, his mouth never leaving Aubrey's, intending to pull his shirt off all the way.

Instead, as soon as his hand felt Aubrey's beating heart under it, Aubrey's nipple going hard against his palm, he stayed there for a moment, feeling the force of his lover's ardor. Part of him would have thought he'd be more interested in slipping his hand down into Aubrey's shorts to stroke his cock—which was definitely interested in the impromptu make-out session—but in that moment, after nearly losing one of the most important people in his life, it was Aubrey's heart that interested Heath.

"I love you," he repeated between kisses, needing to say it and make Aubrey feel it. "You are so much more to me than you could ever imagine."

"I know," Aubrey murmured against his lips, then pulled Heath close to thrust his tongue into Heath's mouth.

A burst of joy, like a firework, exploded in Heath's chest. He pulled back, stared at Aubrey with hungry, teasing eyes, and asked, "You know? Is that what I get for pouring my heart out like this?"

Aubrey laughed, the sound filling Heath with light and bliss. "I'll have you know that that's one of the most iconic comebacks to someone confessing love that's ever been filmed," he said. "You're in the industry, you should know that."

"Fine," Heath said with a mock frustrated sigh, rolling his eyes a little. "I love you and you know. Now kiss me, you ginger bastard."

Aubrey laughed again, and instead of simply accepting another kiss, he took the upper hand by grasping Heath's suit jacket and spinning them so Heath's back was against the wall. More than that, he shoved Heath against the wall with a little more force than was strictly necessary. That only sent a wave of lust more powerful than Heath had ever known through him. Maybe he liked being pushed around by Aubrey more than he'd anticipated.

Those potentially kinky thoughts were drowned out entirely as Aubrey practically attacked his mouth, slanting his over it and treating Heath to a deep, wet, probing kiss. He plastered Heath against the wall with his body while simultaneously unbuttoning his suit jacket and tugging his shirt out of his trousers. Heath let it all happen, giving up whatever struggle to maintain dignity and the upper hand he might have been tempted to put up.

It felt so good. It felt amazing to have Aubrey yank him forward so he could rip Heath's jacket from him and throw it aside. It felt like heaven when Aubrey mirrored what he had done moments before and slipped his hands along the bare skin of Heath's torso to touch him as much as possible. Their mouths barely left each other for more than the space of a breath as they groped and pawed at each other. Heath's cock strained so hard in his trousers that he wouldn't have been surprised if he burst his zipper entirely.

That giddy thought set him over the edge, and he started laughing as Aubrey kissed his way along his jaw to his neck. Aubrey's hands were also busy unbuttoning Heath's shirt.

"We shouldn't do this here," Heath laughed, filled with joy. "We need to go upstairs if we're going to fuck each other into oblivion. I wouldn't want Eugenie or my mother to find us like this."

It was as if he'd flicked a switch that shifted Aubrey into an entirely different setting. Aubrey pulled back abruptly, staring at him with a surprising frown. "Where is Eugenie anyhow?" he panted.

Heath was momentarily distracted by Aubrey's kiss-red lips and flushed cheeks. He was captivated by the sparkle in Aubrey's emerald eyes.

Until the importance of his question hit.

He blinked and let out a breath. "Eugenie isn't here?" he asked.

"No," Aubrey said, shaking his head. "I only got here about ten minutes before you did. I was just looking for her."

Heath was instantly on alert. "My mother has been watching her today," he said, pushing away from the wall, although he hated separating from Aubrey as he did so. "She said she'd be here all day, until I got home. She's probably taken her out shopping or something."

His phone was in his jacket pocket, and so was Aubrey's. He bent to retrieve it, fishing around and taking out Aubrey's to hand to him, too.

"Where did you get this?" Aubrey asked, eyes wide. "Are the pics still there?"

"No," Heath said, walking into the living room so he could toss his jacket over the sofa. "I ended up at The Chameleon Club this morning, and it's a long story that we don't have time for now, but there's a high-ranking detective that's a member of the Brotherhood, and apparently he took care of everything for us."

Aubrey gaped at that and at his phone, though he looked afraid to open it.

Heath wanted to explain more, but he'd already tapped to dial his mother, and she picked up within a single ring.

"Mother," Heath said with urgency after she said hello. "Where are you? Where is Eugenie?"

The momentary silence that came from the other end of the call turned Heath's stomach inside out, even before his mother said, "I thought she was with you."

"What?" Heath suddenly couldn't catch his breath. "How? I left her here with you, and I've been at the office all day."

"Oh, dear," his mother said in a weak voice. "I knew it was some sort of ploy, I *knew* it. I should have called you to confirm, but she had a recording of you telling me it was alright, and then your father called to say his car had been broken into."

"What is she saying?" Aubrey asked in a whisper, most likely in response to the way Heath's eyes went round with horror and his hand began to tremble. "Where is Eugenie?"

"When did all this happen?" Heath asked, his voice hoarse. "And what do you mean, she had a recording of my voice?"

"Gemma?" Aubrey asked, still whispering, but instantly furious.

"Heath, I'm so sorry. I wasn't thinking," his mother began to cry on the other end of the call. "She said the two of you had met for lunch and sorted things. She seemed so contrite and apologized so much. She confessed to her wrongdoings and said that you'd taken your phone to the police, like Aubrey had with his, so that I wouldn't be able to call you. Then she played a recording that she told me you'd made, saying it was alright to let her take Eugenie to the park this afternoon."

Heath would have cursed, if he hadn't been talking to his mother. He began to pace the hall as Aubrey watched him anxiously. "When did all this happen?" he asked.

"About an hour and a half ago," his mother said. "The recording sounded so real, darling. And then I got the call from your father. I...I can see now that was part of her mischief. I was too frazzled to think things through."

"It's alright, Mother," Heath said, even though it was everything but alright. "I believe Gemma has some sophisticated people working with her. They could easily have faked a voice message from me. I'm going to call the police now, and if they contact you, you'll need to tell them everything you know."

"Yes, of course," she said, then added, "Eugenie seemed alright with her today, if that helps. She went to her willingly, and they were playing nicely together when I left them."

It was a small consolation, but not much of one.

"Thank you, Mother," Heath said. "I'll let you know the moment we find out anything."

He ended the call, and before he could do more than turn around, Aubrey said, "Does Gemma have her? Has she kidnapped her? I'm not a violent man, but if she's harmed Eugenie in any way, I'll wring her neck."

The feeling was mutual, so Heath let it go without comment.

"Apparently, Gemma spun some sort of lie to my mother about how I gave her permission to watch Eugenie for the day," he said instead. "She manufactured a fake message of me giving permission and played it for Mama. Then she must have arranged for someone to interfere with my father's car so she would be distracted and called away."

He started down the hall for the kitchen, tucking his shirt back into his trousers as he went.

"That's diabolical," Aubrey said, following him. "If Gemma put as much time into something useful and productive as she puts into being a conniving, manipulative bitch, she might have gotten somewhere in this world."

Heath noted the past tense of Aubrey's statement as he reached the kitchen and turned to him. Aubrey was right. Gemma would be finished in every way once he was done with her.

He wished he'd thought to get Geoffrey Bolton's phone number when he'd been at the club earlier, but since that hadn't happened, he called Oakley instead.

Oakley answered his call with, "Mother's just told me."

Heath dispensed with greetings as well and said, "Do you have Geoffrey Bolton's number? I need to contact the police before Gemma has a chance to do something rash."

"I do have the number," Oakley said, "but I'm not sure what the police can do. Gemma has visitation rights, and she is Eugenie's mother. They might not be able to consider this a kidnapping case until they've been missing for more than twenty-four hours."

"I don't care," Heath said. "Gemma isn't going to have twenty-four hours left, as soon as I get ahold of her."

"Understood," Oakley said. "I'll find the number and text it to you. Better still, I'll call Geoffrey and explain the situation so that you can focus on going after Gemma."

"Thanks."

Heath ended the call, then lowered his phone. He was furious, panicked, and deeply afraid for his little girl. Gemma wasn't violent by nature, and Heath didn't think she'd harm her, but he didn't know who Gemma had been working with to torment him and Aubrey for the last few days. Someone who was capable of loading up Aubrey's phone with child porn might be capable of far more than Gemma had accounted for.

That thought sent Heath into a spiral. He dropped his phone on the table, then let out a vocal breath that didn't quite manifest into words. His knees threatened to give out.

But Aubrey was there a second later, sweeping him into an embrace and lending him strength.

"We'll find her," he said. "Gemma's not as smart as all that. She can't have gone far. I have some contacts too, and everyone knows the situation. We'll work together, and we'll handle this and find her, I promise."

Heath nodded, then leaned into Aubrey's embrace. He trusted Aubrey with his life, and with Eugenie's life. They'd find his little girl, and Gemma wouldn't get away with things this time.

TWENTY

DURING HIS CHILDCARE TRAINING COURSE, Aubrey had actually studied what to do if a child's parent or legal guardian attempted to kidnap them or keep them away from the parent who had legal custody. It was information he'd hoped he would never have to use, but that he was deeply grateful he knew.

"I've texted Eugenie's picture to all of my nanny friends," Aubrey said as he came back into the kitchen after making a few private phone calls. "Have you been able to file the travel notice?"

He wasn't asking Heath. Only half an hour had passed since they'd realized Eugenie was missing, but already, Heath's lawyer and assistant sat at the kitchen table, along with his mother. They were making calls, filling out paperwork restricting Eugenie from foreign travel—which would make it that much harder for Gemma to take her out of the country—and making lists of Gemma's family members to contact about her whereabouts.

"We're almost there," Heath's lawyer said with a surprisingly reassuring smile. He turned to Heath and said, "Don't worry, Mr. Manfred. This is all precautionary right now. For all we know, Gemma will walk back into the house any moment now, and we'll all have a laugh about this."

Aubrey very much doubted that.

Heath didn't look like he was particularly certain either. He got up from the table and walked around to the doorway, where Aubrey was standing. Aubrey didn't have to ask to know what he needed and pulled him into an embrace that was reassuring and intimate, despite the unfamiliar people in the room.

Sure enough, both the lawyer and Heath's assistant, Sara, raised their eyebrows at the obvious connection between Aubrey and Heath, though neither of them said anything.

"It'll be alright," Aubrey said, willing himself to believe it. "This is just another cheap trick on Gemma's part. You know she isn't smart enough to pull this off."

"It's not Gemma I'm worried about," Heath mumbled against Aubrey's neck.

Aubrey knew what he meant a little too well. He was worried about whoever Gemma had hired to do the tech work behind her mean stunts. People who knew how to do things like that were capable of all sorts of horrid things. There was a chance Gemma didn't even know how wicked those people were. She was that stupid.

And Aubrey was letting his imagination run away with him. They didn't really know enough about the situation to panic yet.

"Come on," Aubrey said, taking Heath's hand. "You need some fresh air and peace."

Heath only nodded, and Aubrey led him out of the kitchen and down the hall to the back entrance so they could sit in the tiny back garden for a moment. It was strange that the entire rest of London seemed to be going about its usual business as Aubrey and Heath sat on the stairs, holding hands, listening to distant, ordinary sounds of traffic and sirens. None of it sat right with Aubrey.

"This day has been a ridiculous emotional roller coaster," he said, stroking Heath's hand, like they were in some Dickens novel and Heath was an old woman on her deathbed who needed a respectable touch. "But I'll never forget it as long as I live."

"Neither will I," Heath said in a shaky breath, still looking stunned.

"That's not what I meant," Aubrey said, managing a small smile. When Heath glanced questioningly at him, he said, "I'll never forget it, because it's the day you told me you loved me."

Heath burst into a smile, despite everything, then turned more fully to Aubrey so he could hug him. "I do love you," he said. "I'm sorry that I didn't say it sooner."

Aubrey laughed and hugged Heath in return. "It's not as though we've had loads of time for romantic declarations."

"No," Heath said, touching his forehead to Aubrey's for a moment. "But I knew it weeks ago, before the picnic at Swanmore, even. It was only my pride and confusion and past hurts that kept me from bringing it up. I should have said something sooner."

"It doesn't matter," Aubrey said, looping his arm around Heath's shoulders. "We're together now, and I, for one, am deeply interested in seeing if we can extend that togetherness as long as possible."

Heath smiled, then rested his head against Aubrey's. "I hope so, too."

They sat there for a moment, just being together. Aubrey did what he could to radiate love and support to Heath.

He was about to say something, maybe to prompt Heath to go back inside and face the continued search, when his phone pinged in his back pocket.

Heath straightened and looked at him questioningly. "You turned your phone back on?"

"I needed my contact list to help with the search," Aubrey

said. Lindsey had sent him a message, but before he tapped on it, he grinned at Heath and said, "I got your text from the other night."

Heath blushed a sexy shade of pink. "I meant it then, too."

Aubrey was tempted to toss his phone and make out with Heath, but too much was going on.

A moment later, as he opened Lindsey's message to find the link she'd sent him, he gasped so hard he nearly choked.

"What is it?" Heath asked as Aubrey shot to his feet. Heath came with him.

"It's Gemma's Instagram feed," he said, grabbing Heath's hand with his free hand and pulling him back into the house. "Lindsey sent it. Gemma just posted a pic of herself with Eugenie in St. James's Park."

Everything moved lightning fast from there. They stopped by the kitchen, where Aubrey handed his phone over to Sara, and with only the briefest of explanations, the two of them dashed out of the house, heading for St. James's Park.

It was maddening that the fastest way to get there at that time of day was to take the Tube, but public transportation did its job well. They darted into the park within fifteen minutes, racing down one of the paths to the spot where Gemma had taken her selfie. Lucky for them, she'd staged the pic so that Buckingham Palace loomed large in the background, and several other notable features had appeared with it.

"It's like she wants us to find her," Aubrey said as they raced toward the spot of the pic.

Heath laughed humorlessly. "It's not us she wants, it's her fans and admirers."

Sure enough, and mad though it was, they were able to spot Gemma with Eugenie on one of the sloping lawns toward the Mall side of the park because she had about a dozen overdressed, impressionable young women who also wore too much make-up taking turns posing for selfies with her. At least she had Eugenie with her, though the closer they got, the more apparent it became that Eugenie wanted nothing to do with the social media moment. She fussed and wriggled and tried to get down as Gemma alternately scolded her and posed for her fans.

The moment Eugenie spotted Heath and Aubrey, Gemma's moment of publicity was over.

"Eugenie!" Heath shouted, pushing past a few fans to get to his little girl.

"Daddy!" Eugenie screamed, and even Gemma's death grip couldn't stop her from getting down. Gemma nearly dropped her, and probably would have if Heath hadn't swooped in and picked her up.

"How dare you take Eugenie without permission!" Heath boomed, glaring at Gemma.

Eugenie burst into tears, but Aubrey couldn't blame Heath for shouting. He wanted to do much more than shout.

"She's my daughter, too," Gemma said, losing some of her color and bravado. The trouble was, she seemed far more concerned about what her fans might think of her than she did about Eugenie's health or comfort. So much so that she added, "He's been keeping my own daughter from me," for the benefit of those fans instead of speaking to Heath directly or, God forbid, apologizing.

Heath ignored the gasps and glares from the silly fans. "You deceived my mother in order to take my child," he said. "After attempting to destroy my boyfriend's life and turning me against him."

Aubrey's brain buzzed for a moment when Heath referred to him as his boyfriend, right out in the open, where everyone could hear.

"There's no law that says I can't take my little girl out for a walk," Gemma said, still clinging to her warped perception of the situation. "I'm her mum."

"You'd better believe that once this all gets sorted, there

will be a ruling that says you have no right to see her unsupervised," Heath continued to shout. "My lawyer is working on it right now."

Gemma made an indignant sound that in no way matched the intensity of the situation. "That's so unfair, Heath."

Heath's eyes went so wide that Aubrey was afraid they'd pop right out of his head. If not for Eugenie, Gemma probably would have been blasted straight back to hell, where she'd come from.

Aubrey stepped in, standing just slightly in front of Heath, as if to protect him. "I don't think you have any idea what sort of trouble you're in, Gemma," he said, talking down to her just a bit.

"*I'm* in trouble?" Gemma gave him an indignant look that deserved an Oscar. She glanced to the young women around her as if to play up her plight to them, but the poor things just looked confused. "*You're* the one who waltzed in and tried to steal my husband."

Aubrey ignored every one of the stupid things about her statement. "Do you even know what kind of people you're dealing with that helped you mess up my phone and create that deep fake of Heath's voice that you played for his mother?" he demanded. "You're dealing with real criminals."

Out of the corner of his eye, Aubrey noticed more of Gemma's fans backing away, though they were riveted to the argument, and several other people inching forward to see what was going on. One gruff, middle-aged man seemed to be a little too interested.

Gemma made a scoffing sound. "They aren't criminals. It was just my brother, Ted."

"You had *Ted* send that stuff to Aubrey's phone and make the deep fake?" Heath asked, incredulous.

"Yes," Gemma said with a shrug. "He's good at that sort of thing."

"Where did he get the images, then?" Aubrey asked.

"He—" Gemma stopped, and for the first time, a panicked look came over her face. "I don't really know where he got them."

"Perhaps you could introduce me to him and we could talk about it," the worrying, middle-aged man said, stepping into the conversation.

Aubrey was about three milliseconds away from going off on the man for being a creep when Heath said, "Geoffrey. What are you doing here?"

The middle-aged man smiled. "I'm here to help." He reached into his pocket and pulled out something that looked like a thin wallet, then opened it to show a warrant card to Gemma. "DCI Geoffrey Bolton," he introduced himself. "Let's take a walk, Miss Stone." He kept his smile in place as he nodded off to one side.

Gemma turned, and so did Aubrey and Heath. They were close enough to the road to see a police car with a uniformed officer waiting.

"What? No!" Gemma said, panicking even more. "I didn't do anything wrong. Eugenie is my daughter. I have every right to take her for a walk. I didn't send those things to Aubrey. I…I don't even know what you're talking about."

Strange as it felt, Aubrey breathed out in relief as Gemma danced around, like she was going to make a run for it. He was confident at last that the situation was well in hand.

"Miss Stone, I am authorized to use force if necessary," Officer Bolton said, though Aubrey wondered if he really was or not. "I don't think you want your fans to see that."

Gemma went rigid, glancing to the small crowd of onlookers who had gathered to see what was happening. More than one of them had their phones raised and were evidently recording the potential arrest. She squealed, then said, "I'll behave."

Aubrey wanted to laugh. He was certain that was the first time Gemma had ever spoken those words.

Officer Bolton gestured for the police car and started to walk Gemma toward it. After only a few steps, he turned to Heath and said, "I'll be in touch to help put this thing to bed once and for all. For now, I advise that you take your daughter and your nanny home."

"Thank you," Heath said, smiling gratefully at Bolton.

Aubrey stepped in to help with Eugenie as soon as Gemma and Bolton walked away. Eugenie was in no mood to get back into her buggy, which Gemma had evidently brought with them, but she did let Heath hand her over to Aubrey. Aubrey noted that a few people snapped pictures of the three of them together, and of the quick, unthinking kiss of reassurance he gave Heath.

"I hope you're ready for our relationship to go public," he said as they headed back toward the Tube station, "because a lot of people were taking a lot of pictures just now."

"I don't care," Heath said, his voice heavy with emotion. "Let them see what they want. I'm not planning on hiding our relationship at all."

Aubrey smiled, touched beyond telling. "Neither am I," he said, reaching over and patting Heath's backside just before they crossed the street. "Who was that DCI Bolton guy back there anyhow?" he asked as they navigated their way into the Tube station.

Heath sent him a strange smile filled with relief and bafflement. "He's a member of the Brotherhood."

Aubrey nodded slowly and made a slow sound of understanding. "I'm going to have to officially join up if that's the kind of miracle members are able to perform for each other."

The journey home seemed to take forever, though it couldn't have been more than minutes. Aubrey's nerves were shot, and Eugenie had no respect for that. She had been through an ordeal as well, and missed her naptime on top of it.

Once they reached home, there were explanations to give

and messages to send out to everyone they'd alerted earlier, saying Eugenie had been found and was safe at home. Heath's mother was relieved to the point of tears—which seemed very unlike her usual dignity—then demanded Gemma's head on a silver platter.

She got her wish, to a degree.

"I've just got off the phone with Bolton," Heath announced, walking into Eugenie's bedroom as Aubrey finally tucked her into bed later that evening, after everyone else had gone home. "He wasn't able to charge Gemma with anything, but her brother, Ted, has been arrested on child pornography charges, among other things."

Aubrey let out a low whistle. "Sounds like Gemma ruined the wrong man's life."

Heath huffed. "Ted isn't exactly a choir boy. He's had it coming for years. Bolton has advised Gemma to leave the country for a while, and from the look of her Instagram feed, she's already on her way to Paris."

"Isn't that a bit dodgy for a police officer?" Aubrey asked.

Heath shrugged. "It got rid of Gemma."

"Then good for him," Aubrey said with an ironic arch of one eyebrow.

They finished tucking Eugenie into bed, kissed her goodnight, then headed downstairs to Heath's room. In Aubrey's mind, there wasn't any question about where he wanted to be that night.

"Davison already prepared the change in custody paperwork before he left earlier," Heath said as the two of them stripped for bed. He was in the bedroom with the door to the en suite open as Aubrey brushed his teeth and washed his face. "Going forward, Gemma will only have supervised visits with Eugenie."

Aubrey rinsed and spit, then straightened to ask, "Do you think she'll actually try to see her?"

Heath looked serious as he walked into the en suite in just

his boxers to take his turn at the sink. "Part of me feels awful for saying it, but no, I don't think she'll put much effort into seeing her. She never wanted Eugenie to begin with, and something tells me this whole thing will make her want to forget her daughter entirely."

"That is awful," Aubrey said, resting against the edge of the sink and watching as Heath brushed his teeth. "But it also means we won't have to worry about her interfering anymore."

Heath finished brushing, then turned to Aubrey with a smile that was almost bashful. "I like the way you say 'we'," he said. "I like the idea of us raising Eugenie…together."

Aubrey's heart fluttered and he sucked in a breath.

Heath must have noticed, because he quickly blurted, "Is it too soon to say that?"

Aubrey smiled. He reached for the band of Heath's boxers and used it to pull him closer. "It's not too soon at all," he said.

He slipped his arms around Heath and slanted his mouth across Heath's minty-fresh one, kissing him with all the love and exhaustion, relief and hope that the day had brought them. Heath kissed him back with a vocal sigh that went straight to Aubrey's cock. Aubrey was born to take care of people, and the way Heath leaned into him and threw himself into their kiss, he understood that that need to care extended to Heath as well.

"Bed," he whispered against Heath's lips, then shifted to grab Heath's hand and lead him into the other room.

They were too tired for anything acrobatic or chaotic. Aubrey didn't need that anyhow, and Heath most certainly didn't. Instead, they simply shed the last of their clothes, slipped between the cool sheets, and tangled up in each other. They needed kisses and touches, tongues stroking across necks and fingers teasing nipples. They needed to arch their hips into each other so that their stiff cocks rubbed together. That was more than enough.

"In case I didn't make it clear earlier," Heath said between kissing his way over Aubrey's Adam's apple to the hollow at the base of his throat, "I love you."

Aubrey hummed and threaded his fingers through Heath's hair. "And in case I didn't respond adequately before, I love you, too. Madly."

They both laughed, low and soft, the peace of the moment wrapping itself around them both. Aubrey shifted them so that they lay side by side, stroking each other's cocks while kissing deeply. It was amateur stuff, and on most nights, it wouldn't have been enough to give him what he needed. But on that night, in that moment, it was everything he needed and then some. He and Heath were on the same page, so attuned that when Heath came with a sudden gasp, that pushed Aubrey over the edge, and he joined him in satisfaction.

It wasn't the best orgasm he'd ever had, but those would come later. It was the orgasm he needed, that they both needed. And as they settled their overheated bodies together, letting go of everything they didn't need, Aubrey felt as though he'd found the place where he belonged and the person he belonged to.

EPILOGUE

FIVE MONTHS LATER...

"ARE YOU READY FOR THIS?" Oakley asked Heath as the two of them stood in the corner of The Chameleon Club's ballroom.

The room was still decorated for Christmas, but some of the members were switching out a few of the blatantly Christmas-themed decorations for New Year's ones. All of the decorations were bright and glittery, and whether they were red and green or blue and white and gold didn't matter. The ballroom-slash-dining room was absolutely gorgeous and filled with promise. The ancient, stuffed chameleon that always sat on the mantle of the room's enormous fireplace looked on at the activity with his clever smile.

Heath glanced around, taking it all in with a deep breath, then turned to his brother. "I'm ready," he said. "I think I've been ready for this for ages, from the moment I first met Aubrey, at least."

Oakley smiled, then thumped his shoulder. "Good, because I think I can hear them coming."

Sure enough, the sound of Eugenie's cheerful chatter

echoed in the hallway. Aubrey's laughter sounded along with it. The two sounds together filled up Heath's heart in a way he'd never thought anything could. Especially since the sound of Aubrey and Eugenie together felt so perfect and so right. Gemma might have turned out to be a selfish cow, but Eugenie would grow up with a father who loved her desperately.

Hopefully, she would grow up with more than that. That was partially what the next few minutes would determine.

"There'd Daddy," Aubrey said with a bright smile for Heath as he rounded the corner, Eugenie in his arms. "And look, Uncle Oakley is here as well."

"I didn't think children were allowed in The Chameleon Club," one of the older, stodgier members muttered as he crossed behind Heath and Oakley on his way to the buffet.

"It's a special occasion," Oakley snapped at him.

Heath sent him a brief look of thanks, but was more interested in Aubrey as he and Eugenie approached.

"Don't you look stunning," Aubrey said, glancing up and down Heath's form. "Did you wear that to work?"

Heath usually wore a suit to work, but he was dressed in one of his more formal suits, like he wore to weddings and special occasions.

Which was apropos, all things considered.

He was stopped from replying to Aubrey as Eugenie reached out for him, nearly spilling out of Aubrey's arms in the process. Heath had to catch her to stop her from tumbling to the floor. His nervous energy caused him to laugh a little too loud as a result.

"We saw a poly bear, Daddy," Eugenie informed him with wide eyes.

"A what?" Heath blinked and smiled at her.

"It was a large stuffed polar bear at the toy shop we passed on our way here," Aubrey explained with a laugh. "Of course, Eugenie wants it for Christmas."

"Tell Santa, Daddy," Eugenie said, her eyes bright with excitement.

"Christmas just happened, darling," Heath explained. "It won't come around again for another three hundred and sixty-two days."

"But tell Santa," Eugenie insisted anyhow. She squirmed a little in Heath's hold, making both Heath and Aubrey laugh.

"Are we here for lunch?" Aubrey asked, eyeing the buffet to one side of the room longingly. "I know my membership was only approved last month, but I'd love to take advantage of the perks."

Heath grinned. It had been a matter of course for Aubrey to join the Brotherhood. Casper had offered to sponsor his membership, but that was clearly Heath's privilege. Aubrey was welcomed with open arms, of course, especially after his role in protecting Heath and Eugenie from Gemma's machinations.

"We'll eat lunch in a moment," Heath said, struggling with a wriggling Eugenie. "But first, I want to—Eugenie, could you stop for a moment?"

Heath was forced to put his daughter down, but that proved not to be the wisest move. Somehow, Eugenie knew he had something in his jacket pocket. She'd kicked it a few times while Heath held her, but the second Heath put her down, she dove for his pocket.

With surprising dexterity for a little lady who had just turned four, she reached into Heath's pocket and pulled out the velvety ring box. Without missing a beat, she pried the box open.

"Eugenie, no," Heath said, more startled that his daughter had spoiled his surprise than angry.

"Ooh! Pretty!" Eugenie gasped as she looked at the diamond band inside the box.

Aubrey moved in to help Heath get Eugenie under

control, but his eyes went wide at the sight of the ring. "It that —" He stopped, his mouth open.

Heath glanced sheepishly at Aubrey and cleared his throat as he plucked the ring from the box before Eugenie could grab it.

"Excuse me, darling," he said to Eugenie, sinking to one knee. He peeked up at Aubrey, a flush heating his face, then looked at Eugenie again. "Would you like to help Daddy ask Nanny Aubrey a question?"

"Yes," Eugenie said at once, no idea what she was agreeing to.

"Very well," Heath told her. "Kneel down like Daddy is."

Eugenie struggled a bit, managing to sit on the floor at Heath's side, staring at him questioningly.

Heath leaned over and kissed her forehead. "That's it." He then glanced up at Aubrey, holding up the ring.

Aubrey knew exactly what was happening, and his face was already filled with his answer, before the question had even been spoken. He beamed, radiating joy, and his eyes were shining with happiness and possible tears.

"I guess the cat's out of the bag," Heath said apologetically, then got right to, "Aubrey Kelly, you came into my life by accident. None of this was supposed to happen. There will never be enough words for me to tell you how glad I am that you pushed me into letting you move into our house. You did so much more than just take a room in it, you made it into a home."

"Oh, Heath," Aubrey said, placing a hand on his heart.

"I was a little broken when you found me," Heath went on, rushing a bit, due to the sudden, overwhelming emotion that was threatening to turn him into an embarrassing, blubbering heap, "but you took care of me, and Eugenie, and you fixed me. I cannot imagine my life without you now, and you would make me the happiest man alive if you would be my husband."

Heath offered up the ring he'd had specially made for Aubrey.

"Yes!" Aubrey gasped with hardly any hesitation. "Definitely, yes."

Heath started to rise, desperate to get the ring on Aubrey's finger and to kiss him, especially now that the other Brotherhood members who had been secretly watching them the whole time had burst into applause.

"And here I was planning to propose to you on New Year's, at midnight," Aubrey laughed as Heath slid the ring on his finger.

"Really?" Heath asked, blinking.

"I have a ring for you at home and everything," Aubrey said.

Heath didn't know what to say to that. He was too touched and too overjoyed to find words.

Fortunately, he didn't have to. Aubrey tugged him into his arms, and the two of them kissed with enough passion to melt the decorations all around the room.

In her youthful exuberance, even though she couldn't grasp what was really going on, Eugenie threw herself at Heath's and Aubrey's legs, hugging them together. That burst the heat bubble that was building between Heath and Aubrey to the point where Heath ended their kiss and, laughing, bent to scoop Eugenie into his arms.

"What do you think?" he asked Eugenie. "Would you like Aubrey to be your papa instead of just your nanny?"

"Yes," Eugenie said, throwing her arms up.

Heath's happiness and courage faltered a bit as he glanced to Aubrey and said, "Do you think you would like to have a little brother or sister as well?"

He lifted his eyebrows, asking Aubrey. The question was even more important than asking Aubrey to be his husband, in a way. It was because of Aubrey's amazing way with Eugenie that he'd been thinking so much about doing whatever it might take to bring another child, or perhaps two, into their family. He had whispered a few hints to Aubrey here and there, but they hadn't truly talked about it yet.

But Aubrey beamed and said, "I think another baby, or two or three, would be wonderful."

That answered that. Heath let out a small sigh of relief, then let Aubrey pull him and Eugenie both back into his arms.

"I love you," he told Aubrey, kissing him as best he could with Eugenie wedged between them.

"I love you, too," Aubrey laughed in return.

Heath smiled for all he was worth. They were a true family now, and he would do everything in his power to make his family happy for the rest of his life.

———

I hope you've enjoyed Heath and Aubrey's story! I've always loved busting myths about who should be taking care of children and whether men are meant to have emotions or not. And I love seeing stories about good parents. Now, if you'd like to learn more about The Brotherhood, I have more than one Historical Romance series that deals with the 19th century past of The Brotherhood, including how the organization was created! You'll find a lot of familiar things if you dive into the creation of The Brotherhood, starting with the book *What a Duke Desires*.

And on top of that, if you're curious about the After the War series, well, the television series that Heath was working on in this book (and that will make more appearances in future Brotherhood: Legacy books) is completely based on my MM Regency Romance series of the same name! If you'd like to read about that, start with *Between His Lover and the Deep Blue Sea*.

. . .

What's up next for the modern Brotherhood? Well, Oakley needs his story, of course. What happens when a serious accident leaves Oakley broken, both physically and mentally. Will he be able to heal and find love with the physical therapist nurse who is hired to take care of him? Find out next in *Billionaire Breakdowns*!

If you enjoyed this book and would like to hear more from me—as Merry Farmer or my other identities, MM Farmer (MM Omegaverse) or Em Farmer (Contemporary Romance) please sign up for my newsletter! When you sign up, you'll get your choice of a free, full-length novella. One choice is *A Passionate Deception*. It is an MF romance, but it has a strong MM secondary character, who gets his own book in my May Flowers series. Part of my West Meets East series, *A Passionate Deception* can be read as a stand-alone. Your other choice is *Rendezvous in Paris*. It is an MM Victorian story that is part of my *Tales from the Grand Tour* series, but can also be read as a standalone. Pick up your free copy today by signing up to receive my newsletter (which I only send out when I have a new release)!

Sign up here: http://eepurl.com/cbaVMH

Are you on social media? I am! Come and join the fun on Facebook: http://www.facebook.com/merryfarmerreaders

I'm also a huge fan of Instagram and post lots of original content there: https://www.instagram.com/merryfarmer/

ABOUT THE AUTHOR

I hope you have enjoyed *Nanny Negotiations*. If you'd like to be the first to learn about when new books in the series come out and more, please sign up for my newsletter here: http://eepurl.com/cbaVMH And remember, Read it, Review it, Share it! For a complete list of works by Merry Farmer with links, please visit http://wp.me/P5ttjb-14F.

USA Today Bestselling author Merry Farmer—who writes Omegaverse as MM Farmer—is an award-winning novelist who lives in suburban Philadelphia with her cats, Justine and Peter. She has been writing since she was ten years old and realized one day that she didn't have to wait for the teacher to assign a creative writing project to write something. It was the best day of her life. She then went on to earn not one but two degrees in History so that she would always have something to write about. Her books have reached the Top 100 at Amazon, iBooks, and Barnes & Noble, and have been named finalists in the prestigious RONE and Rom Com Reader's Crown awards.

ACKNOWLEDGMENTS

I owe a huge debt of gratitude to my awesome beta-readers, Melinda Greathouse and Jolene Stewart, for their suggestions and advice. And double thanks to Julie Tague, for being a truly excellent editor and to Cindy Jackson for being an awesome assistant!

Click here for a complete list of other works by Merry Farmer.

Printed by Amazon Italia Logistica S.r.l.
Torrazza Piemonte (TO), Italy